# The Ragged Mudlarke's Christmas Miracle

# NELL HARTE

©Copyright 2024 Nell Harte

All Rights Reserved

License Notes

This Book is licensed for personal enjoyment only. It may not be resold. No part of this work may be reproduced in any form or by any electronic or mechanical means including information storage and retrieval systems, without written permission from the author.

*Chapter Nineteen* ............................................. *193*

*Chapter Twenty* ............................................... *199*

*Chapter Twenty-One* ...................................... *211*

*Chapter Twenty-Two* ..................................... *223*

*Chapter Twenty-Three* ................................... *231*

*Chapter Twenty-Four* ..................................... *241*

*Chapter Twenty-Five* ...................................... *247*

*Epilogue* ........................................................ *259*

*PREVIEW* ....................................................... *275*

   The Little Orphan's Christmas Miracle .............. 277

*PREVIEW* ....................................................... *288*

   The Midnight Watcher's Christmas .................. 291

# Chapter One

*London, 1849*

The sky above the city of London shifted from velvet black to the navy hue of earliest morning, the first embers of the dawn tingeing the darkness with smoky streaks of orange, as if a great fire was raging somewhere in the distance. Frost glistened on the riverbank, the mud frozen, while the Thames made its sluggish way toward the sea, carrying with it all sorts of treasures and detritus.

The trick was knowing which was which.

"We'll have us a fine feast on Christmas Day with this," Kenneth Martin said, tucking the dirtied sack of filthy river plunder under his bent knees. He wore a rare smile today, and Betsy thought it might be the greatest treasure of them all.

At four-and-ten, she had been accompanying her father to the riverbanks of the Thames for as long as she could remember. Even before that, or so her father liked to tell her.

*"I'd have you strapped to my back, talking to you as I worked. You never made a fuss, and you'd stick out your bonny little fingers, over me shoulder—if I followed 'em, I'd always find the finest treasures. Born to be a mudlark, you were,"* he would often say, his brown eyes bright with memory.

"Do you think we might have some goose?" Betsy asked.

Her father gave his familiar, dry chuckle. "I wouldn't set your hopes so high, mouse. But we'll have us a chicken at least, maybe a pheasant or two if I can get John to part with what he's poached upriver."

"And those golden potatoes that ma used to make? I'm going to get them right this time." Betsy's mouth watered at the thought, her mind filling with the daydreams of Christmases past. There had been more than a few stark years, and one very sad year that had not felt like Christmas at all, but she had schooled her memory into forgetting those.

Her father nodded. "Might have us some honeyed carrots and parsnips an' all. A figgy pudding if we can get us one more of something shiny before the sun comes up proper."

Betsy was ready to get up there and then to scour the softer muck of the riverbank for hidden prizes, but her father seemed to be in no rush. He had that wistful look about him that let her know he was about to tell one of his stories, and though she was eager for her family to have the sort of Christmas feast that would leave their stomachs swollen and more than satisfied, she could not resist her father's tales.

She tucked her muddied knees up to her chest, the stink of the sludge and river water so familiar that she no longer noticed it, and rested her chin in the dip between.

Meanwhile, her father opened the flap of his weathered leather satchel to take out their breakfast. A simple repast of sharp, crumbly white cheese, half an apple each, and two chunks of barely stale bread, wrapped in old cloth.

As he passed her portion to her, he began to talk and the air around the pair went still, as though even the blackbirds and gulls and wading birds were listening intently.

"When I was a young'un, and winter howled into the city, so bitter cold you couldn't feel your own nose after a few minutes outside, these riverbanks would be filled north to south with people. Not just the riverbanks, neither, but the river itself," he said, his voice as melodic as music to Betsy's ears.

"It used to freeze over back then, so thick you'd think it were a road," he continued. "And people would flock to it, bringing their barrows and wares, putting up stalls right out there on the ice. Rich and poor alike, they'd all be here to enjoy the Frost Fair. Some of 'em would find an empty bit of ice and skate, moving so quick and so graceful you'd think they was angels."

Betsy's eyes widened with every word, her gaze turning out to the slow-moving river, trying to imagine what he had seen back then. Her imagination struggled, for it seemed impossible that anyone would ever be able to walk on water like that, frozen or not. She, herself, knew she would be too afraid to even set foot on such a thing.

"Me and me brothers would cause all sorts of mischief, sliding up and down, knocking folk over 'til our pa clipped us 'round the ear. Ma—bless her soul—slipped us a ha'penny and off we went, wandering around every stall and barrow 'til we found something worthy of our coin. But with Bert being the oldest, he got to choose. We had us a mince pie each that day, hot enough to burn our tongues but we couldn't wait for 'em to cool. And so sweet it made us wilder than hens when there's a fox loose." He laughed quietly, his eyes misted over as if he, too, was seeing the scene appear before him.

"Every year after 'til I was ten or so, I'd ask me ma and pa when the Frost Fair was coming back. It never did, though, and there's no way of knowing if it's ever likely to," he carried on, taking a bite of his cheese and apple. "It has been thirty-five years since then and I've never seen the river so much as try to freeze again. The winters are still bitter cold, but not cold enough."

Betsy ripped a piece of bread off with her teeth, staring forlornly at the traitorous Thames, wishing that it might freeze over there and then so she could experience a Frost Fair for herself.

Her father must have noticed the sadness in her gaze, as he nudged her in the arm. "There are still parts of the river that freeze, or so I hear," he said. "Just not this far into the city. You have to go out into the counties to see a Frost Fair these days."

Betsy hung her head, envious of the country folk who got to have such delights, while she was left digging in the hard-packed mud for treasures that paled in comparison to such an event.

And that was not all—while they probably had fresh white snow that stretched for miles across fields and woodland, she got brown slush that had been trodden in a thousand times or run through by carriage wheels. And where they had a beautiful frozen river to skate on, she had to be wary of ice-slicked cobbles that would sweep her clean off her feet and leave her winded. It hardly seemed fair.

"So," her father said in a low, conspiratorial tone, "how about I take you upriver next year? I can buy us a mince pie each and we can try to skate, wherever we find us a frozen bit."

Betsy gazed up at her father, all her melancholy complaints vanishing in an instant, awestruck by the offer. She did not need a hearty Christmas feast or any sort of festivities or to envy others if she could have a gift like that. Indeed, she told herself she would ignore this year's Christmas altogether if it would make the next year arrive quicker.

"Do you mean it?" she gasped.

Her father raised an eyebrow. "Have you ever known me to be a liar, mouse?"

"Not ever," she confirmed giddily. "Most honest man I know."

He laughed softly. "Exactly, so you keep that in your mind whilst we finish the morning. I can buy you a new scarf or a pair of gloves to keep you warm. I might even give you a ha'penny to buy yourself whatever you might desire. What do you say to that?"

"I say, I can't wait until next year," she told him, chewing contentedly on her hunk of bread, though the tough texture made her teeth hurt and her jaw ache. She would bear it all and worse if she could go to a Frost Fair once in her life.

They sat in companionable silence as they ate the rest of their humble breakfast, both lost in their own thoughts. Every time Betsy glanced at her father, he had the same distant expression, his brow furrowed and his eyes darting, as if he were following the movement of something on the river. She was not certain she believed in ghosts, though her father had stories about them too, but his gaze was undeniably haunted at that moment, visited by memories of those who had raised him and shaped him, now gone.

Not wanting to disturb his reverie, Betsy sat quietly long after she had finished her breakfast. But though the dawn grew brighter and brighter, the sky a painter's palette of pinks and purples and oranges and reds, it had not grown any warmer. And sitting still, the vicious cold took its opportunity to creep in, bone-deep and so numbing that it ached.

When Betsy could not feel her hands or feet anymore, she knew she had to intrude on her father's quietude. The last thing she wanted was for either of them to fall ill before Christmas, when it was so deliciously close. Three days until they could wake late, eat scrumptious food, and spend a whole day together as a family, worrying over nothing but whether or not they should have another pick at the roasted bird, whatever it might be.

"Sun's almost up," she said by way of distraction.

Her father shook his head as if to dislodge something from his mind and lumbered to his feet without a word.

He took a moment to stretch out stiff legs and arms, bracing his hand against his back as he bent back and forth to relieve the rigidity in his spine.

Betsy jumped up, grateful to be moving again. "I have a feeling I'm about to find the greatest treasure of them all."

"If anyone can, mouse, it's you," her father replied, stifling a yawn.

She was about to slide back down to the softer mud that blended into the lapping, frothing river water, when the flicker of lights that did not belong to the rising sun caught her eye. Bobbing lanterns moved along the embankment, headed in their direction, and even in the gloom of not-yet morning, she knew precisely who those lanterns belonged to.

"The Rat Boys are back," Betsy whispered.

*Always scuttling around, stealing what isn't theirs.* She did not know if they had an actual name for their band of miscreants, but she had chosen to call them the 'Rat Boys' and the name had stuck between her and her father.

Her father grabbed the sack of goods they had scrounged from the mud over the past few hours and stuffed it as best he could into his leather satchel. It spilled out of the top, prompting her father to whip off his belt and lash it around the satchel, holding everything more securely inside. The two of them had learned many a lesson about how to keep their treasures safe after the Rat Boys had started to target them, a few months ago.

"We'll move along the bank," her father urged, pushing Betsy with a firm hand. "If we don't find anything before the sun pokes through that gap between the warehouses over there, we'll leave."

Betsy was not sure it was a wise idea to linger at all, with the Rat Boys so close and getting closer, but she was in no position to argue with her father. If he thought they would be fine, she trusted him.

A few stumbling paces through the thick, sucking mud, and Betsy froze. Sticking out of the mire, the round edge of something unmistakably gold gleamed dully in the low light.

Trying her best to be discreet, she crouched down and scraped away the rancid slurry of rot and decay, and pulled out the golden object. Smearing some of the mud away with her equally dirty thumb, it revealed itself to be a pocket watch. She turned it over, praying to the heavens for good luck.

*Not inscribed.* Her heart leapt with excitement, knowing what a price it would fetch. It was rare to find pocket watches at all, rarer still to find one that was not marked as belonging to anyone. People were wary of buying things that could be mistaken as stolen.

"Papa, look," she whispered, her voice trembling as she flashed the precious item up to her watchful father. His face paled, but before he could respond, a shout echoed across the embankment. The Rat Boys had spotted them—too close for comfort. "Quick, girl!" he hissed, his eyes wide with panic. The lanterns bobbed closer, their light bouncing off the frozen riverbank as the gang closed in, fast. Her heart slammed in her chest. One wrong move, and they'd lose everything. The ground beneath her felt treacherous, the frozen mud threatening to pull her under with every step.

"Go to the pawnbroker and do not stop for anything," her father hissed, slinging off his satchel and throwing the strap over her head. "Run, Betsy. Run!"

THE RAGGED MUDLARKE'S CRHISTMAS MIRACLE

# Chapter Two

Betsy scrambled up the slippery embankment, digging her hands into the mud, clawing with all her might to get to the top. Breathless, her limbs still stiff with cold, she crested the bank and took off as fast as her numb feet would allow. The satchel thudded against her thigh with every desperate movement, hindering her, but she would just have to suffer the ensuing bruises. She would not let her father down, not when he had put the fate of their family's Christmas onto her shoulders.

She hurtled up a smaller embankment onto the road and, dodging past a few people on their way to begin their day, she headed for the labyrinth of alleyways and passages that crowded together to form the parish of Limehouse.

Annoyed dockworkers and swaying drunkards bellowed at her as she raced by, weaving around anyone who dared to get in her way, sprinting on with her lungs on fire and her heart beating in her throat.

But it was not long before she heard the thud of pursuing footfalls, and one frightened glance over her shoulder told her she was not mistaken.

A young man was running after her, and running quickly, gaining on her no matter how many other people she tried to put between herself and her pursuer.

"Give it up, girl!" the young man called to her. "You'll not be able to run faster than me, so you might as well stop and hand it over."

Bursting with a strength she did not know she possessed, spurred on by absolute desperation, she ignored his taunts and gritted her teeth. If she could just make it to St. Anne's, she could dart into the church and hide there, seeking sanctuary until the Rat Boy went away. He might have been able to outrun her, but he could not outlast her stubbornness, and she would stay in the church for as long as it took to make sure her and her father's tireless work was not for nothing.

Cutting down another street, the grim terraced houses and soot-stained workshops seemingly leaning in toward her as if they too would halt her in her tracks, she nearly cried out in relief as she saw the dirty white belltower of St. Anne's Church. The gates stood at the very end of the narrow street, wide open in a gesture of welcome.

*Almost there. Almost there,* she told herself, giving everything she had to make those last fifty yards.

The break between the street and the gates was fast approaching, the footsteps of her pursuer getting ever louder. She was going to make it. She was going to make her father proud. They were going to have roasted pheasant on Christmas Day, with crispy golden potatoes, rich with dripping, and honeyed carrots and roasted parsnips and figgy pudding with just a soak of brandy over the top to make the flame turn blue when it was lit.

They were going to have a happy, hearty Christmas, and nothing could stop her.

Just then, two constables strolled across the opening at the end of the street, and an almighty cry went up from behind her.

"Thief! Stop the thief! Thief!"

Betsy's eyes widened in horror as the constables whipped around, their expressions contorting into masks of bitter distaste as they saw her charging towards them. There were no alleys or passageways to dart through to get off the street, just brick walls and closed doors on either side of her.

But the gates—they were just behind the constables. If she could weave past them, even they would not be able to stop her, as long as she reached the church doors in time.

Betsy refused to slow, flinching every time her pursuer called out the same unkind word of 'thief,' she raced on. What else could she do? The constables would not listen to her explanation, nor believe it, regardless of the fact that she was covered up to the waist in crusting river mud.

A couple of paces from the braced constables, she veered to the left and, with soaring relief, realised she had made it past the first. But the second was faster and sharper. He lurched forward and his foot shot out, catching her ankle.

She barely had time to register the pain that ricocheted up her calf before she was falling, tumbling to the ground with all of the precious treasures in the satchel clinking and clattering as she did. She landed on her side with a brutal thump, wincing at the sound of things breaking as her slim body crushed whatever the hard cobbles had not.

A rough hand grabbed her by the scruff of her threadbare dress, hauling her to her feet as if she weighed nothing at all.

"What's the meaning of this, eh?" the constable who had tripped her asked, his cruel eyes making disdainful view of her.

He let her go and dusted off his hands as if he had touched something rancid, while the other constable moved to block the church gates, no doubt guessing what Betsy might do to escape them.

Shaking with the shock of the fall, her palms scraped where she had tried to ease the impact, her eyes prickling with hot tears at the satchel full of broken trinkets, she explained in an urgent, trembling voice.

"I'm a... mudlark," she wheezed. "I haven't stolen anything. I... found these things, and this man wants to take them from me."

She looked at her pursuer properly for the first time. He was perhaps a few years older than her, and dressed well in a clean shirt, a tweed waistcoat and woollen trousers, his somewhat aged greatcoat grazing the ground as if it were meant for someone bigger. A woollen cap sat at a jaunty angle on his head, raven black curls peeking out from beneath.

Had she met him in the street or at the pawnbroker or at the public house, she might have thought him handsome, with defined cheekbones, a sharp jaw, a sloping nose that looked like it had only been broken once or twice, and piercing grey eyes: the colour of the fog on the river on a summer's morning, just before true dawn.

His lips quirked into a sly smile, as if he knew what she and the constables were thinking—who would believe a filthy urchin over someone so presentable?

"The pocket watch is mine," the young man said confidently. "I don't know about the rest, but she likely stole that too. Straight out of my hand, she took it. Was only checking the time to see the hour, so I could go and meet my sister at the matchstick factory. Can't have her walking alone when it's not yet light outside. It's not safe. All sorts of thieves and brigands wandering around."

The constable closest to Betsy turned up his nose in increasing disgust. "Where's the pocket watch?"

"But it's not his, sir," she pleaded. "I found it, fair and square. He's one of the Rat Boys. All he does is steal what the mudlarks find. He's been doing it for months with the other Rat Boys!"

The young man snorted, and played it off as a cough, banging on his chest. "I don't know about any Rat Boys, sir. All I know is I haven't long until I need to meet my sister, and that wretch took what's mine. I must've chased her for miles, and if an honest man can't keep what's his, what is this city coming to?"

"Honest?" Betsy spluttered. "Why, it's a mystery that your tongue hasn't rotted off with all the poison lies that spill off it!" She looked back to the constable, clasping her hands together. "Please, sir. If you let him have that pocket watch, you'll be handing it to worse than me. I just found it; I swear. It's still caked in the river mud where I plucked it from."

The constable frowned as Betsy produced the golden item, her heart sinking as she realised that the glass front had cracked in the fall. It would not fetch nearly so great a price now, but that did not mean she would let the Rat Boy have it.

"You see," she urged.

But the constable seemed to have made up his mind, with or without the evidence before him. Betsy's appearance was enough for him to decide who would be granted the pocket watch that meant the difference between a truly festive Christmas and a starker one. Especially now that the Rat Boy, by proxy, had also destroyed everything in the satchel—at least, it sounded like everything had been destroyed. He had certainly assisted in diminishing what it all might have been worth.

"Give the pocket watch to him," the constable commanded. "And don't start your whining and whimpering again. Just do as you're told."

Betsy gaped at him. "But..."

"Do as you're told." The constable raised his hand as if he meant to strike her. "I won't say it a second time."

With her hopes dashed, her knees and palms skinned, and her heart cracking in her chest, Betsy dipped into the apron she wore, where she had stowed away the pocket watch. Hands shaking and bloody, she took the item to the waiting miscreant, wishing she had the strength to smack the insidious smirk right off his face.

"Now, you make sure you don't do something so wretched again," the young man chided mockingly, as he wrapped the dirty pocket watch in a handkerchief and tucked it into his pocket.

That done, he tipped his hat to the constables. "Merry Christmas to you, sirs, and thank you for the kindness you've done today."

The constables seemed pleased with the praise, puffing their chests.

"You go on your way now. Make sure you get to your sister," the one nearest said, while the second nodded his agreement.

Betsy doubted there *was* a sister, but what could she say? The constables had judged her and given their sentence, favouring the wicked creature with the nice clothes and the trickster's smile. It boiled her blood, making her want to lash out and protest, but she kept her mouth shut, thinking of what her father would tell her to do. He would urge silence, not causing a fuss.

*"There'll always be more treasures in the mud, mouse,"* he would say, more terrified of anything happening to her than the loss of some trinkets.

The young man tipped his cap a second time and strolled off, whistling to himself. A sound so annoying that it took everything Betsy had not to chase after him and swing at his head with her father's satchel. There was enough in there to leave him with a headache he would not soon forget; that was for sure.

"Now, what are we to do with you?" The second constable stepped away from the gates as he spoke, but Betsy no longer felt like running. There was no point.

The first tilted his head to one side, nose wrinkling. "Could take her to Bow Street. See if that won't stop her thieving again. A couple weeks at Newgate Prison might be what's best for her."

"No!" Betsy gasped, her head spinning. "I swear on all I hold dear that I wasn't stealing. If you were to come to the riverbank every morning, you'd see me there, digging for whatever I can find. Please, don't take me to Bow Street! Please! It's nearly Christmas!"

All of the emotions she had been holding back suddenly sprang forth, bursting out of her in a torrent she could not ease. Tears spilled down her cheeks, cutting rivulets through the dirt streaked there, filling her mouth with the taste of salt. She knew her tears would not affect these two men, but she could not stop them, her pleas becoming an intelligible babble of desperation.

"Enough!" the first constable bellowed, shaking his head. "One more wail out of you and I *will* take you to Bow Street."

Betsy clamped a hand over her mouth, shivering from head to toe as she stared in silence at the constable, willing him to show some festive mercy, some good will to all men—and girls who were only trying to help their family.

The second constable cleared his throat. "Might be that she *is* a mudlark. She smells like one, and there's river mud all over her."

*Now you say that?* Betsy kept her hand clamped over her mouth, fearful of whatever else might pour out if she released that seal. All the things she wanted to say would assuredly lead to a spell in a prison cell.

"Could be, but a mudlark shouldn't be stealing other people's things from the riverbanks anyway," the first constable replied with a shrug. "They ought to give it back."

The second constable seemed more pitying, all of a sudden. "It's probably hard to do if it doesn't have a name on it." He paused and gave Betsy a light shove in the middle of her back. "You run along now, but don't let us catch you thieving again, else there'll be no leniency."

She got the feeling he did not actually believe that she had stolen anything, and hated that he had not spoken up sooner, but the relief of being released was far greater than her ire.

She did not hesitate, lest the first constable disagreed, and took off at a clip, heading back the way she had come.

At the first right turn, she veered away, knowing that part of London as well as she knew the tides of the river. For despite the upset, she still needed to get to the pawnbroker in Whitechapel, and prayed that he too showed a sort of festive mercy when he looked over the ruined goods in her satchel.

Treading carefully across the icy cobbles, ignoring the remarks of loafers and inebriates who had begun their revels early, Betsy wended her way through the underbelly of Whitechapel and hugged the satchel closer to her side.

The sun was almost entirely awake, promising a clear and crisp day, but it always seemed to be dark in the streets of Whitechapel.

The buildings were too cramped, the daylight never piercing the alleyways and passages, whilst the inhabitants seemed to be in a state of perpetual night, stumbling out of the public houses and lurking on street corners. Betsy had never been able to explain it, but it was as if the sun did not dare to illuminate the vice and degeneracy that existed in that grim corner of London, not realising that at least half of those people were simply trying to feed themselves and their families however they could.

"Merry Christmas!" a lout called from outside the White Hart pub.

Betsy put her head down and pressed on.

"Oi! I said 'Merry Christmas'!" the man called again, as footsteps began to follow her for the second time that day.

She quickened her pace, slipping and sliding on the ice, but as she rounded the corner onto the next street, all of her fears melted away like a light dusting of snow on a sunny winter's day.

Her father stood outside the pawnbroker with an anxious look on his weathered face, glancing this way and that as he tapped his foot. When he looked in her direction, his expression softened into relief and he came running toward her, enveloping her in a tight hug.

"You had me worried, mouse," he said quietly.

"I had some trouble, but all's well now," she replied, quickly giving him the short version of what had occurred. "Some of the things got damaged and the pocket watch was taken, but there'll be enough for maybe one pheasant and perhaps a partridge too."

Her father put his arm around her and steered her into the pawnbroker's shop, murmuring softly, "It doesn't matter if we have nothing for Christmas, so long as you are safe." He smiled down at her. "Saying that, we'll find a way to have our feast. Don't you worry about that."

And stepping into the relative warmth of the shop, Betsy was *not* worried anymore. After all, her father never lied.

# Chapter Three

"Merry Christmas, love," Kenneth said, smiling his half smile as he set a carving of a robin down in front of the headstone of Penelope Martin. 'Penny' to those who loved her dearly. 'Ma' to the one who loved her wholly.

Betsy crouched down and adjusted the little robin with its red-painted breast, setting it more precisely among the others that crowded the grave. Always birds, one on Christmas, one on her birthday, one on the day that Kenneth and Betsy lost her. She had an entire flock now, after six years.

"Merry Christmas, Ma," Betsy whispered, pressing her fingers to her lips before pressing that kiss to the cold stone.

In the nearby yew tree, a robin chirped and hopped along one of the crooked branches, singing its cheery song. Betsy gazed up at it with delight, her heart filling with joy at the thought that it was her mother, wishing them a 'Merry Christmas' in return. Even her father's smile warmed, as he closed his eyes and listened to the robin's sweet tune.

Betsy would always miss her mother, the same way she would have missed a limb if she awoke one day to find it gone. But time passed and time healed, and though life had never been the same without Penny, the grief was not as crippling as it had been six years ago. It was lighter now, more reflective and nostalgic—a thing of fond memory rather than cruel pain.

"I really was going to get those potatoes right this year," Betsy told her mother, as she moved a carved blackbird taking flight into the centre of the headstone. "Next year, I'll bring you one and see what you think. We didn't get any pheasant either, but Pa says we'll still have us a feast to remember."

Her father offered his hand to help Betsy up. "Speaking of which, we ought to be going. We can't be late." He paused. "But we can come back this way, and you can tell your ma all about it."

Betsy got to her feet and dusted off her hands, taking one more moment to admire her mother's resting place. No other grave in the cemetery was as well attended, the birds looking like they were holding a constant vigil over the precious soul below. It cheered Betsy's spirits, making it easier to leave each time they visited, knowing her mother was not alone.

"Lead the way," she said, weaving her arm through her father's as they made their way up toward the church.

The robin followed them for a while, chirruping and trilling as it fluttered from tree to tree, headstone to headstone, as if Betsy's mother had decided she did not want to wait for the stories; she wanted to see where her husband and daughter were going with her own eyes.

They had just passed a row of proud mausoleums and weeping angels, stepping over the thick, serpentine roots of an ancient yew, when Betsy heard it—the most beautiful sound, drifting towards her from the imposing white church up ahead.

The choir was singing, their angelic voices warming Betsy, body and soul, against the vicious wind that whipped through the city and nipped at every speck of bare flesh it could find. She almost wanted to stand there for a while, away from the church but amongst the lost souls all around her, to enjoy that heavenly music.

"Your ma had the sweetest voice," Kenneth said, clearing his throat. "But she would only ever sing for us. I'd urge her to sing when we'd go to the tavern of a night, but she never would. Do you remember her singing carols?"

Betsy nodded. "I would forget to breathe; it was so beautiful."

"Me too." He smiled at her, his eyes misty.

After a moment or two, they carried on toward Christ Church. An exquisite structure in the heart of the Spitalfields parish that was anything but. Betsy had always liked the Gothic tower and the striking porticoed porch with its curved pediment and Tuscan columns, and how brightly white it all shone despite the ingrained grime of the city. It made every visit feel special, as if she were entering a palace or an ancient temple, instead of just their nearest church. Even before they had buried her mother there, it had felt like truly hallowed ground.

A long line of people trailed down from the portico, shivering in the cold and blowing into frozen hands, many with faces half buried in woollen scarves.

The poor of Spitalfields, come to feel the mercy of the church on Christmas Day.

"Merry Christmas to you!" a woman in a too-large overcoat and holey shoes cheered as Kenneth and Betsy joined the line. It ended a fair distance from the porch steps, but close enough to smell the delicious aromas that wafted out of Christ Church.

Betsy smiled back. "And a Merry Christmas to you too!"

The woman had two small children with her, who were making a game of chasing each other up and down the steps. Their laughter was loud and unapologetic, fond smiles following their joyful sprints back and forth, perhaps reminding a few people of themselves at that age.

By rights, the people in that line should not have had much to be cheerful about, relying on the charity of the church because they had nothing of their own. Yet, there was a magic in the air that rippled down the line, a festive spirit that passed from person to person, bringing faces out of their scarf hideaways, urging the waiting people to speak to their neighbour and offer words of good cheer.

"I hear there are mince pies," a young woman behind Betsy and her father said, as her two children took off to play with the ones who were still racing up and down the steps.

The man beside the woman—her husband, presumably—flashed a delighted grin. "I haven't had a mince pie in years. I wouldn't be surprised if the high-and-mighty of Mayfair could hear me stomach growling!"

"And potatoes," the woman in front chimed in. "They're serving proper meals, not the watery soup you get at St. Anne's."

The man groaned, rubbing his belly. "Don't get me hopes up. If there's potatoes, I'll have to be dragged away like a feral cat after the Sunday pie."

Betsy chuckled and her father smiled, his arm around her shoulders.

Soon enough, Kenneth fell into conversation with the man, talking of the price of coal and whether the heavy, dark clouds in the distance were carrying snow or sleet. Betsy hoped for the former as she stood patiently at her father's side, getting closer to the church in slow increments. No matter how numb her hands got or how wretchedly cold their lodgings became in the winter, she could never resist snow.

Just then, someone started to sing, further down the line.

Betsy's eyes darted toward the sound, finding a large family of ten or so, standing like a group of carol singers in their Sunday best. Freshly scrubbed, their hair neat, their clothes threadbare but clean, they had their pride despite their poverty. And their sweet voices carried twice as loudly as the church choir, singing a jaunty rendition of 'I Saw Three Ships' that soon had other voices joining in.

Unable to help herself, beaming from ear to ear, Betsy took a breath and sang with them—shy at first, but growing in confidence as more and more of the line joined in, from the exquisitely melodic to the rich and rumbling baritones to the folk who could not carry a note in a bucket, but had enthusiasm.

Betsy liked to think she was somewhere between the sublime and the ridiculous, letting her inhibitions drain away as everyone's voices filled the air.

People walking by on the adjoining streets stopped to listen, and some began to sing, the magic of Christmas capturing anyone and everyone who came near enough to its enchanting spell. It was, perhaps, the most heartening moment of Betsy's life, her eyes welling with happy tears as her body responded to the astonishing beauty of it all, her skin prickling into gooseflesh, like it knew this was something very special indeed.

*Can you hear me, Ma?* Betsy noticed the robin hopping along the curve of a nearby headstone, and knew that her mother could.

By the time she and her father passed through the doors of Christ Church, the line had moved through several carols, and were in the midst of singing 'The First Noel.' It mingled with the hymn that the choir were singing for a short while, before the thick stone of the church drowned out most of what was taking place outside.

But Betsy was no longer thinking about carols as she looked at the glorious display arranged in front of her—a Christmas feast as good as anything she had imagined. Better, perhaps.

Roasted goose cut into generous slivers, crispy golden potatoes that would never be as good as her mother's but made her mouth water regardless, sweet parsnips cut fine enough that the ends were slightly burnt and would be deliciously chewy, and vivid orange carrots covered in rosemary and the roasted in the goose fat. There were also what appeared to be tiny cabbages, steaming from their time in the boiling pot, and a rich gravy to pour across everything.

Betsy took her full plate and headed over to the tables and chairs that had been set up for the occasion, joining the woman and children who had been in front of her.

Kenneth sat down a moment later and clasped his hands together to say a prayer. Betsy echoed his movements, the two of them having their own personal conversation with the Lord, before they opened their eyes and flashed a smile at one another.

"Didn't I tell you we'd have a feast to remember?" her father said, eyes shining as he looked over the delicious meal.

Betsy nodded eagerly. "And I never doubted you for a moment."

"Well," her father said, "you just make sure you leave some space in your stomach for pudding."

Betsy looked over at the tables where they were serving food. "I don't think they have any figgy pudding, Pa. No mince pies, either."

"Still, you save some room," he told her with a cheery glint in his eye. "You never know what sweet treats might be waiting for you."

Excited and already as giddy as a child with a penny in their hand, Betsy prepared to tuck into the Christmas feast, grateful beyond words for the blessings that had come to them despite the mishaps that had gone before.

The moment she had handed the satchel of river pickings to the pawnbroker a few days ago, and he had all but scoffed at the shattered goods, she had been certain that Christmas was ruined.

When the pawnbroker had offered no more than tuppence for it all, she had been even more convinced. But she should have known better, should have known that all would be well, for her father would never, ever let her down.

*You are my Christmas blessing and my Christmas wish, Pa. You always will be.* She sent up her silent gratitude and, with that, she began to eat.

With full bellies and high spirits, Betsy and her father wandered the streets of London in the grey of early evening. The nights grew dark quickly in the winter, and the streetlamps had already been lit, illuminating the path that father and daughter walked together in a warm apricot light that chased away any ominous shadows.

They had been wandering for some time, heading westward, and though Betsy was content to just amble along with her father, he seemed determined to reach a particular destination. Now and then, he muttered to himself as if he might be lost, but soon found his way again.

Gradually, Betsy began to recognise the area around her. She had not been so far from the east of the city in a long time, but the half-enclosed market of Covent Garden was something that could not be easily forgotten.

"Oh, look at that!" Betsy gasped at the extraordinary scene before her.

Her father nodded. "It's always pretty this time of year."

'Pretty' was something of an understatement. Covent Garden had been transformed into a magical otherworld, the colonnades wrapped with green and red bows, while wreaths of holly and ivy adorned every stall and wall, and colourful tinsel had been draped between the stalls and over the balconies of the market's upper floor. Two Christmas trees had been placed in the piazza at the front of Covent Garden, overlooked by the imposing grey stone of St. Paul's Church, and those trees had been just as beautifully decorated.

Indeed, it seemed that Betsy and her father were just in time, because the small tree candles had recently been lit, sparkling like the stars in a clear night's sky.

"Are we here to see the trees?" Betsy asked, for though she had often wished that they could have a tree of their own, it was simply not possible.

Her father smiled and shook his head, leading her away from the breathtaking piazza, through an arched passageway, and down a narrow alleyway that ran parallel to the buildings that flanked the market square.

They were halfway down the alleyway, when her father stopped. "Smell that," he said.

Puzzled by the request, Betsy inhaled... and gasped in delighted surprise. A window had been opened in the wall, letting out the glorious scent of burnt sugar—like sweets and bonfires combined.

"What *is* that?" Betsy whispered.

Her father chuckled. "Confections, mouse. All the confections you could dream of."

There were actual bricks-and-mortar shops along the side of the market square, though she had not paid much attention to them. She realised they must have been outside the kitchens of a confectionery, with the confectioners hard at work, making treats and delights for the festive season, even on Christmas Day.

"You stay here and enjoy that sweet scent," her father told her. "I'll not be long."

Betsy frowned. "Wait here? Why?"

She did not like the notion of being left by herself in an alleyway, not after her recent encounter with the Rat Boys. One, in particular.

"You'll see," her father replied, and with that rare smile of his, he hurried back the way they had come, leaving Betsy standing in the dim alleyway, surrounded by the scent of sugar and the muffled sounds of someone in the kitchens singing carols as they worked.

She leaned against the wall and closed her eyes, imagining the twinkle of the Christmas trees as she revelled in the aroma of festive luxuries, wondering what on earth her father was up to.

## Chapter Four

Betsy must have drifted off, sharply awoken by someone shaking her by the shoulders. Her eyes snapped open to find her father in front of her, a paper bag stuffed under his arm.

"Come on, mouse," he urged, steering her quickly up the alleyway, away from the window that poured out such delicious smells.

Still half dazed, she did not ask questions or wonder why they were hurrying; she followed her father blindly, reassured by his hand on her arm, tugging her along.

Her belly was full, and she still had that lingering sleepiness that came from knowing she had eaten well. Nothing could have removed the heartened smile from her face.

They emerged through an arched passage, back onto the main market square of Covent Garden.

Betsy marvelled at the decorations and the twinkling candles of the trees in the piazza, her heart swelling with greater joy as the bells of St. Peter's Church began to chime out the hour, adding its music to the lively chatter of the sellers and buyers, and to the different carols that sprang up from pockets of stalls.

"Hurry, mouse," her father urged, snapping her out of her festive trance.

She bowed her head and quickened her pace, though her stomach began to ache with the rushed movements.

Cutting through the array of stalls and coming out the other end, back onto the open streets, a sudden pinch on Betsy's cheek prompted her to look up. A gasp slipped from her lips as she realised what the cold bite was.

"Papa, it's snowing!" she whispered reverently, sticking out her tongue to try and catch a snowflake. As sweet to her as any confection.

But instead of her father's voice replying, a loud, angry voice barked down the glass-covered arcade of the market. "Stop that man! Stop that thief!"

A strange feeling came over Betsy, wondering if she had been transported back to the labyrinth of Limehouse, running with all her might toward St. Anne's with a Rat Boy in fierce pursuit behind her.

She shook her head as the yell came again, more insistent this time. She had not been transported back in time; it was happening again.

"Run home, Betsy," her father urged, stuffing the paper bag of sweets into her arms. "I'll meet you there. Don't you worry about nothing. It's a misunderstanding."

Betsy might have believed him if he had not used her name. She had come to realise that he only did that when they were in dire trouble, and he needed her to obey without question. Otherwise, he called her "mouse."

"I have coin," she fumbled to say. "I have ma's ring. I can—"

"Just go, Betsy!" her father snapped, his eyes wild with worry.

All the while, footsteps thundered towards them.

She hated to leave him, hated to think what might happen to him, but she could not disobey him. With a protest lodged in her throat, she discreetly veered off to the left, walking quickly but not suspiciously down the road. There, she blended into the crowds that were making their way to the church or to the market to purchase a treat or a gift for that special day, and only when she was past the throngs did she break into a run.

Not once did she look back, terrified of what she might see.

In the sickly light of a solitary lantern, the glass panes ingrained with soot and the last candle dwindling quickly down to a useless stub, Betsy waited for her father in her corner of the dingy lodgings.

She and her father shared the draughty tenement room with three other families—a corner each—and Betsy observed the meagre festivities of those other souls with bleary eyes.

The mother and son in the far left corner had already gone to sleep, curled up together beneath a blanket of sewn-together potato sacks. But the other two families—the Westons and the Holbrooks—were seated around the fireplace on the back wall, talking in low voices as they ate the remnants of two wood pigeons and a bowl of oily carrots and potatoes.

The hearth technically belonged to the Westons, who paid more for the privilege, but they were never stingy when it came to offering the use of it. As long as someone used their own coal and wood, they could do with it as they pleased, whether to cook or to just keep warm in the bitterest months.

"Betsy, love," Gemma Weston said. "Why don't you come and have something to eat, eh?"

She was the mother of the Weston family. A robust woman of five-and-twenty, with four small children climbing all over her at any given time of day. Oftentimes, Betsy would entertain the children whilst Gemma rested or tended to the evening meal. They had already tried to play with her, but Betsy was in no mood to smile and laugh and pull silly faces to amuse them.

"I ate already," Betsy replied, her chin to her chest.

"At least come and warm yourself by the fire," insisted Marianne Holbrook, who just had the one child, and a husband who doted on her.

It had been a long while since Betsy made it home, her ears pricked for the distant church bells every time they tolled to let the people of London know the hour. Soon enough, it would be four hours since she left her father at Covent Garden. He was never away for that length of time. He *should* have been back ages ago, and with each passing moment, her fears grew.

"I have something I need to do," she said, getting to her feet and grabbing her threadbare cloak, "If my pa comes home before I'm back, let him know I went to the market."

Marianne gasped. "You can't be going out, Betsy. You'll catch your death."

"It's snowing, love. Best to stay here in the warm," Gemma agreed.

But Betsy would not be dissuaded. Fastening her cloak tight to her throat, she took out a small handful of the boiled sweets that bulged in the paper bag and handed them to Gemma. Her mother's ring would be enough to pay for those, while the rest would never be eaten.

"For Christmas," Betsy said, turning her attention to the children who stared at the sweets with eager awe. "Suck them slowly. That way, they'll last longer."

Marianne stood up, dusting off her hands. "Betsy, I really don't think you should go out. Your pa will be back soon enough. Stay and eat these with us, eh?"

"I won't be long," Betsy lied, having no notion of how long she would be.

With that, she skirted around Marianne's reaching hand, and darted out of the gloomy lodgings before anyone could force her to stay.

After all, she had what those shouting men had likely been after, and she would not let anything bad happen to her father because he wanted to make sure she had something sweet to finish their Christmas Day feast.

She had known the moment she walked away from Covent Garden that the sweets were stolen, but she had not thought of turning back to return the goods until she was already at their lodgings.

Had she seen sense quicker, perhaps all of this might have been avoided, but there was no changing it now. All she could do was make it right.

She walked quickly through the night dark streets, the amber glow of the streetlamps silhouetting the fat flakes of snow that silently drifted down.

A fair dusting already covered the ground, the snowflakes lavishing Betsy with icy kisses as she bowed her head and tried not to notice.

There was nothing she loved more than snow, and she had been eagerly waiting for the first snowfall of the year. But she would leave her enjoyment of that magical white until she was heading back to her lodgings with her father at her side. *Then*, she would marvel at it, hoping that when she awoke in the morning, it would be thick enough to make a snowman or to declare a snowball battle with as many families in the tenement as possible, as they had done in years past.

It seemed to take forever to reach the glowing lights of Covent Garden, her lungs hurting with every cold drag of air she took in, the collar of her cloak moist with the puffing condensation of every breath she expelled.

Her legs were sore, and her mood was at its lowest ebb, unaffected by the pretty sight of the Christmas tree candles still flickering, or the rustling tinsel in all its bright colours, or the beautiful wreaths that smelled of balsam when she passed by.

Taking a steadying breath, tucking the paper bag of sweets into the pouch of her apron, she marched right up to the door of the confectioner's shop and let herself in.

A bonny young couple were perusing the iced buns, already sharing a paper bag of what appeared to be candied fruits. They were well dressed in garments that would have cost more than Betsy could scrounge from the riverbank in a lifetime, the sound of rustling silk like cruel whispers to her ears.

She tried not to loathe them for their good fortune, tried harder not to scowl at their backs, and wandered up to the counter.

"What can I get for you?" the smiling assistant asked, a slight frown appearing between his eyebrows as he looked her up and down.

Heart pounding, Betsy took out the ha'penny that she kept for lean days, so he would not think she was a thief.

His expression relaxed at the sight of the money. "A quart of boiled sweets?"

"You must have to worry a lot about thieves," she said clumsily, uncertain of how else to broach the subject of her father.

The young man sniffed. "All sorts of chancers and troublemakers come in here. It's not often I don't catch 'em before they get away."

He gestured back at the huge glass jars of sweets. "Had a fella in here before who almost got away, but we got him caught."

"That's awful," Betsy choked. "I heard about it whilst I was outside just now. Couldn't find out what happened to him, though."

The assistant smirked. "What do you think happened to him? The constables came and took him to the Old Bailey. Expect they'll hold him there 'til he stands in the dock this week. It'll be quick, I reckon. Cut and dry." He paused, shrugging. "Anyway, what do you want?"

She already had what she came for, but wondered if she ought to buy the sweets that she had given to the Westons and Holbrooks, so she could offer up the full bag in exchange for her father's freedom.

"Ten sweets, please," she said, handing over her precious ha'penny.

The assistant took it and brought down one of the big jars of colourful boiled sweets. He scooped a full quart into a new paper bag and pushed it across the counter to her with a wink.

"As it's Christmas," he said by way of explanation.

Betsy picked up the sweets and held the bag to her chest, muttering "thank you" before she turned on her heel and left, stepping out of the warm, sweet world of the confectioner's and back into the icy chill of the market square.

*If you can give me more at no cost, why did you have to chase my pa?* It made no sense to her, as she stopped on the snow-blanketed flagstones and turned this way and that, not knowing where to go. She could return to her lodgings and wait for news of her father's trial, but what if she missed it?

Steeling herself, she headed east, towards the Old Bailey and the shadow of Newgate Prison that loomed beside it. A place that she prayed her father would not have to go.

---

Huddled against a wall in a recess between the courthouse and the prison, Betsy wrapped her cloak around her legs and tried to think warm thoughts. She pictured the majesty of St. Paul's Cathedral, which she had passed on her way to the Old Bailey.

She always forgot how enormous the cathedral was, with its dome and spires and golden statues up so high that it looked like it was scraping the heavens. The structure screamed a wealth that somehow never made its way to the poor, but it was beautiful to behold. It had been all aglow, a choir singing angelically within, but the doors had been closed, as if to say, "No more room." Rather fitting for the purpose of Christmas Day, she supposed.

Taking out a single sweet, she popped the sugary treat into her mouth and sucked on it slowly, determined to make it last. Savouring the fruity sugar, she closed her eyes and rested her head against the icy stone wall, not meaning to fall asleep.

But slumber or the cold must have knocked her out for a while, for she stirred to the sound of cruel laughter. Blinking open tired eyes, she could not make out the figure who loomed over her, the shadows too thick in the recess where she had hidden herself.

The voice was unfamiliar too.

"What a pretty thing you are," the man said in a gruff, sly tone. "You don't need to be on the streets, girl, when you'd do so well at one of my establishments. Why don't you come with me, eh? We'll give you a warm bed for the night, and you can warm some beds in return."

As her eyes grew accustomed to the dim, she could make out a coarse beard and glinting eyes. "No, thank you," she replied curtly. "I'm waiting for my father."

The man was certainly big enough to carry her away unwillingly if he had wanted to, but he simply shrugged and continued on with his cruel laughter, as if her rejection were the most amusing thing he had ever heard.

"Very well. You come to me when you've lost your high-and-mighty attitude. Ask for Don Durham, and you'll not be disappointed," he said. "Or, maybe, I'll find you, already on a street corner with all your value gone."

At that moment, Betsy realised there was a second figure. A young man, standing a short distance behind the first, just bathed in the orange light of a nearby streetlamp. She would have known that face anywhere, though he would not look at her.

The Rat Boy who had taken the pocket watch that could have prevented any of this from happening.

"I said no," Betsy snarled, though she was not looking at the big, grizzled man. She was looking at the one who was to blame.

The unpleasant specimen in front of her shrugged again. "Suit yourself. But don't be surprised when you do find yourself before me, begging me for a bed. It's a bitter cold winter, girl, and it's only going to get colder."

The man walked away and as he passed under the streetlamp, she saw he was the size of a bear, dressed well in expensive clothes, with a shaggy mane of dark brown hair. A monster to avoid, undoubtedly. The King of the Rats, perhaps.

Betsy turned her attention back to the Rat Boy, glaring at him though he probably could not see her ire.

He moved to follow his master, but as he left, something landed in a small drift of snow. It gleamed in the apricot light, just as it had done when she had first spotted it in the mud.

Betsy waited until the Rat Boy and his King were out of sight and scrambled toward it, snatching it out of the snow before the wet pile could cause any further damage. Turning it over and over in her hand, there could be no mistaking it—it was the same pocket watch, the glass cover cracked, that might have saved her Christmas. All too late.

## Chapter Five

Coughing and spluttering, the cold weather heavy on her lungs, Betsy hurried through the stormy city to get to the Old Bailey. Her cloak flapped behind her like a bird's wings, the vicious wind biting at her face, all the snow of Christmas Day turned to slush and black ice underfoot; the pretty drifts replaced with sleet that burned like needles on bare skin.

She had only had to wait outside the courthouse until the morning after Christmas Day to be told when her father would be standing trial, but that one tense night had been enough to make her sick.

Not that any ailment would have been enough to keep her from rescuing her father from the law. Still, for the past four days she had slept close to the smoke-belching fire of her lodgings, tended to by Gemma and Marianne and the children, who fed her broth when she was awake, and left her to sleep when fatigue claimed her again.

*Tomorrow begins a new year, and my father will be there to celebrate it,* Betsy told herself, pausing to cough. Great wheezing, wracking coughs that left her ribs aching. The moment she could catch her breath again, she hurried on, barging past anyone who thought to get in her way.

---

From the front row of the sparsely occupied gallery, Betsy fidgeted on the hard bench, constantly checking the contents of her apron pouch: she had the sweets, and enough coin from the pocket watch to buy her father's freedom if it came to it. She was not certain how it worked, but if what had been taken could be returned, and there was money enough to pay for the trouble caused, she did not see why her father could not leave the Old Bailey with her that day.

"Six months in Pentonville," the judge said in a bored voice, slamming down his gavel as he sentenced a young shipwright who was accused of stealing a roll of canvas.

An older woman, seated at the end of the bench where Betsy sat, held her head in her hands. Her wails drifted down to the man in the dock, who peered up at the gallery, clearly trying to get the woman's attention. But she would not look at him, instead comforted by the older man at her side, who put his arm around her and held her as if the young man in the dock had been sentenced to death instead.

Betsy pitied what she assumed were the shipwright's parents, but the sentence had given her some confidence in her father's fate. If the young man had only received six months for stealing an entire roll of canvas, surely a bag of sweets would be a week or two at worst, no sentence at all at best.

"Mr. Kenneth Martin of Spitalfields," the bailiff announced, bringing a painfully familiar figure up to the dock.

Betsy's heart lurched. Her father looked pale and exhausted, one of his eyes swollen shut with livid bruising. A recent blow, judging by the colour. It had not yet begun to yellow.

"His crime?" the judge asked, stifling a yawn.

"The theft of four pounds of boiled sweets from Milton's Confectionery," the bailiff replied.

Betsy gasped at the outright lie, drawing the attention of her father. His face fell as he saw her there, and he dropped his gaze, staring down at his feet instead of at her.

"Is the complainant present?" the judge asked in that same dreary monotone.

Another man stepped up into the plaintiff's box, unfamiliar to her. She did not know why she had expected to see the assistant there, when he clearly just worked for the confectioner. This man had a severe look about him, with sharp features, thinning white hair, and cold blue eyes. Not at all what she would have thought a confectioner might look like. Surely, someone who made sweets and delicacies should be portly and jolly, with pink in their cheeks and a ready smile.

"This man stole from me on Christmas Day, and when asked to give back what was stolen, he attempted to run," the confectioner said in a gravelly, unpleasant voice. "He is the dozenth miscreant to try and steal from me in a fortnight or more. I shan't let it lie again."

Betsy shot up from her seat, her shaky voice trembling out into the cavernous courthouse. "I have what was stolen!" she called out. "I have the sweets, and I have money to pay you for the trouble!"

"And you are?" The judge arched an eyebrow.

"I am this man's daughter," she replied, a lump in her throat. "Please, sirs, I have no one but my father. If he is taken away, I'll be alone. I sold what I had to pay for his freedom, and I have the sweets here! Please. Please, in the spirit of mercy and good will to all men, before it becomes a new year, might you spare him?"

The judge's expression seemed to soften, his bloodshot eyes turning to the confectioner. "Will you accept, Mr. Milton?"

Betsy's heart soared, daring to hope that there was a Christmas miracle to be had, even so many days past that celebration.

But the wiry, sharp-faced man scowled up at Betsy from the plaintiff's box, and her hopes deflated.

"No." The confectioner looked back at the judge. "This thievery can't be left unpunished again. An example must be made. I don't care about the sweets or whatever meagre coin this wretch's daughter can offer; I care about justice, and about preventing this from happening week after week with no repercussion for the criminals."

The judge sat up straighter, a haughty expression on his face. Clearly, he did not like to hear that he had not been delivering the measure of the law properly, the insult flaring in his eyes.

"Had he apologized and given what he stole back at the time," the confectioner continued, "perhaps an agreement could have been made, but that time is long past."

The judge shot a dark look at Betsy's father. "Do you have anything to say for yourself?"

"No, Your Honour," Kenneth replied, head still bowed. "It was a moment of madness, but I'll accept my punishment."

"Pa, no!" Betsy shouted, drawing snickers from some of the others sitting in the gallery.

Her father raised his gaze, a small, sad smile on his lips. With his hand on his chest, he mouthed, *All will be well, mouse.*

But how could it be when he was not fighting for his freedom? He had always been a proud and honourable man, someone who she had believed would never lie to her, but one little lie did not unravel his integrity. She had already forgiven him. What use was there in being separated for the sake of a bag of sweets? Did he not understand what his imprisonment would mean for her?

"Very well," the judge said with a weary sigh, his gavel raised. "If there are no arguments or concessions to be made, then I declare that Mr. Kenneth Martin of Spitalfields is sentenced to two years of hard labour at Pentonville Prison."

The collective gasp resounded around the courthouse, as loud as the wind that screamed in through gaps in the window frames. Even those who had been snickering at Betsy halted abruptly, their faces frozen in open-mouthed shock.

"For a few handfuls of sweets?" someone whispered, horrified.

Another shook his head in disbelief. "That shipwright got six months. What's Bobby going to get for nicking that coin pouch? A decade?"

But Betsy barely heard their mutterings, her head spinning. She knew what she had heard, and flinched as the gavel came down, but she could not process it. How was it possible? What was she supposed to do without him for two years?

The confectioner smirked, no doubt thrilled by the sentence.

Meanwhile, the judge looked up to the gallery. "Let this be a warning to you all, and to the miscreants of London, that petty theft will no longer be leniently punished. And let it never be said that Justice Roan is feeble with his judgments."

Betsy's last crumb of strength disintegrated, and like the older woman before her, she held her head in her hands and keened for the absolute *in*justice that had been delivered. Her father was a good man who had made a mistake; he did not deserve to lose two years of his life for what he had done. What he had done for *her*.

Suddenly, firm fingers closed around her wrist, pulling her hand away from her face. Another touch settled beneath her chin, tilting her head up.

"Keep your chin up for your father," a familiar voice hissed. "Don't let him see you weep for him. It'll only make it harder for him. Keep your head up and watch him leave. Give him courage."

She opened her teary eyes, and kept her gaze fixed on her father, her hand on her heart, as the bailiffs took him down. He watched her the entire way, shaking his head and mouthing, *I'm sorry, mouse.*

All too soon, he was gone, swallowed up by the unforgiving courthouse. Only then did Betsy turn to see who had helped her, though she already knew whose face she would see, staring back at her. She would never forget those grey eyes, the colour of the sky before a storm and the fog on the river that she would now have to witness alone.

# Chapter Six

"Why?" was Betsy's only question, as she smeared the tears from her cheeks.

The Rat Boy sighed, standing up without a word. He opened his mouth like he was about to say something, but must have thought better of it as he started walking quickly towards the narrow door at the top that provided the only escape from the gallery.

*Not this time...* Betsy leaped up, running after him.

She chased him down the winding stone steps, her footfalls echoing, and gained some ground as he slowed to cross the foyer of the courthouse without arousing any suspicion.

At the entrance, however, he took off at a clip, bursting out into the bitter winter storm that lashed the wide steps and the boxy sandstone structure of the courthouse. Betsy tore out after him, her lungs on fire as she urged her legs not to fail her, running faster than she had ever run before to catch up to that wretched man.

Had it not been for a patch of slush that had turned to treacherous ice, a short distance down Newgate Street, she doubted she would ever have caught up to him. But fate seemed to be on her side, the dirty dark slick sweeping the man's feet out from under him.

He yelped as he went down, crashing onto his back to the delight of a trio of urchins who were selling the dismantled parts of withered Christmas wreaths, turning them into sparse posies, on the other side of the street.

Betsy picked her way over the dangerous stretch to stand over him, glowering down at him with her hands balled into fists, as bruised snow clouds swelled above her.

"Why?" she repeated, breathing hard as a vicious bout of coughing threatened her chest, tickling in the back of her throat.

He glared back at her. "Why what?"

"Why bother to help me?" she replied. "Why drop the pocket watch? Why keep my head up like that?"

He sniffed and shuffled back, sitting up with a wince. "I don't know what you're talking about. I didn't drop any pocket watch, and sure as anything haven't helped you."

There was a note of something like guilt in the last part of that sentence, his eyes flitting away from her.

"Turn out your pockets then," she demanded. "I reckon we'll find that you don't have that pocket watch anymore."

"Aye, 'cause I sold it," he shot back, his accent laced with a lilt of the north. Scotland, perhaps, or somewhere close to the border. Just a hint of some other place. "And I lifted your head up 'cause you were embarrassing yourself."

"Why would you care if I was?"

He shrugged. "Don't know. Moment of madness, same as your father had when he took them sweets. It's gone now, so, if you don't mind, I'll be on my way."

"Off to escort your sister from the matchstick factory?" she snapped, folding her arms across her chest.

The man lumbered to his feet, bracing a hand against the small of his back as he bent this way and that, his face twisting in pain. But it did not stop him from smirking at Betsy as he said, "I don't have no sister."

"I know," she retorted.

He brushed the wet crumbles of snow off the seat of his trousers and expelled a deep sigh that puffed a plume of breath into the cold air. "Look, girl, I didn't help you and I'm not in the habit of it." He paused. "But I took something from you, and you're clearly not going to leave me be 'til you get something back. So, take this advice—it's more valuable than anything else I could give you. That man who bothered you the other night. Don't ever accept his offer, and don't ever find yourself out in Whitechapel after dark. He doesn't like to be rejected twice."

"Does your master know you're warning girls away from him?" Betsy spat, stunned by his idiocy. As if she would ever be compelled to accept an offer to sell herself. Did she really look so naïve to him?

The Rat Boy's lip curled. "He's not my master."

"You could've fooled me."

He pulled back his shoulders and gave her another curt look. "Take my advice or don't, but that's all you're getting from me."

He made to move past her, managing just a few steps before he turned back. "And maybe don't go mudlarking on the river anymore."

"I beg your pardon?" Betsy stared at him, astounded by his audacity.

He groaned and came back to her. "If you've got to do it, make sure you're gone well before dawn. That's when we arrive, when the sun is coming up. The other lads don't like to be there when it's still dark; they're usually sleeping off the night before."

"Did you knock your head when you fell down?" she asked. "One minute, you're telling me you don't care either way. The next, you're giving me *more* advice—that I didn't ask for, by the way."

Startling her, he grabbed her by the hand. "I don't like to see folk left alone, that's all. Think what you want of me, but I'm just doing what you were doing with that offer you made to the confectioner."

"And what's that?"

He shook his head. "I'm trying to make one thing right before the new year starts." He gripped her hand tighter. "So, let me walk you to your lodgings, and we'll say we're even."

"My pa is going to be in prison for *two years* because he didn't have the coin to pay for what he took. Coin he would've had if you hadn't chased me. You think some advice and escorting me home is going to make us even?" Her voice snagged on that perennial tickle in her throat, and the next thing she knew, she was bent double, coughing and wheezing as she fought to catch her breath.

Her eyes bulged, her head pounding, her lungs desperate for the air she could not get.

The Rat Boy's hand rested between her shoulder blades, his other hand dipping pickpocket-quick into the pouch of her apron. Before she could glare at him or hit him for stealing, he shoved the sweet into her mouth. She sucked it out of startled habit, coughing all the while, but as the sugar melted into a syrupy thickness, it slid down her throat, easing that aggravating tickle.

A short while later, she could breathe again, the boiled sweet coating her throat, making it feel less raw than it had in days.

"Better?" the Rat Boy asked bluntly.

She nodded. "We're still not even. Not a little bit."

"Fine, but I'm walking you back home," he insisted. "Can't have you keeling over in the street. And it's New Year's Eve, after all. It's pitiful to be alone on New Year's Eve."

She was about to tell him that he was at least partially to blame for her newfound isolation, but he was already tugging her down the street, and she was already following him. Deep down, after what had just happened and what would be waiting for her at home, she would have taken any company over the crushing devastation of sitting in her lodgings, knowing that her father would not be coming back that day.

"How do you know where you're going?" Betsy asked suspiciously, her hand warm in her unexpected escort's.

He laughed tightly. "I was in the gallery, remember. 'Mr. Kenneth Martin of Spitalfields' sort of gives away where you're from."

"Oh..." She had forgotten about that, her heart clenching at the sound of her father's name.

It still did not feel real that she would not see him again for two years, and she sensed that it would take a long time before it did. In the back of her mind, she somehow believed that he would be waiting for her when she walked into the tenement room, and that this was all just a terrible dream.

The longer she stayed away from the tenement, the longer she could keep reality at bay. Perhaps, that was what possessed her to say, "Can we sit for a while?" as they passed the gates of Christ Church, where she had spent such a wonderful Christmas Day. Half of it, anyway.

"Here?" the Rat Boy glanced up at the white-walled church, turning up his nose.

"What, are you afraid you might burst into flames if you get too close?"

He snorted, a crooked smile appearing on his lips. "We can sit awhile. I've got no place to be, and I'd wager you don't either."

"Your master won't be wanting his pet back?"

He narrowed his striking eyes at her. "Keep saying things like that, and I'll stop taking pity on you. I'll leave you to sit alone."

She withdrew her hand from his, feeling the absence of that warmth immediately, and headed through the gates. She made her way around to the side, wandering through the greenery and graves, stepping over the gnarled roots of the familiar yew tree, until she came to a rickety bench. She had no idea if the young man was following, or if he had decided to abandon her, but she sat down and fixed her gaze forward regardless, plucking out a sweet.

The bench groaned as a heavier body sat down beside her.

"You know there's a perfectly good church that we could shelter in instead. I'd prefer an inn, but needs must," the Rat Boy said grimly, pulling his greatcoat tighter around himself as the fierce wind tossed his curly, dark hair.

She shook her head. "I don't want to be inside just yet."

"With that cough of yours, you ought to be." He hunched his shoulders, tucking the lower half of his face into the collar of his greatcoat.

Too numb to pay the biting wind and stormy drizzle any mind, Betsy took out another sweet and held it out to him.

He eyed it like it was a dead mouse, but shrugged and took it, popping it into his mouth. A moment later, a smile spread across his face. "I haven't had one of these in years," he said, almost to himself. "Thank you."

"It's just a sweet. It's not forgiveness," she told him, in case he got the wrong impression.

He chuckled and stuck out his hand. "Clifford Kinross. 'Cliff' to most."

"Pardon?"

"It's my name. I'm introducing myself," he replied, rolling his eyes.

"Oh..." She took his hand and shook it. "Betsy Martin."

He nodded, his cheek bulging where he had pouched the sweet. "Nice to properly make your acquaintance."

"I'm not sure about 'nice,' but at least I won't have to keep calling you 'Rat Boy,' even if that's what you are."

"Why 'Rat Boy'?" Clifford asked, amused despite her remark.

She gazed out across the windswept cemetery, spying her old robin friend as it hopped from slushy snow mound to slushy snow mound, pecking at it and shaking any crumbles from its feathers. "Because you take what doesn't belong to you and scurry away with it."

"I can't argue there, though I'm not certain I've ever scurried," he said, following her gaze. "Your pa will be all right, you know. That's why I told you to look at him when they took him down—as long as he's got the memory of you to hang onto, he'll come out just fine. It's those who get taken down with nothing to encourage 'em that wrecks 'em."

Betsy crunched down on her sweet. "I hope you're right."

As they sat there together, sharing the now-useless bag of sugary currency and watching the robin, the snow clouds began to drop their feathery, delicate flakes down onto the earth below. The wind whipped and whirled the snowflakes, tossing them like blossoms in spring, and as the first icy flake kissed Betsy's cheek, the reality finally hit her.

Her father was not there to share the snow with her and would miss two Christmases to come. Perhaps, their recent Christmas Day would be the last they ever shared, for despite Clifford's encouraging words, she had heard enough awful stories of prison to know that not everyone came out alive.

*Ma,* she looked toward that decorated headstone, *what am I going to do without him?*

The robin chirped, having no answer she could understand.

# Chapter Seven

*February, London, 1850*

Crouched low like a furtive creature, covered in mud and so cold she could no longer feel her limbs, Betsy's intent gaze scoured the riverbank. To anyone watching, she likely resembled something that was not quite natural, not moving a muscle as if waiting to strike upon unwitting prey. But her hunt had no victims, and only she would suffer if she could not make a prized catch.

A glint snared her attention, close to where the grimy river tongued the slick shallows at the bottom of the bank.

Betsy was on it in an instant, hands scrabbling through the foul muck for that glitter of promise. Once she had it safe in her palm, she moved her hand back and forth through the murky water to wash away the last of the detritus that clung to her prize.

Only then did she allow her fingers to unfurl to reveal whatever she had captured.

Her numb heart leapt into her throat, witnessing the resplendent twinkle of a sapphire as big as a ha'penny coin.

It was the pendant to a necklace, the chain snapped, and possibly the most valuable thing that she had ever found in the treasure trove of the Thames. So valuable that she immediately tucked it into her father's worn satchel, and glanced around warily, fearing that the Rat Boys might suddenly emerge from the gloom to steal it from her.

With the nights still winter-long, she had more time to mudlark before those miscreants arrived with the dawn, but she never allowed herself to be complacent. They could appear at any moment to take what was hers, as they had done without warning over the past weeks. On several occasions, it seemed they had simply wandered from the tavern to the riverbank in the early hours of the morning, still reeking of liquor, to fulfil their task of intimidating her and robbing whatever she had acquired.

*When Spring comes, I'll have to find other work...* She was already considering splitting her talents for finding lost treasures between mudlarking and toshing--sifting through the maze of London's sewers for anything that would bring a good price. But she had not yet taken the plunge, fearing the suffocation and danger of the sewers.

Still, what she *was* making in income was not nearly enough, and difficult choices would need to be made soon. The pawnbroker constantly undermined her, giving her far less than something was worth without her father there to argue, and despite working twice as hard, she was struggling. After paying her rent for the lodgings she refused to leave—the lodgings that had been home for her and her father for years—she rarely had much left for more than a meagre meal each day. Maybe two meals, if the Holbrooks and Westons took pity on her.

She could manage until the days lengthened again, or so she kept telling herself. But even if she had to starve, she would not give up her home, for her father deserved to return to somewhere familiar when he was finally released from jail.

Thanking the heavens for the gracious gift she had already found, she continued on along the riverbank, pausing every so often in that hunter's crouch, eager to spot another glitter in the mud.

The past month-and-a-half of lone mudlarking had served as a brutal education for Betsy, but there were lessons that she still had not quite learned. Namely, that if she had one glorious prize, there was little use in risking it to find something lesser or nothing else at all.

As such, she did not hear the sound of footfalls getting closer, murmuring voices snatched away by a deceitful wind. Nor did she see the shielded glow of lanterns, for three sides had been painted black and the encroachers had the light turned towards themselves. If she had glanced over her shoulder just once, she would have been able to pick the figures out of the darkness.

But another gleam had caught her eye, and, like a magpie, she was transfixed. Not with greed, but with survival.

She had managed to free half of a gilt hand-mirror from a particularly stubborn chunk of mud, when someone tapped her on the shoulder.

"I think we'll be taking that," a gruff voice declared, "and whatever's in that bag of yours."

Betsy went rigid, not daring to turn, uncertain of which direction would be her best chance of freedom.

The figure behind her crouched down, his booming voice becoming a whisper. "It'll be easier if you just hand it over. But if you must fight, then make it convincing."

She finally turned to face the thief, a strange feeling pinching her chest. Clifford had not been a part of the band of Rat Boys who came to plague her very existence over the past weeks, likely busy with other tasks set for him by the Rat King, Don Durham. And now that he was right there, crouching so close, she could not help thinking of sitting on the cemetery bench with him, sharing a bag of sweets, feeling less alone.

Since her father's incarceration, she *had* seen Clifford here and there on the streets of Spitalfields and Whitechapel, but they never spoke, like enemy ships passing in a fog. They barely acknowledged one another's existence, in truth.

"I don't care what's easy," she seethed, her eyes flaring with ferocity.

He reached for the satchel and Betsy instinctively yanked it back, thinking of the glittering sapphire within. She should have stuffed it into her apron pocket or in the little drawstring bag that she had tucked down the neckline of her muddied dress, having been taught this lesson before. Why she had not was a mystery that she cursed herself for, as Clifford grabbed for the bag again.

"What's taking so long?" another masculine voice called down from the embankment.

The Rat Boys never liked to get themselves dirty if they could help it, always sending in one unlucky member to do the job.

Clifford wrenched the satchel out of Betsy's grip and had it up and over her head before she knew what was happening. Helplessly, she lurched for the precious goods, no longer caring much about the snapped necklace; she could not lose her father's satchel. She would not. It had been at his side for as long as she could remember, always filled with their carefully prepared breakfast, as well as the more expensive pieces they found.

"Give it back!" Betsy howled, but as she lunged, Clifford stepped away... and she fell, face first, into the muck.

The other Rat Boys higher up laughed cruelly at her misfortune, the sound bristling up her back with the burn of a nettle rash. She tasted the foul mud in her mouth and in her nostrils, her hands slipping and sliding as she fought to get back onto her feet. As long as the Rat Boys had her father's satchel, she would not be defeated.

"Give that back!" she spluttered, smearing her eyes with her sleeves, making her vision worse.

But Clifford was already walking away from her, the satchel over his shoulder, not even deigning to look back.

She struggled upward on all fours, but the riverbank had decided to turn on her. Her caked shoes could not get purchase, her slicked hands unable to grasp any of the spiny reeds or lumps of harder earth that could have helped her up, her body straining uselessly as she collapsed into the mire again and again.

By the time she was on the embankment, she truly *did* resemble something unnatural: a grim, dripping creature freshly emerged from the river, like the villain of a fable, told to scare children into doing as they were asked.

Meanwhile, the Rat Boys were already headed towards the dim lights of Limehouse, where they would easily be swallowed up by the streets and alleyways.

Betsy had lost the sapphire, and she had lost the last thing she had of her father's.

Sinking to her knees, she covered her dirt-smeared eyes with her filthy hands and sobbed as a bitter wind whipped across the riverside, bringing with it the sting and scent of a frigid autumn.

---

Betsy stepped out of the public washhouse as an entirely different person to the wretched creature who had entered it. Her dress was still damp, though it had been put through the wringer for what seemed like an eternity, but it was clean and so was she. Her scrubbed-pink skin smelled of harsh soap and her wet hair was tied up with a ribbon, the bright late-winter morning keeping the locks from feeling like she had icicles growing from her head.

The washhouse in Goulston Square was a fairly recent addition to Whitechapel, having only been there for a few years, and though she tended to avoid that part of London like her life depended on it—unless she had to deal with the pawnbroker—she had not been able to think of anywhere else to go. She could have returned to her lodgings, she supposed, but she did not want to waste water or coal on a bath, or bring the stench of the river in with her.

So, although it had cost her a precious ha'penny, she had soothed away her woes amongst the safety of women: old women, young women, prostitutes, beggars, factory workers, seamstresses, and every woman in-between. She probably would have stayed there all day, amidst the steam and soap and chatter of those women, if she had not had her next employment to face. Employment that rather made bathing herself seem like a foolish endeavour, for she was about to—at last— exchange the riverbank for the sewers.

Mr. Holbrook had told her of a man he knew who was always looking for willing workers to scour the sewers. All Betsy now had to do was find him at the public house he apparently frequented near Saint Pancras. First, however, she needed to traipse all the way there: an hour's walk at least.

She had taken no more than five paces before she heard a whistle.

Her head turned sharply, to find a familiar figure leaning against the soot-stained wall of the alleyway opposite. He still had her father's satchel slung across him, his greatcoat still too large for him.

Clifford beckoned and retreated into the shadows, knowing that she would follow. How could she not, when he had her prized possessions? And if it was a trap, then so be it; she did not care anymore.

"How many times have you cursed my name this morning?" Clifford asked as Betsy approached through the gloom, to where the alley branched off in two directions.

Betsy sniffed, folding her arms across her chest. "You'll find out at the end of your days, I expect."

To her surprise, he seemed to flinch at that.

"I'm... glad you got all that mud cleaned off you," he said, a moment later.

"Why? Are you taking me to Mr. Durham now?" She sounded a lot more defiant than she felt, some of that diminished pride shining through like a rainbow through heavy rain.

He pulled a face. "What would I do that for? You'd only refuse him again, and I'd get my ears boxed for it." He unslung the satchel and held it out to her. "I came to give back what's yours. Been waiting a fair while an' all—thought you'd drowned in that washhouse, considering the time it took you to come out."

"You *followed* me?" She glared at him.

He shrugged. "I didn't have aught better to do."

"You didn't need to take what you stole back to your master?" she said drily, suspicious of the good deed he was offering. It was the only reason she had not snatched for the satchel at once.

Clifford smiled but it did not reach his eyes. "Don doesn't care for worthless trinkets, Betsy. He cares about letting people think he'll take everything they have."

"Then, aren't you defying his wishes?"

"Maybe I am, maybe I'm not. Look, do you want the bag or not?" he pressed, shaking the satchel in the air.

Betsy took it hesitantly. "Why do this? You said you had nothing to do with the pocket watch, though we both know that's a lie. You said you weren't in the habit of helping. You said you wanted to do one good thing before the new year, but it's past the new year now and you already reached your quota the last time we spoke. Is this you getting your new good deed in early, so you don't have to worry about cutting it fine when December comes?"

"I just..." He paused, taking off his woollen cap to run a stressed hand through his dark locks. His hair was thick and wavy and clean, and looked like it might be soft to the touch. It seemed unfair that such a crooked man could be so extraordinarily handsome, though perhaps that was why he was so skilled at his work; the constables had proved without a shadow of a doubt that his looks and demeanour made him appear more trustworthy than an innocent like her.

A familiar ache surfaced, that he couldn't quite explain, she was alone. In that way, she reminded him of someone else. The memory of a coach door slamming shut flickered in his mind—his last glimpse of her. He pushed the thought aside before it could take hold. He expelled a strained sigh. "I've been seeing you around, Betsy, and I don't like that you're alone. I don't like that you have to do so much to gain so little. I don't like that what you *do* gain has a half-and-half chance of getting taken off you." He met her gaze. "When was the last time you ate?"

"What business is that of yours?" Her tone had a bite to it, but inside she was in a strange turmoil. Why did it sound like this miscreant cared about what happened to her? Was she imagining things?

He nodded to the satchel in her hand. "We'll take that to Kimpton's first, then I'm taking you for breakfast. You're naught but skin and bone."

"You're not coming anywhere with me," she protested, hugging the satchel to her. The dried mud flaked off and drifted to the slippery cobbles underfoot.

All of a sudden, he was standing right in front of her, leaving barely a hand's breadth between them. He was breathing hard as if he had just run the length of London and back, his lupine eyes shiny, his handsome face twisting into an expression akin to pain.

"I don't know what I started when I helped you before, but I can't stop whatever it began in here," he replied thickly, banging on his chest. "It's a feeling of... responsibility, and it won't go away. I've tried to make it, believe me. So, I want to keep helping you, Betsy, however I can. I know you'll not believe me, and I probably don't blame you, but it's the truth. It *is* partially my fault that your pa is in jail, and since I can't undo that, just... let me help you, for Pete's sake!"

She blinked at him in astonishment, stunned by the earnest nature of his outburst. It was as if he had been afflicted by something and she was the remedy, able to kill or cure him with one word of rejection or agreement.

"But... why?" she murmured.

He groaned, rolling his eyes. "Because you don't have anyone, and I took what you had. Truth be told, it makes me feel sick with guilt when I see you wandering by yourself in Whitechapel, getting thinner and thinner each time I see you." He shook his head slowly. "Until you've some meat on your bones again, I'm not going away."

"And when I have, you'll leave me be?" she replied, not quite knowing what to make of the situation. Indeed, if anyone had told her that the young man who had lied in front of constables to take her pocket watch would have been offering, sincerely, to help her, she would have laughed or recommended them to an asylum.

He shrugged. "Sounds like a fair enough exchange to me."

"And you won't steal from me again?"

He hesitated. "I can't stop the others from stealing from you, but I won't steal." He took a small step back, giving her some space again. "With that in mind, you need to be more careful when you're down by the water. Anyone could've crept up on you like I did."

"I was tired and cold and hungry," she muttered, by way of an excuse. A poor one.

"Well then, let me take care of the hungry part." He took hold of her arm, just above the elbow, and steered her down the left-hand branch of the alleyway.

As he walked her to the pawnbroker's shop, he cast her a sideways glance, adding, "By the way, that necklace you found—it's not worth much."

"You *looked* through my bag?" she snapped.

He smirked at that. "Call it professional curiosity. Actually, I saved you embarrassing yourself at Kimpton's. The pendant is glass, not sapphire—costume jewellery. The chain might fetch you a bit, but I wouldn't bet your rents on it."

She fought to hide her disappointment, refusing to believe Clifford until the pawnbroker himself told her the same thing... which the wretched man did, twenty minutes later.

Indeed, Mr. Kimpton of Kimpton's Pawnbrokers all but laughed her out of his shop.

"I told you," Clifford said, leaning against the wall wearing a lopsided grin as she came back out into the street.

Betsy glowered at him, not in any mood for japes. "And as it was probably the first honest thing you've ever said to me, you'll excuse me for thinking you were lying through your teeth."

"You're excused." He offered her his arm. "Now, how about we soothe the wound to your pride with some breakfast?"

She thumped him in his proffered arm. "I'm still not convinced the two of you haven't conspired together to share the riches between yourselves."

"After all I've done to get that bag back to you, why would I do a thing like that?" he asked, quirking an eyebrow. "I'd have just taken the necklace to Kimpton myself."

She eyed him closely, searching for any signs of deceit in the twitch of a muscle or the slight curve of a grin or the flicker of his eyelids, but he looked more offended than anything else.

"Eggs and toast," she said quietly, still distrustful but infuriatingly curious about the man who had helped her thrice now.

His eyebrow came back down, furrowing into a frown. "Eh?"

"I want eggs and toast." She straightened up and pulled her shoulders back, habitually feeling for the slightly plumper coin purse in her apron pocket. It was not the fortune she had anticipated, but it would see her through another week at least.

Clifford's face relaxed into a smile. "Eggs and toast it is. As much as Her Ladyship desires."

He laughed as he grabbed her hand and pulled her urgently down the street and out of the danger of Whitechapel where anyone might see them together.

# Chapter Eight

*Christmas Day, London, 1850*

"It hurts to move, Clifford," Betsy complained, holding a hand to her engorged belly. "When I said a walk might be nice, I didn't mean we should wander half of London."

Clifford halted by the stone balustrade of London Bridge, pulling himself onto the top of it in a boyish fashion that was immediately and infuriatingly endearing. He waited for her there as she waddled along through the slush, struggling to catch her breath. A few carriages went by, but it was almost ten o'clock in the evening and those with any sense were indoors with their families, enjoying the festivities and the last hours of their guaranteed day off.

"It's good for your digestion," Clifford insisted, chuckling as she paused beside him. "I *did* warn you not to eat that third mince pie or to have second helpings of the goose and potatoes."

Betsy groaned, uncomfortably full from the delicious Christmas feast she had devoured at Christ Church.

Surrounded by others like her, who either had nowhere else to go or had no coin to spend on such luxuries, it had been a bittersweet repetition of the year before.

Clifford's appearance, however, had been an unexpected surprise. She had been standing alone in the line leading up the church steps, discussing the possibility of more snow with a pleasant brother and sister who were just in front of her, when she had felt a tap on her shoulder.

*"You talked about it so much, I thought I'd see what all the to-do was about,"* Clifford had said with that charming grin on his face.

There had been some disgruntled mutterings when he had joined her in the line instead of going to the back, as would have been polite, but the transgression had soon been forgotten.

There had been carols and stories and good cheer all around, rising with the foggy breaths of those who awaited their Christmas dinner in the cold, and though Betsy had suspected that Clifford could have had a fine meal elsewhere, his company was not unwelcome. In truth, for a while, it had helped distract her mind from the stark absence of her father. Whenever she had experienced a moment of sadness, memory hitting her like a slap to the face, Clifford had swooped in with a joke or a remark about the wonderful array of food, smoothing the rough edges of her sorrow.

*"You can't cry on someone else's birthday, Betsy. It's not proper, and you wouldn't want people thinking you're a brat, now, would you?"* he had said, eyes twinkling. It might not have seemed like a lot, but it had been enough to snap her out of any looming melancholy.

"The ladies *forced* me to have two more mince pies," Betsy argued, resting her elbows against the balustrade, turning her gaze out towards the Thames that gleamed below. "And they gave me the second helping of goose and potatoes. It wouldn't have been right to refuse."

"I told you, it's because you're still skin and bone. One look at you, and no one can help trying to feed you up." Clifford slid down and came to stand beside her, both of them looking out across the river and the two sides of the city together.

The amber glow of lights stretched and wavered across the black surface of the water, as if the north side and the south side were trying to bridge the divide and join hands, forgiving old quarrels because it was Christmas Day.

"I'm *not* skin and bone," Betsy insisted, feeling suddenly shy at his closeness. His arm brushed hers, but instead of pulling away, they both instinctively leaned into it.

"Aye, you are," he retorted. "Doesn't matter what I do, there's not a bit of meat on you. I'd say it probably has something to do with the fact that you don't sleep, you just work yourself half to death, but what do I know?"

Betsy rolled her eyes, for this was an old quarrel of their own. "I don't have a choice, Cliff, and I *do* sleep. I sleep plenty. You can ask Mrs. Holbrook and Mrs. Weston if you don't believe me." She paused, her heart lurching into her throat. "Speaking of which, they've invited you to have dinner on New Year's Eve. Won't be much, but they're keen to meet you."

"Whatever for?" He glanced at her.

She shrugged. "I suppose they want to make sure that the man who keeps bothering me isn't going to cause me any harm."

"Bothering you?" He tutted loudly, turning his back to the river, a smile on his lips. "Maybe I'll stop."

"You've been saying that for almost a year now," she reminded him, discreetly scooping a large handful of fresh snow off the bridge's balustrade.

While he was not looking, his attention fixed on the opposite side of the bridge, she compressed the snow between her motheaten gloves, ignoring the icy chill as she turned that glittering snow into a perfect ball.

"Fine," he said with a huff of foggy breath. "I'll come to this dinner on New Year's Eve, but not before we've had our sweets at the cemetery."

Betsy's eyebrows shot up. "You want to do that again?"

"Of course I do," he replied, pushing off the low wall. "A tradition isn't a tradition unless you keep doing it. I like sweets, I like to watch the robins, that bench is comfortable enough—I don't see any reason why we shouldn't carry on as we were last year. Might even be better, now that you don't hate me so much."

"I don't hate you, Cliff," she said gently, rethinking her desire to hurl a snowball at him. He might take it the wrong way.

He laughed, almost to himself.

Not saying a word, he began walking again, heading for the south side of the river that cut London in half.

He had made it just a few paces when Betsy let the snowball fly, unable to resist the impulse any longer. She had never been much of a thrower, so it was quite the surprise to watch the snowball arch perfectly through the air... and strike Clifford squarely in the back of the head.

He stumbled and whirled around, eyes wide. "Why, you—!"

"It wasn't me!" she replied, chuckling. "It must've been someone in the carriage that just passed us."

Those startled eyes of his narrowed with playful menace, as he scraped snow from the balustrade and balled it between his bare hands. "It's not proper to lie, Betsy. You could've knocked me out."

"With a snowball?" She snorted. "I doubt it."

"Well then, I hope you realise you've just started a war," he said.

Flashing a wicked grin, he took aim and hurled the snowball in her direction. She felt the air vibrate as it sailed past her shoulder, but whether it had been a deliberate miss or not, she was in the mood for a festive battle.

"Brace yourself!" she shouted, scooping up another ball of snow.

"The same to you, soldier!" He grinned, his eyes alight, his expression warm, as he also prepared his ammunition.

To anyone watching from the windows of the passing carriages, they must have looked like two overgrown children, laughing and crying out giddily as they launched snowballs at one another.

They ducked and dived and feinted out of the way of their opponent's attacks, grabbing more snow on the way, until their laughter and their shouts of playful delight drifted out across the night-darkened river. Lost in their own world, it was the first time in an age that Betsy had felt so free.

And not for the first time that day, she found herself sending up a prayer of gratitude to the heavens, for without Clifford, she knew it would have been a very different Christmas. A sad, lonely affair, without a speck of joy in it. Thanks to him, she was pink-cheeked and laughing as if all was well and she had lost nothing. And *that* was a Christmas gift to be grateful for.

---

Clifford rubbed the back of his head as he and Betsy wandered arm-in-arm through the empty streets near Borough Market, on the south side of the river. He winced a little, casting her a sideways glance and pouting, to ensure that he had her sympathies. But it only made her laugh, quite against her will.

"You're amused that you probably dislodged half of my brain?" he chided, clicking his tongue.

She smiled and gave his arm a tender squeeze. "I told you I was sorry. I didn't know a snowball could be that hard. Please, say you forgive me."

A small fragment of ice inside one of the snowballs had brought their battle on the bridge to an abrupt end. The moment Clifford had called out in pain, she had run to him... and he had captured her in his arms, crushing the last of his snowballs against the back of her head; the snowy dust crumbling down her collar, sending chills down her spine. A dastardly trick, or so she had thought, until he said, *"That actually did hurt a bit, Betsy. I think it was old snow. Best we end with my victory now, so I can tend to this mighty bruise."*

Of course, she had argued that it ought to be a stalemate, and, after she had gathered up a fresh snowball as leverage, he had conceded.

"I forgive you," he said, his face cracking into a smile. "I'm just enjoying the sympathy for a while. It didn't even hurt that much."

She batted him lightly on the arm. "You're wicked sometimes, do you know that?"

"Not *so* wicked, I hope," he replied with a strange softness in his voice. Wistful, almost.

"No... not so wicked, I suppose."

Just then, the hazy glow from a shop window captured Betsy's attention, drawing her like a match girl to the blaze of a brazier on the coldest of nights. Letting go of Clifford's arm, she hurried towards it.

An array of delights sat upon finely decorated plates, set on a grand cake stand of vined metalwork, enthralling Betsy with the same envious pleasure that struck her whenever she wandered past the tearooms in the centre of the city.

She had not the smallest amount of room in her stuffed stomach, but her mouth watered regardless as she practically pressed her nose to the windowpane. There were sweet treats and fancies of all kinds: perfect little cakes, golden madeleines, glistening fruit tarts, a variety of French-inspired cream cakes; and shortbread biscuits that had been beautifully iced—shaped to resemble Christmas trees, stars, bows, and there was even a rudimentary donkey that made Betsy chuckle into her gloved hand.

But it was a currant bun, off to the left of the main display, that made her mouth water the most, reminding her of that well-dressed couple who had been choosing one at the wretched confectionery in Covent Garden. It was thick with decadent white icing, and though she could not taste it, she knew how gloriously sugary it would be, tempered with the tartness of those little currants.

"I'd have to mudlark for two weeks and not eat a thing to buy that," she mumbled with a sigh, eyeing the price etched elegantly on a little card beside it. It was not as expensive as some of the bakeries she had viewed with longing, but it was still too expensive for her.

Clifford approached, though he did not move to stand beside her. Instead, he leaned in behind her and rested his chin upon her head as if he had done it a thousand times before. An informality, a casual act, that pushed the air right out of Betsy's lungs, for he had *never* done that before.

"Which cake?" he asked, apparently oblivious to her racing heart and the shock that surely must have been written across her face.

In a daze, she pointed to the currant bun.

"So many beautiful cakes, and *that's* your choice?" he said, his chest almost flush against her shoulders.

She nodded, unable to breathe. "I've always... wanted to try one."

"I could try the lock if you *really* want one?"

"No!" she gasped. "Goodness, no."

He laughed softly. "I was only teasing, Betsy."

"Well, I never know with you," she replied in defence, her skin suddenly flushed as if she had a fever, warming her against the biting cold of the Christmas night. It would snow again soon; she could feel it building in the air, preparing to fall to end the day perfectly.

A gasp escaped her lips as his hand slipped into hers, his fingers interlacing with her own. He lowered his head and whispered close to her ear, "When I have made my fortune, I'll buy you one. I'll buy you so many that you'll never be skin and bone again."

Before she could say a word of thanks or protest or wonder, he was dragging her away from the bakery, his pace so hurried that she had to half-run to stay level with him.

"What's wrong?" she asked, noting that his expression had darkened.

He shook his head. "Nothing, Betsy. I've tired of this side of the river; that's all."

But she did not believe him. As he continued to pull her along, she glanced back in time to see four men emerging from the front of Borough Market.

They did not seem to have noticed Betsy and Clifford, but dressed in long greatcoats and woollen caps, she knew them even without seeing their faces: The Rat Boys had come looking for easy pickings... and had almost sniffed them out.

# Chapter Nine

*Christmas Eve, London, 1851*

"Anything shiny for me to pinch?" an amused voice called down from the top of the embankment, the shape of him barely visible in the dark before dawn.

Betsy raised her lantern so Clifford would be sure to see her mock-withering look. "No, but I've just sent for the ratcatcher, so you ought to make yourself scarce. Those terriers will think it's Christmas Day already, getting to chase you down!"

"I thought I heard barking. Figured it was you trying to scare off the gulls." Clifford raised his own lantern, grinning from ear to ear. "You coming up for your breakfast or are we swallowing half a pound of river mud with it?"

Betsy chuckled. "Let me just dig this out and I'll be with you."

"Seriously, anything good?"

She shrugged. "Broken bit of something silver. Not much but not nothing."

"Well, get digging then." He laughed and vanished back into the darkness, retreating to the spot that had become theirs over the past two years: A stretch of rickety pier that jutted out into the Limehouse Basin, where nothing ever moored for fear of the old wood collapsing.

Wedging her makeshift shovel into the frost-hardened mud, she levered up the broken half of a silver candelabra. The pawnbroker would still give her less than it was worth, but every coin made a difference to the growing cache she kept hidden behind a loose brick at her lodgings.

Pleased with the morning's treasures, she dropped the candelabra into her sack, now bearing more patches than it once did, and pushed *that* into the leather satchel that she refused to part with. After all, her father would want it back when he was freed from Pentonville, so they could carry on as if nothing had ever happened.

Whistling the tune to 'Deck the Halls,' she scrambled up the slippery embankment and paused to scour the near horizon behind her. There were no ominous lanterns coming along the riverbank, her lesson well and truly learnt. But one could never be too careful.

Crossing a stretch of road to get to the Limehouse Basin, she found Clifford by his lantern, hooked on the end of the pier. The sight of it warmed her in a way that would have appalled her two years ago, but she had found an unexpected friend in the Rat Boy who continued to 'bother' her, sticking to his promise to keep her fed.

"Took the liberty of pouring the water for you," he said, nodding to a bowl he had brought with him.

She sat down, her legs dangling merrily off the end of the pier. "You're too kind."

Putting the bulging satchel on her left, looping the strap around her thigh, she dipped her hands into the water, washing off the filth of the river. All part of the routine they shared at least twice a week. And she would have been lying if she had said she did not look forward to hearing his voice calling down to her from the embankment, letting her know that she did not have to worry about at least one meal that day.

As she dried her hands on a cloth, Clifford cleared his throat and dug into his own satchel, glancing at her shyly as he handed over a waxed-paper parcel. "Here. I got you something."

"What is it?"

He rolled his eyes. "That's the surprise. You're supposed to open it."

"Well, forgive me for not being used to gifts," she replied, chuckling.

Carefully, she peeled away the waxed paper, her eyes widening as they fell upon a currant bun, adorned with thick white icing and a solitary candied slice of strawberry.

"From that shop near Borough Market?" she gasped, remembering the snowy winter's day last Christmas, when they had walked together after enjoying a feast at Christ Church. How that glow in the bakery window had drawn her in, moth-like, and how Clifford had leaned in to see what had captured her eager attention.

If she thought about that moment for too long, she could still feel the warmth and weight of him pressing against her back, and the casual hand he had put on her arm. The tickle of his hot breath against her cheek, and the rumble of his laughter when he had noticed the price.

*"When I have made my fortune, I'll buy you one. I'll buy you so many that you'll never be skin and bone again,"* he had promised, taking her by the hand and dragging her away from the torment of the shop window.

Although, it had not been the currant bun that had worried him. Whether or not the Rat Boys had ever mentioned seeing the pair that night, a year ago, she did not know, but Clifford had not appeared with any new scars or bruises, so she assumed they had managed to get away in time. Indeed, that Christmas, she had spent her wish on him, pleading with the heavens to ensure that they *had* gone unnoticed.

Clifford smiled. "I know it's not Christmas Day until tomorrow, but I thought I'd spoil you early, since we won't be feasting together this year."

"We won't?"

He frowned. "Your pa is getting out tomorrow, isn't he?"

"Well, yes, but... that doesn't mean you're not invited," she insisted, wondering what her father would make of Clifford. She doubted he would mind once she had told him about Clifford's help and companionship; her father might even be glad that she had found a friend like Clifford.

Clifford shuddered. "With respect, I'd rather not. You've waited all this time; I'm not about to intrude. Next year, maybe."

"Well... thank you," she said softly, plucking off the candied strawberry and crunching down on it. She did not want to show how disappointed she was that they would not be continuing their new tradition, knowing she ought to be nothing but grateful that she would be with her father again.

As for the rest of the bun, she tore it in half, her fingers sticky with the snow-white icing, and passed the larger piece to Clifford.

"It's for you," he said, laughing. "You can't give back a gift. It's rude."

She shrugged. "I'll be rude then." She forced the half a bun into his hand. "And as it's my gift, I can share it with whomever I like. Besides, I haven't got you anything yet, so this can tide you over until I can think of something."

He bit into the bun and his eyes closed dreamily. "You just think about seeing your pa again," he said between blissful chews. "I don't need anything else."

It was because of him that she knew that her father was due to be released from Pentonville Prison on Christmas Day. He knew someone in the prison in possession of that kind of news and had relayed it to her a month ago. She had been counting down the days ever since, knowing that it would be the greatest Christmas gift she could dream of, to have her father back with her.

But the bun was not to be dismissed as inferior, nor was the gift of Clifford finding that news out for her. Indeed, she was not sure if she would ever be able to pay him back for all the kindness that he had shown her since her father was taken away.

They sat together, legs swinging, contentedly eating the bun, as well as the boiled eggs and bread and dripping that Clifford had brought. They spoke of the weather, the contents of Betsy's satchel, and of last Christmas, when she had almost knocked him out with a snowball to the head.

Betsy spoke of the Weston and Holbrook children, and how eager they were to see Clifford again, whilst he grimaced at the thought, declaring, "I still have a bit of hair missing where they pulled it out."

"Will you work less when your father gets out?" Clifford asked, finishing off the last part of a hard-boiled egg.

Betsy gazed down at the shimmering water as it reflected the first tinges of sunrise. "I hope so, but we'll see."

It had not been easy to bridge the income lost after her father's sentencing, but she had managed, working all the hours possible without collapsing under the strain. From noon until dinnertime, she toiled in the sewers; from evening until the early hours of the morning, she worked at a music hall near Drury Lane, serving drinks and fetching things; from the early hours until just before dawn, she picked through the riverbank. And between dawn and noon, she slept, delaying that blissful sleep for blissful breakfast on the days where Clifford visited her.

There were days when she had wanted to give up, too tired to see or think straight, but the promise of showing her father that she had taken care of herself well and had held onto their home kept her going. Moreover, she hoped to treat him to the delicious Christmas feast they had not been able to have two years ago, and that required a decent sum of money, especially as she intended to feed the Westons and Holbrooks too. She would not have survived without their generosity, just as she would not have been able to survive without Clifford's.

"Are you excited?" Clifford began to pack away the remnants of their breakfast.

Betsy took an unsteady breath. "Nervous would be the word I'd use."

"Why?"

She dipped her toe into the water, ripples distorting the streaks of orange that mirrored the sky above. "I have waited and wanted this for... what feels like an eternity, sometimes, and I just... I won't believe it until he's here, you know? I raised my hopes when his trial came, and they were dashed. I don't want to make that mistake again, so... I don't feel like I *can* be excited. Not yet. Not until I see him."

"You don't trust me?" Clifford sounded sad, but she could not see his face, his concentration fixed on putting away the breakfast things.

"I trust you," she told him, meaning it, "but I don't trust the prison and the authorities. They put a man away for two years for stealing a quart of boiled sweets. I have no reason to trust them."

Clifford nodded. "I understand, but you've got no cause to worry. Your pa *will* be free on Christmas Day. I've had it assured." He leaned in, putting his arm around her. "I promise you. I told myself that New Year's Eve that I'd make at least one thing right, and until he gets out, I can't keep my promise to myself either."

"Thank you," she murmured, resting her head against his chest. "If I live to be a hundred, Cliff, I'll never be able to repay you."

To her surprise, he bent his head and kissed her hair softly. "I don't want repaying. Consider this... I don't know, the cost for my immortal soul being saved or something."

"That worries you?" She peered up at him, remembering when she had said he would find out how much she had cursed him at the end of his days. She had not known it was actually something that concerned him.

He smiled down at her. "Sometimes." He released her slowly. "Now, get yourself to bed, lass. Sun's coming up."

"Will you walk with me?"

He flashed a wink and got to his feet, offering his hand to her. "I can't have you walking alone when it's not yet light outside. It's not safe. All sorts of thieves and brigands wandering around."

"Imp," she muttered, nudging him in the ribs. "How *is* your sister? Still working at the 'matchstick factory,' is she?"

He chuckled drily, his arm slipping around her shoulders once more. "I told you; I don't have a sister."

---

Betsy's teeth chattered uncontrollably as she bent near double, ploughing on through the blizzard that had seized London in its icy grip. It seemed too cruel that the snow she loved most could be turned into vicious, stinging pellets, turning the world so white that it was near impossible to see more than an arm's length ahead.

She wished she could have stayed in the relative comfort of her lodgings, offering to put more logs on the fire, but she made the majority of her income from the music hall. It was the employment she hated the least when the clients were polite, and the performances were at their liveliest. And, being the festive season, with everyone looking forward to Christmas, the atmosphere in the music hall became something akin to magic.

*I should have gone to the bathhouse another day,* she lamented silently, her wet hair frosting over where it had been teased free of her headscarf by the wind. The music hall proprietor liked his girls to be clean and presentable, but half-frozen was probably not his preference. It would take her an hour to thaw out.

"Oh..." she gasped, her heart suddenly cheering.

She heard the music hall before she saw its bright lights, a bawdy version of 'While Shepherds Watched Their Flocks' drifting towards her through the blizzard, like a dockworker clanging a pan in dense fog, calling a ship safely home to port. She chuckled at the change of words, and tutted in the next moment, wondering if there was anything sacred that drunken men would not twist with their affinity for rudeness.

A short while later, the music hall's glow filtered dimly through the haze of white. She followed it all the way into the warmth of the establishment, shedding her layers of woollen clothing with a smile on her face. It was going to be a good night; she could tell. And once the night was over, no matter how tired she might be, she would go directly to Pentonville Prison to wait for her father's safe return.

"Betsy!" A blur ran down the sultry red hallway, wrapping her up in an eager embrace. "I was worried you wouldn't make it. Half the girls aren't here, so we're a little thin tonight. Mr. Crawley is tearing his hair out, but that's nothing new."

Betsy hugged her friend, Victoria. "We'll manage. We always do."

"That's what I keep telling him, but he doesn't listen," Victoria muttered, pulling back. "You went to the bathhouse, didn't you?"

Betsy had to laugh. "I'll comb all the frost out before I begin and hope I don't accidentally snap my locks off whilst I'm at it."

The two ladies headed up the hallway of draped crimson velvet, adorned with holly-studded wreaths, twists of tinsel, big green bows, and folded paper stars. Out in the music hall proper, Mr. Crawley had made of point of making the establishment as festive as could be, with no fewer than five trees, every table having its own centrepiece of pine fronds, ivy, and holly, and tinsel and bows draped from every balcony and along the upper gallery.

The evening revue was also aligned with the season, with carol singers, a folk play about Father Christmas; and all the singers and dancers leaned into the festive spirit, their costumes vibrant and trimmed with white fur.

Even the humourists adapted their jokes and jests to fit Christmastide, though by the time they took to the stage, the audience would have laughed at anything.

Betsy and Victoria were just about to enter the dressing rooms, so Betsy could put on her own festive costume, when a grating voice barked down the hall, "Miss Martin, I need you!"

Betsy halted as Mr. Crawley, the music hall proprietor, marched down the hallway towards her with a face like thunder.

"What can I do for you, Mr. Crawley?" Betsy asked. A dangerous question in other such circles, perhaps, but not at the music hall. Mr. Crawley viewed his 'girls' as a necessary nuisance, rather than a menagerie to pick and choose from.

The red-cheeked man with his thin moustache and scraggly hair puffed out an angry breath. "Theodora isn't here. *No one* is here. And we have the most important clients we might ever have, short of the Queen herself paying us a visit, sitting in the private box with nobody to tend to them. *I* am having to serve them, but they will leave if it stays like that. I am not what they were expecting."

"Important in what way?" Betsy asked bluntly, cold water dripping down her face as her hair thawed.

Mr. Crawley shrugged in exasperation. "Sickeningly wealthy. More money than sense. Rich as Croesus. If we treat them well, they'll come back, and that can only be good for us all."

"Wealthy and generous, or wealthy with short arms and deep pockets?" It was vital to know the difference, because if it was the former, Betsy knew she could add a considerable amount to the sum she had been squirreling away. And just in time for Christmas, too.

Mr. Crawley clapped his veiny hands together. "Wealthy and generous."

"Give me... ten minutes to make myself look more respectable," Betsy said, sliding into the dressing room with Victoria behind her.

"Five!" Mr. Crawley shouted as the door swung shut.

Betsy split the difference, hurrying to throw on her festive costume: a gown of brushed red satin with rabbit fur trim on the hem, sleeves, and neckline which was not, under any circumstances, to be taken from the building. She combed her hair into a slicked bun and grabbed a few sprigs of holly and ivy, pinning them into her hair to improve the look. A scrap of gauzy red fabric finished the improvised ensemble, acting as a half veil that covered her eyes.

She looked at her reflection, dabbed a little rouge onto her lips, and headed out.

A long corridor took her to the door of the private box. She waited outside for a moment, smoothing down the skirts of her dress and taking a steadying breath, whilst muffled chatter drifted out.

Fixing on a smile, she knocked and entered... and immediately wished she had stayed at home.

# Chapter Ten

"A woman, at last!" The bearded, grizzled, belligerent man shouted, slamming his tankard down on the mahogany table.

Betsy bowed her head and hoped that the makeshift half-veil and vivid garments would prevent Don Durham from recognising her. Since her brief and unpleasant encounter with him outside the Old Bailey, she had mostly managed to avoid him, heeding Clifford's warnings.

But she had not been entirely successful.

At least thrice, she had run into him whilst walking through Whitechapel in the broad daylight. Once, when he had emerged from the White Hart pub, puffing on a pipe with a pleased look on his face. She had turned around and walked in the opposite direction, not knowing if he had recognised her or not.

The second time, she had just crawled out of the sewers, half-drowned after a sluice gate had opened unexpectedly, sending a violent wave of filthy water through the underbelly of the city without warning.

It probably should have killed her, but she had held on to an iron bar sticking out of the ground, surviving to live another day. As such, the very last person she had wanted to see was Don Durham. He had frowned at her, a flicker of recognition in his eyes, and had swiftly moved on.

The third time, however, had happened on the first of October, just a couple of short months ago. Clifford had offered to take her to the Great Exhibition at the Crystal Palace, as it was soon to close, and she had leaped at the chance. They had wandered through that ethereal world of glass and invention, marvelling at the creative minds of those who were putting their ideas and discoveries on display for all to see, dumbfounded by innovations that seemed to belong to another planet.

It had been one of the best days of Betsy's life, made all the better by afternoon tea in Hyde Park afterwards. The pair had been walking back to Spitalfields, at least one of them giddy with the pleasures of the day, when Clifford had suddenly shoved her into an alleyway. She had not known why until Don Durham approached, pausing to have a few clandestine words with Clifford.

She did not think Don had seen her in that alleyway, crouched low with her back turned, but having him so near, remembering what he had offered her, had ruined the gorgeous day completely. She had been a nervous wreck when she had finally crept out of the alleyway, and even Clifford had walked on the other side of the street until they were closer to Betsy's lodgings.

"Apologies," she said quietly. "The snowstorm has caused no end of trouble tonight, gentlemen, but I'm here now. What might I get for—"

She froze, seeing another familiar face in the far corner of the dimly lit room. Clifford slowly shook his head, his eyes wide to the whites. A look of panic if ever she had seen one.

"What might I get for you?" she repeated, snapping her attention back to Don.

The smirking, silver-toothed man eyed her from toe to crown, a fat tongue rolling across his lips as if he could taste something sweet in his coarse, grey and black beard. "What a pretty thing," he said, brown eyes glinting. "*Still* a pretty thing, I should say."

Betsy's heart plummeted into her stomach. He recognised her.

"So, you chose a music hall over my establishments, did you?" Don clicked his tongue. "I suppose it's not so different. Mercy, it's a pity though. A fine-looking woman, isn't she?"

He glared around at his cohort of Rat Boys—nine in total, including Clifford—and they all sat up straighter in their brocade chairs that Mr. Crawley insisted were exact imitations of the chairs at Versailles.

"Yes, Mr. Durham," they chorused, all staring at Betsy.

If any of *them* recognised her as the mudlark they used to steal from regularly, they did not even let the thought pass across their faces.

"Finer-looking now, I'd say," Don purred, lighting up his pipe. Inhaling, he puffed a plume of bluish smoke in her direction. "How old are you now, girl?"

Betsy cleared her throat. "Six-and-ten."

"Cease!" Don clutched a dramatic hand to his chest and, for a moment, Betsy hoped it was an apoplexy. "You're too perfect. It'll kill me not to have you in my collection of rare birds."

She kept her gaze low, her heart thundering in her chest, not daring to peek at Clifford as she said, "I don't much care for cages, Mr. Durham. Gilded or otherwise."

During her tenure at the music hall, she liked to think she had learned the most common characters that came through the doors. There were gentlemen who liked to be made to feel like kings, there were gentlemen who cared for nothing but the constant flow of drinks, there were gentlemen who were besotted with a different dancer every night, there were gentlemen who did not want to be talked to at all, and there were gentlemen who appreciated bold banter from their female attendant. She prayed she was right in thinking that Don was the latter.

The Rat Boys blinked in horror, and Betsy's confidence floundered.

A second later, Don burst into bellowing laughter. The Rat Boys joined in, nervously at first, until the tension dissipated.

"Oh, I like you!" Don roared. "Why, you've got me thinking I might have to steal you away!"

"I am as good an escape artist as I am at serving drinks," she replied, hoping he could not hear the tremor in her voice. "To find out how good I am at both, why don't you order something?"

Don wagged a thick, scarred finger. "If I can't cage you, I'll still hear you sing. Come and chirp a little ditty for me."

It was not a request.

Betsy moved to the balcony of the private box and peered over the side. The music hall was barely full, not at all as packed as it usually was, and there was a lull as the stage awaited its next performers.

Swallowing to help her dry throat, she began to sing a carol. A favourite of hers that she had heard for the first time in that joyful line outside Christ Church, and had loved ever since as a reminder of that brief spell of absolute happiness.

It began with 'Once in Royal David's City...' and she hoped she would not forget the words as her voice carried not just across the private box, but down to the main hall. Confused faces looked up as she lilted through the song, their bemusement turning into serene smiles.

A few began to sing along, much to the obvious distaste of Don, whose pocked brow furrowed into a grim frown. But Betsy took courage from the voices that blended and jarred with hers, and soon enough she was singing without fear, her voice high and sweet and strong.

Still, as she reached the last verse, it could not have come soon enough. "Not in that poor lowly stable with the oxen standing by, we shall see him: but in heaven, set at God's right hand on high, where like stars his children crowned, all in white shall wait around."

A moment of silence ensued, and Betsy's heart lurched into her throat. Then, to her relief, the men below began to applaud. Not one to be left out, Don thudded his meaty palms together, his dark gaze simmering in the dim light.

Clifford and the Rat Boys followed their master's lead, and Betsy dared to dip into a curtsey, careful to ensure it did not look like she was mocking Don.

"A charming voice," Don growled. "Wasted on a pitiful song like that, but charming nonetheless."

"It's Christmas tomorrow, Mr. Durham. I thought you might prefer something festive," she replied.

"Christmas is a farce," Don snarled back. "A day for idlers and pretenders. All that talk of God on high and decking halls and good will to all men. No man ought to be celebrated for being born. It's what a man does with the rest of his life that matters. Can't abide all these simpering fools."

Betsy blinked at him, horrified to hear anyone say such things out loud. Then again, she supposed she should not have expected anything less from a man who had clearly made his fortune off the backs of desperate, downtrodden, destitute women. A man who sold bodies to other men and called himself successful.

It made her sick just looking at him.

"Can I fetch you any drinks now?" she asked, putting a tight smile on her face.

Don sniffed. "Three bottles of your finest brandy and one of whatever whisky you have."

"Of course." She dipped into another curtsey and walked out of the room.

She had never been more grateful for the sound of the door closing behind her, putting solid wood between her and that wretched beast.

Taking a few seconds to swallow her anger and gather herself, she set off in search of the bottles Don had asked for, fully intending to take as long as possible. In fact, if it were not for the fact that she needed all the money she could make, she might have walked right out into the blizzard and returned home, risking the loss of her employment instead of having to contend with such a vile specimen all night.

"Betsy?" A hushed voice pursued her down the hallway.

She turned, her entire being relaxing as she saw Clifford running toward her. "I didn't expect to see you here tonight. Ever, in truth."

"I didn't know we were coming," Clifford said in earnest. "If I had, I would have found a way to get word to you, to tell you not to be here. Betsy, you have to leave. At once."

She frowned up at him, noting his blanched complexion and the worried creases that furrowed his brow. "I can't leave, Cliff."

"You have to," he urged, glancing back over his shoulder as if he expected Don to stride out at any moment. "It's not safe. I told you that he doesn't like to be rejected twice, and you've rejected him more than twice. What's more, I doubt he was joking when he said that he would steal you. It... wouldn't be the first time."

An uneasy feeling squirmed in her belly as she stared at the man who had become so dear to her. "Why do you work for him, Cliff? Why *would* you work for such a beast, if he does horrible things all the time?"

"I'll tell you, one day," he replied, head bowed.

"You always say that."

In two years, she still had not managed to get him to explain.

He sighed, sweeping a hand through his dark curls. "I know, but... you said you trusted me, didn't you?"

"Yes, but—"

"Then leave now." He dipped into the pocket of his woollen waistcoat, pulling out a pouch of coins. "For this, will you go?"

She eyed the pouch, not elated by the sight, but deeply disappointed. "If I take that and leave this minute, I'll lose my employment. Whatever is in there might last me a while, but until my father is back on his feet, I can't risk losing any of my employment. And if you think I want to rely solely on mudlarking and toshing, you're mistaken. Nor do I want to rely on your charity, Cliff."

"It's not charity, Betsy," he urged. "It's... a Christmas gift. Take it and go, and... and... if I have to, I'll help you find work *like* this. Or I'll speak with Mr. Crawley for you. But I can't have you here tonight. It's not safe. Don... isn't pleased and I don't know what he'll do."

She smiled sadly. "You already gave me a Christmas gift. It was the most delicious thing I've ever eaten." She sighed and reached for his hands, squeezing them gently. "Nothing is going to happen, and I'm telling you, I *can't* leave. I won't. I almost have enough for me and my pa to have a slightly better life, and I would like to maintain that. So, please, don't worry."

"You don't understand," Clifford murmured, shaking his head.

She raised up on tiptoe and pressed a daring kiss to his cheek. "You're here, Cliff. As long as you are, I'll be safe. *That* is what I trust."

"But—"

"I have work to do," she said, letting go of his hands.

Without another word, she left him standing in the hallway, his fingertips reaching up to touch his cheek. And as she passed through the doors into the liquor storage, she touched her own fingertips to her lips, as they tingled with the echoing brush of his skin against them.

# THE RAGGED MUDLARKE'S CRHISTMAS MIRACLE

# Chapter Eleven

"How are you all faring?" Betsy asked, returning to the private box for what felt like the millionth time that night. "Is there anything else I can fetch for you?"

The Rat Boys and their disgusting King had ploughed through all three bottles of brandy and the one bottle of whisky as if it were water, and with every gulp and sloshing glass of the stuff, they became louder and rowdier and more of an irksome nuisance to everyone else. After four more bottles, they were completely feral.

The only one still sober was Clifford, who had been discreetly pouring his measures into a slops bucket to the side of where he sat, but as Betsy looked around the wreckage of the private box—chairs and tables upturned, drapes ripped down, plants upended, paintings tossed over the balcony—she could not find him.

"I want you to drink with me!" Don bellowed, gaining sharp glares from the audience below, who were attempting to enjoy the dancers in their Christmas costumes.

But every time the dancers kicked their legs high in the air, the roars coming from the private box rather ruined the experience.

Betsy smiled stiffly. "I can't do that, Mr. Durham. Mr. Crawley doesn't like his girls to imbibe from his stock."

That was not technically true, but she did not want to drink with Don. She would not have taken a drink if it had been anyone, for fear of the potent liquor preventing her from making it to her important appointment in the morning. She could not risk anything making her sleepy.

"I paid for it, and I say you will drink with me!" Don slammed his glass down on the table so hard that it shattered.

With a shiver of panic beetling up her spine, Betsy went to the spot by the balcony where she had sung for him earlier. Close enough and far enough from that awful man. She still did not want to drink with him, but nor did she want his anger to turn more violent and, worse, to turn on her.

"Just one, then," she said softly, soothingly, hating every word. "But no more, or you'll get me in trouble."

Don grinned, his eyes unfocused. "Just one. Like a good girl."

He plucked the bottle from by his foot, and, with an unsteady hand, he poured a glass of brandy for Betsy. It sloshed over the sides and spilled across the table, but that would not be her problem until later, when she had to clean up the royal mess they had made.

"Drink," Don rasped, shoving the glass into Betsy's hand.

Pinching her nose and willing her stomach to bear it, she downed the measure in one go. And though Don Durham was not someone she would have wasted a Christmas wish on, she wished in that moment that all of the Rat Boys and their abhorrent Rat King would pass out soon.

---

Betsy stumbled between the upturned tables and broken chair legs, fumbling for anything she could use to keep herself upright. She closed one eye and squinted in an attempt to find the exit to the private box, but her vision was butter-slicked, the world around her just a jumble of shapes and muffled noise, as if she were underwater.

She had been in the private box, pouring brandy for the Rat Boys for no more than half an hour since she, herself, accepted the drink from Don. But something was wrong. This was not merely the effects of one measure of brandy; it could not be. Her legs were too wobbly, her entire body not responding at all to what she wanted it to do, her feet feeling as if they were made from blocks of stone.

Halfway to what she hoped was the door, her hand missed the leg of an upturned table. She fell forward, staggering into something hard that knocked into her ribs, winding her. Whether it was the side of a table or a fist, she had no way of knowing; everything was a smudge in her vision.

But she *was* aware of cruel laughter, cackling all around her. The more she stumbled and searched for the door, the louder the laughter grew.

She closed her eyes altogether and tried to concentrate on her breathing, but every gulp of air was sluggish and lacking, leaving her chest tight. *Clifford... Where is Clifford?* He would help her. He would come to her aid. He needed to make things right for the sake of his immortal soul. But where *was* he? She could not remember, nor could she make out anyone's faces from the shadows that danced and swayed around her.

All of a sudden, a booming voice cut through the muffled babble, and a rough hand seized her above the elbow. "Time for us to leave, boys," it said. "Festive delights await."

An explosion of laughter prompted Betsy to try and cover her ears, but her arms would not move, flapping uselessly at her sides. As for her legs—they would not get her anywhere fast, either.

But she need not have worried about that, as a powerful arm grabbed her around the waist, squeezing so hard she thought she might be sick. Whoever that grip belonged to seemed determined to drag her out of the private box, though all she saw of her departure was the shift from gloom to brighter lights and the shine of tinsel glittering from the walls.

*Pretty... So pretty... I wonder if the lights are still twinkling in Covent Garden... I can smell the Christmas tree... I hope Cliff will have sweets with me this year...* Her mind wandered as she was hauled along, and though she was vaguely aware of someone shouting after her, the vice around her waist did not ease at all.

*I think I'm in trouble...* Indeed, her clenched chest and racing heart definitely *knew* she was in danger, but there was not a single thing she could do about it. She had once thought that Don was big enough to kidnap her if he wanted to, and she suspected through the daze of her mind that that was exactly what he was doing.

Out of nowhere, an icy blast struck her in the face, the whip of the blizzard lashing at her cheeks as if it was trying to wake her up and snap her out of whatever was wrong with her. She blinked, rousing from her stupor just a little bit, the cold bite of the snowstorm taking the edge off her confusion.

"I'll take her," someone called out.

"This is precious cargo, so don't you go damaging her before she gets to port," Don's unmistakably gruff voice replied, as she was roughly pushed towards a nearby shape. An animal scent wended its way into her nostrils—sweet and comforting.

"I won't," the voice replied.

New hands, gentler than before, lifted her up to a higher height. A pressure pushed against her stomach, her fingertips touching the rippling side of what appeared to be a horse.

"Merry Christmas," she whispered to the creature.

A soft nicker replied.

"Thank you," she murmured, stroking the horse as carefully as her shaky hands would allow.

She winced and wheezed as someone clambered up behind her, the pressure on her ribs and stomach turning to the throb of would-be bruises as the horse began to move, swaying slowly from side to side as the rider urged it on. All the while, the blizzard whipped and whirled around her, determined to keep her awake despite the pulling desire to fall fast asleep.

"When I say the word," a familiar voice whispered, "I'm going to push you from the horse, and it's probably going to hurt, but then you're going to run. You're not going to stop until you reach somewhere safe. Anywhere safe. Do you understand?"

Still dazed, but increasingly sharpened by the constant blast of frigid air in her face, Betsy made a noise of assent. Her mind was not entirely certain in its foggy state, but her heart knew with *all* certainty that it was Clifford behind her, holding her, keeping her safe before he put himself in quite obvious danger.

Not for the first time, he was prepared to risk Don's punishment to ensure that she survived. And all she could think as she faintly realised that truth was, *I should have left when you told me to.*

# Chapter Twelve

Betsy's mind faded in and out of clarity, like a pool where someone had decided to skim stones. Her awareness rippled and stilled, rippled and stilled, helped along by the bite of the blizzard and the ache in her ribs, where she lay draped over the horse's back.

Through the hazy white veil of driving snow, two streaks of orange highlighted the carriage ahead. Don's carriage, leading the way towards something undoubtedly terrible.

"We are almost at Whitechapel," Clifford's familiar, soothing voice whispered. "You have to run soon. Can you manage it?"

She tried to twist her head to see him, to take comfort from his striking grey eyes and easy smile, but all she could make out was a dark blur. "I can... manage," she told him, hoping she sounded more confident than she felt.

Her memory of why she was going to have to run kept drifting in and out too, a fog slithering on the morning tide, but she trusted in the man sitting behind her.

If he told her to flee, she would. She just had to hope she would not forget the reason *whilst* she was running, without Clifford there to encourage her.

For a few more minutes, or perhaps an eternity, the horse plodded on across snow blanketed cobblestones, the two lanterns on the carriage multiplying into countless dancing orbs of amber. To either side of the horse, other shapes began to appear and disappear: cramped and lopsided terraces, the candlelight and babbling noise of a public house, the darkened fronts of closed shops. In the butcher's window, a sad, solitary, holly-studded goose took pride of place, plucked and prepared for a Christmas feast that no one in Whitechapel could ever hope to afford. No one who made their money through any respectable means, anyway.

*If that has not been stolen before Christmas Day, it will be a miracle,* she mused, passing a greengrocer and a bakery, decorated for the festive season in a similarly stark fashion. The bakery had, at least, made a few loaves and arranged them to resemble a Christmas tree, while the greengrocer had a single Christingle on an old apple crate: an orange studded with cloves, with a candle protruding from the top and a red ribbon tied around it.

If that rare delicacy of a fruit made it to Christmas Day too, she would be doubly shocked. Indeed, she would not have been surprised if that Christingle was not the original, but the descendant of those that had already been stolen and devoured.

She was just peering into the window of the fishmonger, to see if they had bothered with festivities, when Clifford hissed a sharp, "Now!"

He grabbed the back of her dress and yanked her backwards as hard as he could, before she was at all prepared for it. There was a moment of slipping, her hands instinctively trying to grab onto whatever they could to prevent herself from tumbling, but there was nothing to keep her atop the horse. She slid off, falling for half a second before her feet hit the ground with a jarring impact that splintered pain up her left ankle. Her knees buckled with it, and she crumpled to the ice and snow for a fleeting, hopeless span of time that felt like hours.

"Run, Betsy!" Clifford rasped desperately.

Those two words awoke something in her, something habitual and unconscious, driving her up onto her feet. Ahead of her, around the horse, she spied the dark mouth of an alleyway… and took off.

She dove into the shadows, her arms out to either side of her, feeling her way down the grimy, freezing cold walls. Her legs were still wobbly, her head still hazy with a blizzard of her own, but the rest of her body had taken over, and it seemed to know exactly where she was, and where she needed to go. A memorised map that she had unwittingly crafted in her subconscious mind after years of being told to run, after years of being harassed for the smallest spoils, after years of knowing that if she did not lose her pursuer, she would lose far more.

As the alleyway forked into two more passages, she thought she heard Clifford's voice ringing out, bellowing for help, shouting at the top of his lungs, "She got away! She got away!"

*What is he doing?*

Her addled brain did not understand, her heart sore at the thought that he had not facilitated her escape but was merely playing his part in some game that Don wished to play. She had heard that the gentry hunted foxes for sport, but what if vile, crooked overlords of London's underbelly liked to hunt women for sport?

Whatever was afoot, she was not going to allow anyone to play games with her.

Brimming with a potent yet useful wave of panic, she turned right at the fork in the alleyways. As she did, she prayed that Don and his men would expect her to turn left instead, following a path that would lead her back the way she had come instead of deeper into the black heart of Whitechapel.

As she hurried along, her mind played tricks with her. She thought she heard footsteps close behind, fear gripping her as she braced for a hand to seize her. She thought she heard voices where there were none, she thought she heard her father calling to her out of the darkness and might have stopped to heed that call if the alert part of her mind had not reminded her where her father was. And through the thick walls to either side of her, she was certain she could hear girls singing in high, sweet voices—evensong hymns that never failed to remind her of Christmas Eve, surrounded by candles, in chilly churches where she and her father would pay their respects.

At length, the warren of protective alleyways came to an abrupt end, and she stumbled out into the threat of the open streets. Her still blurry eyes darted this way and that, half expecting Don to come surging out of the shadows to catch her, having scented her fear like a hunting dog.

Bowing her head, she made her way down the street at a slower, less suspicious pace, flinching at every carriage that rattled by. Drunkards yelled from the nearby inns and alleys and street corners, each one possessing the face and voice of the man who was after Betsy.

"You all right, love?" Someone finally caught hold of her arm, pulling her to a halt.

Betsy peered up, terrified, only to find herself looking into the worried, black-smeared eyes of a strumpet. The lady of the night wore a ripped and tarnished red dress that might have been beautiful once, with a flimsy woollen shawl around her shoulders, yet she did not seem to feel the cold at all. A jar of 'Mother's Ruin' could help with that, the potent liquor making a body and soul numb to everything.

"You in some trouble?" the woman pressed, looking quickly over Betsy's shoulder.

Betsy grasped the woman's hands. "I need... a church. I need to get off... the street."

*Her* teeth chattered violently, the cold sinking deep into her bones as the blizzard continued to whip and whirl around the city, pummelling down the main thoroughfare of Whitechapel like an invisible battalion of artillerymen, firing at will. The more whatever Don had put in the brandy wore off, the more she felt each intolerably cold sting.

"This way, sweetling," the dollymop said, swiftly pulling Betsy through a narrow doorway.

A thick haze of smoke bombarded Betsy's senses, making her throat tighten and her eyes water, as the unknown strumpet pulled her on through a grim corridor.

Through half-closed doors, Betsy saw things that made her quickly look away, and turned her fleeting relief into a fresh bout of panic. What if this woman was not going to help her, but was planning to trap her in the very thing she had attempted to escape with Don?

Still, Betsy allowed herself to be led, her legs protesting every step of the way, her vision phasing in and out. Following this woman was her only real choice, unless she wanted to run back to the street and attempt to find somewhere to hide in her weakened, disoriented condition, where Don might capture her at any moment.

They wended through a maze of corridors, barely illuminated by anaemic lanterns, until they came to another door. The lady of the night eked it open and ushered Betsy out into a small, bleak yard with another door at the end.

"Take that door out into the alley behind and turn right. Follow it to the end and you'll be ten paces from St. Mary's," the woman said in earnest. "But hurry now. The weather's not going to get no better tonight, and you ought to be warm in your bed at such an hour."

Betsy was halfway across the yard when she turned, remembering her manners. "Thank you, Miss."

"Ain't no thing but what I wish someone had done for me," the woman replied, dipping her head in a small nod.

Betsy hesitated. "Merry Christmas to you."

"Pardon?" The woman's eyes widened.

"Merry Christmas to you," Betsy repeated more shyly. Perhaps, this poor woman had the same feelings about the festive season as Don.

The young woman suddenly smiled, a grin so bright and cheerful it was as if the moon had managed to break through the maelstrom of the blizzard. "Mercy, I can't remember the last time anyone said to that to me. Truth be told, I'd half-forgotten it was Christmas at all." Her voice hitched in a way that tugged on Betsy's heart. "Merry Christmas to you too."

In that instant, for just a few seconds, Betsy could see the girl that the woman had been. Someone sweet and excitable, who had not yet been marked and trampled by the world around her. Someone who had looked forward to Christmas once, but now let it pass by as if it were just another day. But perhaps, this year, she would continue to remember and find some joy in it again. *That* was Betsy's hope for the woman who had helped her, as she let herself out of the back gate and into the alley, following the directions to St. Mary's.

It seemed strange that the old church should be so close to such nests of vice and disrepute, but the woman had not lied. As soon as Betsy made it to the end of the alleyway, it was a short distance to the church that gave the territory of Whitechapel its name, the grey exterior occasionally whitewashed to restore it to its former colour.

She ran that last stretch with everything she had left to give, sprinting up to the doors and pounding her fists upon it. Choral voices rose up together within, communing with the heavens, but the otherworldly conversation ended sharply as Betsy's interruption echoed through the building.

Footsteps scuffed within, at the same moment that footsteps thundered somewhere behind her too.

She did not know if the latter were real, or merely shutters banging in the storm, but it was enough to make her thump more desperately against the doors.

The door opened to reveal a short, thin woman with spectacles and lacquered grey hair. "May I help you?"

"I need safety. I am... not well," was all Betsy could find the strength to say as she slumped against the door.

Another face appeared, belonging to a more robust woman. Without saying a word, both women took hold of an arm apiece and aided Betsy into the glowing, candlelit protection of St. Mary's. And though Betsy did not know which Mary the church was named after, she liked to think it was the one who knew what it was like to have a door closed in her face when she needed somewhere safe the most. Just as she liked to think that there was a reason it was *this* church that she had found her way to, thanks to the kindness of a stranger.

"If you sit here awhile, we'll come and tend to you when we're done," the older woman said gently, guiding Betsy to a pew near the back of the church.

Betsy sat obediently. Now that she was no longer running, she shuddered violently as the true depth of the cold finally hit her.

Noticing the violence of Betsy's shaking, the younger, stronger of the two women who had helped her in went to fetch some blankets. And soon enough, Betsy was wrapped in layer after layer of musty-scented wool and left to warm up in peace as the women returned to the opposite corner of the church, where they appeared to be preparing refreshments.

The choir had resumed already, the loveliest sound that Betsy had ever heard. They were singing one of her father's favourite festive hymns and, in that moment, she finally allowed herself to believe that he *would* be coming back to her when morning came.

"Let it be true," she murmured. "Let my Christmas wish come true."

Lying down on the hard pew, readjusting some of the blankets so no part of her was left uncovered, she closed her eyes and, with that sweet music enveloping her, she succumbed to the wooziness at last. For in that church, a devil like Don Durham could never get to her. She was safe.

*I hope Cliff is not punished. I wish... for his safety,* she prayed as she drifted off, realising with a brief sliver of clarity that he had not let her go only to see her captured again. That was impossible. And she hoped that his kindness would not cost him dearly.

THE RAGGED MUDLARKE'S CRHISTMAS MIRACLE

# Chapter Thirteen

Pale grey daylight tickled Betsy's heavy eyelids, eking them open. She brought a hand to her forehead, groaning as she squinted up at unfamiliar windows. It felt as if someone had stuffed her head full of cotton in the night and tipped sand into her eyes and throat, making her desperate for water.

Slowly, she sat up and looked around, vaguely remembering the night before. Her saviours had gone, the choir had gone, and she appeared to be entirely alone in the empty church.

*Wait...*

Panic struck her like a hard slap to the face, as the hazy fog of her mind allowed a sliver of piercing thought through. It was Christmas Day. The sun had already come up. And she was late. Very, very late.

She jumped up, shedding the layers of blankets like snakeskin as she raced for the doors.

"Stop!" a voice called out from the other end of the church, near to the altar. "Young miss, you must stop!"

Betsy glanced back over her shoulder as a priest began to walk towards her, waving his hands as if that would make a difference.

"You do not need to return out there," the priest urged. "There is redemption for all fallen women, but only you can choose to save yourself. Please, stay here."

He clearly thought she was something that she was not, but she had no time to explain. He was still shouting to her as she burst out of the doors, her stiff legs complaining as she urged them into a run. Her father would be waiting, and that was the only redemption she cared about.

---

The storm of the night before had eased into silent snowfall, fat flakes floating down like the moulting petals of a vast cherry blossom. The sort of snow that Betsy adored with all of her heart, but she barely noticed it as she trudged through the city, her shoes soaked through, the hem of her skirts heavy with moisture, a deep chill shivering from the bones of her toes to the top of her skull. A chill that was not merely caused by the frigid weather, but the fear that she would arrive at Pentonville Prison to find her father already gone, thinking he had been abandoned or that something had befallen his daughter in his absence.

It took almost two hours and several wrong turns before the grey and dismal building appeared in front of her, whilst the church bells in the distance mocked her with three chimes, letting her know it was mid-afternoon already. She had hoped and prayed upon leaving St. Mary's that it was still morning, but it was not to be. She had slept for far longer than she had ever intended to, dragged into a deep slumber by the events of the night before and the intoxicant that had lingered in her body.

Weak and breathless and nauseated, her empty stomach gnawing and roiling, she shambled up to the towering prison gates. There, she turned this way and that, as if she might have missed the sight of her father waiting for her. Or, if not her father, then Clifford.

He had said he would leave her to her reunion, but part of her had hoped that he might show up anyway, to keep her company.

*But I am hours and hours late,* she reminded herself, spotting the guard post to the right of the gates. Perhaps, Clifford *had* come to wait with her, retreating when he had realised that she was not there.

Perhaps, he was searching Whitechapel for her at this very moment. Or worse, that Don *had* punished him, and he was in no condition to take a single step, much less walk all the way to Pentonville Prison.

"Excuse me," she rasped, approaching the guard post.

The uniformed man inside blinked quickly, as though he had been sleeping.

"What?" he said sharply, stifling a yawn.

Betsy clasped her hands together, her fingers numb with the cold. "Might you tell me if any prisoners have been released today? If so, did you happen to see where they went?"

"Today?" The guard barked a laugh. "You've been out in the cold too long, love. It's addled your head."

She frowned. "But... I was told that my father was being released today. Kenneth Martin is his name."

"You were told that your father was being released on *Christmas Day?*" The guard snickered, shaking his head like it was the funniest thing he had heard all year. "No one's that lucky, Miss. Sounds to me like someone's playing a jape on you."

Anger flared in Betsy's chest as she blew into her hands with a fury. "It's no jape, sir. I was told by someone who knows. They wouldn't lie to me. They said that my father was being released from prison today. They heard it from one of the guards in there."

"And you're hearing it from me that you've been misled," the guard replied, his tone sharper than before. "There's no one being released today. You think anyone is going to give a criminal a gift like that?"

Betsy's heart began to sink like a stone tossed into a deep well, tumbling to the fathomless bottom. Perhaps it was the guard's blunt tone, but hearing it framed like that did make it sound unlikely.

But Clifford would not have lied to her. Clifford would not have spent the last two years being her dearest companion, only to break her heart on Christmas Day.

Yes, he had ruined her Christmas once, but that was in the past—those had been the actions of a different Clifford who had not known her as he did now.

Undeterred, she put on her sweetest voice and batted her eyelashes at the guard, echoing one of the characters she adopted at the music hall. "Could you see if there is a prisoner by that name still inside? Kenneth Martin." She paused, sighing wearily. "I realise how foolish I've been, but I've come all this way, and I'd like to leave with the knowledge that my pa is alive, if nothing else. A little gift on this Christmas Day."

The guard observed her closely, his blank expression revealing nothing. She met his gaze and mustered her saddest smile, hoping she was right about the kind of man that he was—someone who could be persuaded by some fawning and the feeling that they would be a kind of hero if he did as she asked.

"You would be saving my Christmas, sir," she added thickly. "I don't have much, but if you were to do this, I would be eternally grateful. I would hold you in my prayers and thank God for your kindness."

The guard pursed his lips and looked back at the door behind him: the gateway between the outside world and the prison underworld. If Betsy could have painted a portrait of reluctance, he would have been the muse.

Dipping into her pocket, she pulled out her coin purse, stuffed fat with the money that Don had been throwing at her last night. She suspected that the wretched beast had planned to take it back when she reached wherever it was that he meant to take her to, but Clifford had saved her life *and* the hefty sum that she had made.

It would have been more than enough for at least two months in nicer lodgings, but if the entire contents of the coin purse was the price for finding out where her father was, then that was the price she would pay.

"Merry Christmas," she said, setting the coin purse on the ledge of the guard post. "You can have all of this if you will just see if my father is still inside. There's enough in here to buy an excellent feast for you and your family, or whatever you prefer."

She kept her hand on the purse, ready to swipe it back if he tried to take it without doing as she had asked.

Greed shone in the guard's eyes as he visibly made a measure of the purse's plumpness. She had been wrong to think that he could be persuaded with prayer and thanks, when he was evidently a man who favoured the weight of tangible coin.

"All of it?" he asked.

Betsy nodded. "A gift from me to you."

"Let me see." He came a step closer, and Betsy removed the purse from the ledge.

Half a pace further back than his arm's length, she opened the purse and showed him the clump of coins that jingled and clinked within. His eyes widened and gleamed, a pleased smile turning up one corner of his thin lips.

"Wait here," he said. "I'll not be long. Kenneth Martin, did you say?"

Betsy nodded. "And I'll know if you've just gone in and come back out without speaking to a soul." Her voice darkened, fuelled by the frustration and disappointment that bubbled in her veins.

"Remember, I know people who know people in there. People you wouldn't want to cross. People who'll come and take back what I've given you if I find out that you've lied."

A flicker of fear crossed the guard's face. "I'll do it properly," he promised. "Don't you go anywhere."

"I don't intend to," she replied, as the guard let himself through the door at the back of the guard post and locked it behind him, no doubt worried that Betsy might try to find her father herself if he did not.

---

The snow fell thicker, the sky bruised and swollen, the sepia light turning the world around her into a moving photograph. She had seen a photograph for the first time not too long ago, and though she knew she could never afford such a thing, she had wondered how nice it must be to have a captured memory of her and her father or her and Clifford. A mark in history to say, "I was here. I existed."

She was just imagining the ridiculousness of putting a photograph somewhere in the dingy lodgings she called home when the door screeched on its hinges, announcing the guard's return.

Gripping the coin purse in her frozen hand, she hurried back to the guard post. "Is he there?" she gasped, her heart lurching into her throat.

The guard nodded. "There's a man by that name inside, imprisoned for stealing confections. Is that him?"

"That's him!" Betsy urged.

"Well, that's your only good news." He held out his hand expectantly. "The bad news is, he's not getting out for another year at least. Bad behaviour, by all accounts: starting fights, stealing food, not doing his work, disrupting the peace, up to mischief, etcetera."

Betsy froze. "My father wouldn't."

"If it's the Kenneth Martin you just said it was, then he has," the guard retorted, tapping his fingers against his palm as if to say, *I gave you what you wanted, now hand over the money.*

But it was not what Betsy had wanted. Not even close. She had imagined the guard returning to tell her that her father was going to be released tomorrow instead, or on New Year's Eve, to make it two years to the day since he was imprisoned. She had not, not even for a second, thought that her father might be incarcerated for another year *at least*.

"Thank you," she said softly, her heart breaking as she set the coin purse on the ledge. "M-Merry Christmas."

"It will be now," the guard replied with giddy cheer as he snatched up his prize and stuffed it into his pocket.

With her head bowed, her chin to her chest, Betsy turned and began to walk away from the looming walls of Pentonville Prison. A tear slid from her eye, cooling on her cheek, as she wondered if the next year would be any different. What if her father was never released? What if they kept finding excuses to keep him there?

*My wish didn't come true...* More tears began to fall, her boots crunching through the blanket of virgin snow, as she thought about the miserable two-hour walk that she had ahead of her. The beginning of another difficult year, alone.

"Betsy!" a voice shouted through the muffled stillness of the snowy, sepia world.

Puzzled, she raised her head. Coming up the road on the back of a chestnut horse, one arm held against his chest in a sling, was a man she did not recognise. His face was bruised and bloodied, one eye swollen shut, his lip split.

"I thought I might've been too late," the man said, bringing his horse to a halt a short distance from her.

He slid down from the saddle and hurried to her, pulling her into his embrace with his one free arm. And as he held her close, breathing hard and pressing his lips to her snow speckled hair, she wrapped her arms around him in kind, realising that he was not a stranger at all, but the only person in the world she wanted to see at that moment.

And as she clung to Clifford, a memory of the night before came wheeling back into her head, and she realised what she had done. She had spent her Christmas wish on *him*, praying more fervently for his safety than the release of her father.

Grateful but torn, she wept into Clifford's shoulder, letting herself be held by the man who, even battered and bruised, had come to wait with her. The man she looked for every morning on the riverbank, just in case it would be one of the mornings where he came to share breakfast with her. The man who had become so dear to her that she no longer knew what she would do without him.

"Where's your father?" he whispered, pulling back.

All Betsy could do was shake her head.

His face fell, and he pulled her into another embrace, sighing as he said, "I'm so sorry, Betsy. I'm so very, very sorry."

# Chapter Fourteen

"I wasn't sure if you'd want to see me," Clifford said, leading the horse back through the eerily empty streets of London.

Candles glowed from every window and sounds of good cheer drifted with the snowfall. No one needed to be out in the bitter cold when they could be inside with family and friends, enjoying the festive day. It was akin to wandering behind the stage at the music hall, hearing the muffled chatter and rehearsed songs of the performers from the dressing rooms; a secret world that Betsy and Clifford were outside of, listening in.

"Why wouldn't I?" Betsy asked, leaning back against Clifford's chest.

She was keenly aware of his injured arm around her waist, holding her steady as the horse's gait swayed them gently from side to side. It must have been hurting him, but he did not wince or complain. And he was warm and sturdy, refusing to let her feel the full bite of the cold weather, refusing to let her fall too deep into her pit of despair.

"I don't know how much you remember of last night, but I was worried you might think I was part of it," he explained hesitantly. "I had to pretend that you had escaped, so I had to alert Don and his men once you had run off. I hated doing it, and I was fretting for hours that they might have caught up to you. I searched your lodgings and the churches, and when I got to St. Mary's, I knew you were safe. That's when I went back to Don. I swear to you, I didn't tell him where you were."

Betsy covered his forearm with hers, sliding her fingers into his. "I think I did suspect you for a while, but that was the delirium talking." She chewed her lower lip, contemplating. "What did he do to you when you went back?"

"Had a couple of the lads beat me," Clifford replied with a light shrug. "Nothing I haven't been through a hundred times before. Honestly, it looks worse than it is."

She gently brushed the side of his hand with her thumb. "How did you get away?"

"I was kicked out. It happens. You get a beating, you get exiled for a few days, then Don remembers that he needs you for this or that and it's like nothing ever happened," Clifford replied.

Betsy swivelled, peering up into Clifford's eyes. "What if you didn't go back? What if you were to stay with me, and we never set foot in Whitechapel again?"

"I wish I could, but..." His gaze clouded over, his attention fixed ahead. For a moment, Betsy thought he might be about to tell her why he worked for Don in the first place. Maybe, he was considering it, but a short while later, it seemed he had decided not to.

"But I thought we might spend Christmas Day together, if you'd like?" he said more brightly. "I've got lodgings of my own where no one will bother us, and I've enough food set by to make us a decent dinner, so we won't have to go to Christ Church... unless you want to, that is."

She smiled. "You don't want to have Christmas with the Holbrooks and the Westons instead? I know the littluns would be pleased to see you."

"With respect, I'd rather eat raw potato peelings and carrot tops on my own," he replied, his quiet laughter ringing hollow.

She shrugged, suddenly shy. "If you've got something better than potato peelings and carrot tops, I won't say no to having Christmas dinner with you."

For some reason, venturing to his lodgings to have dinner seemed like a far more worrisome, far more intimate thing than sharing breakfast at the Limehouse Basin. She *had* been curious about where he lived, but she had assumed that all of the Rat Boys resided together in some form of dormitory or bunkhouse, not in lodgings of their own.

*It wouldn't be a trick. He wouldn't take me back to Don. Not this Clifford,* she told herself as doubts crept in, stirred up by the foggy memory of what she had heard the night before. What Clifford had *reminded* her that she had heard. But he had explained himself and he seemed apologetic, and he likely would not have mentioned it if there was anything nefarious about it.

Besides, on a day where she had no one else, she was not about to start casting foolish aspersions on the one person she *did* have left. A fellow lonely soul, like her.

The Holbrooks and the Westons were lovely, of course, and Betsy deemed them to be good friends, but she did not want to be the sour-faced, gloomy one at the table, bringing down their high spirits. The same went for being at Christ Church. Clifford, on the other hand, would not mind her melancholy.

"Do you still have the coin you earned last night?" he asked, smiling strangely.

She shook her head. "I gave it to the guard for information."

"No matter." He frowned as if deep in thought. "We'll just have to be without another currant bun. Still, I've got plenty to buy a few additional things on our way. It'll be a fine feast; I promise you."

And despite that strange smile that had lasted for a second or two, she believed him.

---

"You were supposed to peel the parsnips, not shave them down to nothing!" Betsy laughed, holding up one of Clifford's carved victims. The parsnip had begun as a thick, hearty vegetable with a few spots of rot that just needed gouging out, but now it was as thin as a hatpin.

Clifford pulled an apologetic face. "I got carried away. The carrots aren't doing so bad, though. And I doubt you've seen a bird so well plucked in all your days. Not a single feather to be found."

He had purchased a chicken on the way to his lodgings on the farthest edge of Spitalfields, surprisingly not too far from where Betsy herself resided. The parsnips, carrots, cabbage, and partially stale bread had also been acquired, alongside a pound of potatoes and a dollop of goose fat that only smelled slightly rancid. Last of all, Clifford had gone into the confectionery to fetch a familiar paper bag that now sat out on the windowsill of his attic residence.

The lodgings were not much, but the attic room was positively palatial in comparison to the room Betsy shared with the Holbrooks and the Westons. He had the space all to himself, with his own fireplace and a wide ledge beyond the single, long window which he had been calling his 'terrace,' much to Betsy's amusement.

"That *is* a finely plucked chicken," Betsy conceded, laughing. "Trouble is, I don't know how we're going to cook it. You don't have a stove up here."

She was surprised to find that she *could* laugh, considering the devastating blow that the prison guard had delivered, but that was the magic of Clifford—if he was in her company, nothing seemed so bad. It was only when she was alone again that she would begin to feel the full weight of her father's prolonged absence, but she was not ready to think about that yet.

"I'll take it down to Mrs. Gourley's," Clifford said. "She's the only one here with a stove and she doesn't mind others using it for a small fee."

Betsy raised an eyebrow at him. "But won't lots of others be using it today?"

"If they are, I'll take it down the street. There's a lad there who cooks whatever you want, but it's slower than Mrs. Gourley's stove."

"Lucky for you, I don't have anywhere else to be."

Clifford grinned. "Even if we don't eat until midnight?"

"Even so."

Betsy sawed off two slices of bread and dropped a pat of butter into a frying pan, holding it over the licking flames of the fireplace. Once the butter started spitting, she put the slices of bread in side-by-side, listening to the cheerful sizzle.

As she waited for the first side to get crispy and delicious, she spoke, "Did your ma cook for you at Christmas?"

"Didn't really have a ma," Clifford replied. "We'd get the same thing as any other day. Thin porridge. Maybe a bit of sausage if there was someone coming 'round to look at the place and us. I'd always give my bit to..." He trailed off, shaking his head like he had a memory to dislodge.

"Look at the place? What do you mean?" Betsy asked, desperate to know who he would have given his bit of sausage to, but she knew she had to be careful not to press him before he was ready.

He shrugged, resuming his more hesitant carving of the carrots. "When I was little, I got handed over to an orphanage by me own ma—ironic, really. Not a good place. The husband and wife in charge of it didn't care a lick for any of us. We were just... chattel for them, sent out to whoever needed labour on the cheap, once we got big enough—*if* we got big enough. They'd take the coin we made; we'd get nothing. So, Christmas wasn't so much of a celebration where I came from."

"I had no idea," Betsy gasped, almost forgetting to turn the slices of fried bread over as she watched him.

"I don't talk about it much."

"No pa, either?"

His jaw tightened as he gouged a hole in the latest carrot. "Don't know him. Could've been anyone. I have this... foggy memory of what my ma looked like, but I have no memory of there ever being a pa around. I reckon that's why she gave us up—easier that way. Not so many mouths to feed."

*Us?* Betsy's heart jumped.

"Your ma must've been a mighty woman if your pa never remarried," he added quickly.

Betsy nodded. "She was. I'd sometimes ask my pa if he was ever lonely, and if he'd ever thought of finding a new love for himself. He'd tell me not to be daft—that he'd had the rarest diamond in the world for a wife, and no one else would ever compare, so what was the point. Once, he said, "If being by myself is the price for having had those beautiful years with her, and a beautiful daughter too, then I'll pay it for the rest of my life without complaint." He doesn't talk about her often, but when he does, you can... feel that love, even so many years after she left us."

"Is that the sort of love *you* want for yourself?" Clifford paused in his peeling, looking at Betsy with an unusual shine in his eyes that somehow felt like fond regret.

Betsy shrugged shyly, pinching the fried bread off the pan and putting the pieces on a nearby plate. "As long as he's kind and can make me smile and thinks the world of me, I think I'd be happy."

"What about a man who brings you currant buns?"

Betsy swallowed thickly, her cheeks flushing with heat as she held his gaze, wondering what on earth he meant. She had long suspected that *her* feelings for Clifford went beyond mere friendship, but losing the friendship was not something she was willing to risk because her heart had some foolish notions. But if *he* also felt more for her, that changed everything.

"It's not kind to tease," she chided uncomfortably, unable to gauge his expression.

His throat bobbed. "You think I'm teasing?"

"I think... I think..." No words would come, her mind entirely blank.

He set down his knife and carrot, and began to move towards her, his eyes soft and inviting.

It was the look that never failed to make her stomach flutter, though she always diligently corralled the loosed butterflies back into a net of reason and sense whenever they appeared.

But it was different in his lodgings, amongst his meagre belongings, where she had been invited to join him. The butterflies would *not* be suppressed, flapping more vigorously in the pit of her stomach.

"What did you mean by gave "us" up? Was it not just you?" she blurted out when he was but a few paces away.

That warm, tender expression evaporated like dawn mist, his grey eyes hardening as his jaw clenched. "It was just a turn of phrase," he said tightly, grabbing the plucked chicken off the lopsided, makeshift counter. "I'm going to go and ask Mrs. Gourley if we can get this cooking."

"But the fried bread is ready," Betsy protested, cursing herself for not letting him come closer, for not seeing what he would do once he was right in front of her.

"You eat my slice," he replied, turning away. "You need it more than I do."

With that, he was gone, leaving Betsy none-the-wiser about who "us" might be or what he had meant by "What about a man who brings you currant buns?"

---

Clifford was gone for hours, to the point where Betsy had considered leaving and returning to her own lodgings several times. But it was Christmas Day, and the man she cared for had gone out with a chicken that they were supposed to eat together, and she would not give up and leave until they *had* eaten their Christmas feast together.

So, she diligently boiled and fried the vegetables, before turning her efforts to the golden roast potatoes that she had dreamed of for years. This year, she would get them right, following her mother's recipe, even if they were cold by the time Clifford returned. After all, he could not stay away from his own lodgings forever, could he?

Outside the window, the world had long turned dark, the snow easing for the time being. Far below, she heard the laughter of families and a few drunken songs to bring some welcome noise to the otherwise silent room. Church bells chimed in the distance and carollers sang out from the streets, prompting Betsy to open the window to hear it better.

Soon enough, the potatoes were spitting and crisping nicely, and as she sat and watched them like a hawk, refusing to let them burn, a sense of cheer swelled in her heart. It was not the Christmas she had expected, but she supposed that was the beauty of the day, making the best of it. None of the Christmases she had spent with her father had gone according to plan either, yet they had never let it stop them from having a memorable time.

As if summoned by her happier thoughts, the door opened and Clifford walked in, stomping the snow off his boots and shaking it from his hair. He carried an old wooden crate in his arms despite his injury; the contents shrouded by a worn piece of burlap.

"That chicken had better be under there, and you need to be more careful with that arm of yours," Betsy said with a relieved smile, both grateful and surprised to see a grin on *his* face too.

"Mrs. Gourley made it perfect," he told her, his voice laced with a boyish excitement that charmed her more than he could have known. "Smells so good it's a miracle I didn't eat the whole thing on my way up. As for my arm—it can hurt another day, once Christmas is over."

A waft of the roasted chicken reached Betsy at that moment, her mouth watering.

"The potatoes are near perfect too," she said, her own excitement rising. "I didn't know when you'd be back, but you timed it well."

Clifford beamed from ear to ear. "About that. I wasn't just sitting idly by, watching a chicken cook. I went out to get you something that I thought you'd like." He whipped off the old burlap, revealing the wavering fronds of a small plant. "I got us a Christmas tree."

Betsy's eyes widened, a gasp slipping from her throat. She hurried toward Clifford and his box of surprises, carefully lifting out the tiny, perfectly formed pine tree. It was the most beautiful, thoughtful thing she had ever seen, but that was not all; at the bottom of the box was a rope of tinsel, a stack of little candles, two red velvet bows and a hastily crafted angel that appeared to be made of old newspapers.

"Where did you find this?" she whispered, as if she were in the presence of greatness.

He winked. "That's for me to know."

Setting the crate on the lopsided counter, he took out the roast chicken and began to carve, whilst Betsy hurried to warm up the vegetables she had already cooked. Before long, they had two plates piled high with delicious food, and sat down on the floor in front of the tiny Christmas tree.

Clifford leaned forward to light the candles, melting them onto the miniature branches so they would stay put. And before the twinkling glow of the prettiest Christmas tree Betsy had ever beheld, they ate their feast as the carols and the bells drifted in through the window, sharing in their own joy with smiles and jokes and stories.

"Do you remember the first time I came back to the riverbank after the necklace incident?" he asked, closing his eyes in blissful satisfaction as he popped a potato into his mouth.

Betsy chuckled, ripping the succulent, dark meat off a chicken leg. "When I hurled a clod of mud at you?"

They had had to make it appear convincing that Clifford was still an enemy of hers, and she had very much leaned into her role.

"Hit me square in the face." He laughed, swallowing. "You've got a mean aim, Betsy."

"Tomorrow, we ought to have a snowball fight in the street," she urged. "Figure out once and for all who the champion is, since you cheated last year."

He paused, his smile softening. "Tomorrow?"

"Oh... um... only if you have nothing else to do, I mean," she said awkwardly, almost choking on a piece of the meat.

He shook his head. "That's not what I meant." His throat bobbed. "I didn't realise I could ask if you wanted to stay tonight. Of course, I thought about asking, but... all things considered and with your own lodgings so close, I assumed... You would have the cot, of course, and I would be quite content on the floor."

"I couldn't," she replied quietly. "It wouldn't be proper."

Clifford nodded slowly. "What might make it proper?"

"Well, we would have to be married," she explained, her heart leaping into her throat, her traitorous stomach fluttering all over again.

"Even if I slept on the floor?"

She smiled. "Even then."

"Am I allowed to walk you back to your own lodgings, at least?" he asked, his eyes bright.

"Of course." Her cheeks grew hotter. "And then, tomorrow, we wage icy war again."

She glanced at the neat cot in the corner, feeling the warmth of the fireplace and the food and Clifford's presence, and wondered if she might make an exception for just one night. They would be at a polite distance from one another, and they could talk until they fell asleep, with their bellies full and their day successfully pulled back from the brink of ruination. That would not be so improper, would it? It was no different to sharing lodgings with others, really.

"Can I get you some more?" Clifford asked, mopping up what was left on his plate with the half stale bread.

Betsy patted her stomach. "I think I'll burst if I do, but we can eat it tomorrow."

"Very well, but I hope you've still got some hunger left—enough for your gift," he said, taking her plate and his to the water bucket.

"I already ate your gift," she pointed out.

He grabbed the paper bag on the makeshift counter and wandered over to the long, narrow window that led out onto his 'terrace.' One foot on the sill, he paused to look back at her, smiling. "We've got to have something sweet to finish the meal, Betsy Martin, and I couldn't get my hands on any mince pies." He turned his gaze out to the darkened world. "Bring us a blanket—I think it's about to snow again."

# Chapter Fifteen

Huddled together in the warmth of the woollen blanket as snow tumbled down around them, Clifford's injured arm around her "to stop her slipping off by accident," Betsy sucked contentedly on a boiled sweet that tasted of blackcurrant. Clifford crunched his and grinned down at her, opening his mouth for another.

"So impatient," she chided playfully, picking one of the red ones that she knew he liked.

"Might as well crunch them whilst I've got the teeth for it," he insisted, laughing as she popped the sweet into his mouth.

It was not at all the Christmas she had expected, but it was one she would never forget. And though she fervently wished that her father could have been there with her, freed from the misery of the prison, she would not insult the heavens by ignoring the wish that she *had* been granted: Clifford's safety. He was alive and well and vibrant, raising up her spirits when, by rights, they should have been in tatters.

"Do you hear that?" he said suddenly, his lips quirking into a fond smile.

She pricked her ears, her heart soaring as the sound of someone singing drifted up through the falling snow to the precarious 'terrace.' It was a soft, slow, bittersweet rendition of 'Silent Night,' the night air bristling with the kind of magic that was rare to find in that city. The kind of magic that could only happen on Christmas, where peace on Earth and good will to all actually seemed possible.

"I wouldn't mind hearing *you* sing again," Clifford said, brushing a snowflake from her cheek. "I had no idea you had such a voice."

Betsy laughed tightly. "I'm surprised I could sing at all last night with all the nerves jumping around in my veins. It's the least at ease I've ever been whilst singing a carol; I can tell you that much."

"He can't hurt you," Clifford whispered, holding her tighter. "I won't let him. I don't care what it costs me; you'll never have to face him again."

"And if he comes back to the music hall?"

Clifford rested his cheek against the top of her head, turning slightly to press his words to her hair in a strange sort of kiss as he murmured, "He won't. If he does, I'll send word to you each and every time. He isn't getting his hands on you. I made that decision two years ago, and my determination has only grown stronger." His hand came up to cradle her face, tilting her head up so she would look at him. "You see, Betsy, I—"

The door to Clifford's lodgings burst open, and three men ran in: one with a blade, one with a bat, and one with a pistol in hand.

Betsy's lungs seized, turning the scream that tried to escape her throat into a strangled gasp of pure horror. She recognised at least two of them from the music hall and, even without the weapons and grim-faced glares, knew to whom they belonged.

"Was this a... trap?" Betsy rasped, staring at Clifford in desperation. There was no way out. Those men were blocking the only escape, and she doubted they were there to wish the pair a 'Merry Christmas.'

Clifford's face crumpled, as if she had struck him with her fist instead of her accusation. "I'd throw myself into the Thames before I did that to you," he replied in earnest, pulling her to her feet and tugging her toward the jagged edge of the wooden ledge. "Climb down. I'll keep them occupied."

"Climb down?" She could barely squeeze the words out. "I can't, Cliff! I'll fall and break my neck!"

Even if it had been the height of summer, the weather fine and dry, she would have thought twice about trying to scale the walls down to the street below. Slanted gables formed a sort of funnel downward, where different parts of the building had been constructed at different times, with sections added and repaired, but the glistening blanket of snow that clung to her 'escape' would surely be her demise.

Clifford glanced between Betsy and the three men, who approached slowly. "Please, Betsy. You have to."

"I... I can't. I can't do it." She grabbed his arm and clung on tight, terrified that he would push her to do what could not be done.

He stood in front of her, his frantic breaths pluming in the icy air.

Behind her, barely half a step remained between her and the fatal drop. She clung on even tighter to Clifford, praying with all her might that he had not orchestrated this; that he was not a gifted performer who had spent the last two years building her trust as he worked towards this finale.

"I've no quarrel with the three of you," Clifford growled at the encroaching men. "If you turn around and leave now, there'll be no harm done."

The first of the men—a young fellow with short blonde hair, sharp blue eyes, and a jarringly handsome face—smirked at the suggestion. "You trying to pretend for Mr. Durham's quarry that you've not led us right to her?" He snickered. "There's no use in that now. The jig is up. So, why don't you save us a task and throw her over your shoulder—bring her out here so we can get back to Whitechapel before the festivities are over with. I've a jar of gin with my name on it."

"Leave her be," Clifford snarled, his hands curling into fists.

The second man, older than the first with a bevy of scars across a pocked and grizzled face, rolled his eyes. "You've got your orders, Cliff, and we've got ours. So, hurry yourself up."

Betsy's hand relaxed on Clifford's arm, her heart a bolting horse in her chest, thundering wildly. She stared up at him as if he were a stranger, though he did not look back to meet her gaze. Why would he, when all she would see was his guilt? He had ensnared her and, what was worse, she had mindlessly wandered into the trap he had set.

"Don't listen to them," Clifford hissed, but it was too late. The scales had fallen from her eyes, and she was seeing him properly for the first time in two years. He was the same man who had tricked the constables and stolen her pocket watch. He had always been that man; he had never changed, not one bit.

*"I wasn't just sitting idly by, watching a chicken cook..."* Those had been his words, and he had been gone for a very long time. Longer than it took to fetch a Christmas tree, she wagered. Had he gone to Don, to let him know that he had Betsy where he wanted her? Had he deliberately lulled her into a false sense of security, so she would be captured more easily? No matter how she thought about it, especially that lengthy absence, it felt like a trick. A trap.

And now he planned to finish the performance by giving her to Don, who would no doubt reward him handsomely.

"Betsy, don't listen," Clifford whispered again.

Her panicked gaze flitted between the ledge's precipice behind and the attic room ahead, frantically wondering which would give her the greatest chance of survival. Neither offered much hope. Still, if she *did* fall and break her neck, at least she would not have to face whatever Don had planned for her.

In truth, there was only one choice.

Steeling herself, she cast one last, fierce glare at the men who wanted to capture her, and one final, sadder look at Clifford's back. Then... she leaped, landing with a thud on the slanted gable roof below.

Her feet began to slide out from underneath her almost immediately, her hands grappling hopelessly for purchase, but as she glided toward the roof's edge, she managed to find some strength in her shaky legs. Pushing upward with everything she possessed, she sprang toward the next gable roof... and the next and the next, leaping ever downward, using the momentum of the slippery surface to her advantage.

Before she knew it, she was at the last jutting ledge, grasping tight to the triangular ridge of what appeared to be someone's tiny larder. It had clearly been a late addition to the building, a crack in the wooden slats showing her rudimentary shelves, sparsely stocked with jars and ceramic urns, covered with cheesecloth.

It was ten feet or so to the ground. Not a great height, but nothing to be sniffed at either. If she landed wrong, she could hurt her ankle and lose her ability to run.

Gathering her breath, refusing to look back up to the 'terrace' she had fled from, she noted where the snow was thickest on the street below. A small bank had formed against the building itself, just beneath where she was holding on for dear life, her feet scrabbling every few seconds for some kind of foothold.

*It is now or never...*

Thinking of what could await her if she lost her nerve, she let go of the gable roof's ridge and let herself slide down. The drop came sooner than she had expected, and, for just a moment, there was nothing but air as she fell.

As she had feared, she landed awkwardly in the snowdrift, which was not nearly as dense as she had hoped. A splinter of pain ricocheted up from her left ankle, her balance threatening to abandon her as she stumbled away from the drift, but with each step she took, her ankle held. With each step, she grew in confidence. With each step, she grew more certain that she could escape Clifford and the Rat Boys, just as she had escaped them a hundred times before.

Ignoring the residual pain, she broke into a run... but the snow that she adored so much had become her enemy, hindering her like churned-up mud on the riverbank. It crunched underfoot, thick in places and thin in others, making it impossible to keep a swift gait. And where it was thin, it had become ice, her feet slipping this way and that, jarring her ankle every time.

"There!" a gruff voice barked.

Terror shivered down Betsy's spine as she glanced back. Four figures were charging towards her through the evening darkness, seemingly unimpeded by the snow that was determined to slow her down. Perhaps, the snow too was in league with Don Durham, willing to give her up for the right price.

She had made it no more than twenty further paces, when a viciously strong arm snaked around her waist.

"Get off me!" she screamed, lashing out in every direction, driving her fists into any flesh she could find.

But the arm was a vice around her, lifting her up off the snowy street and over a broad shoulder. She kicked and punched and flailed and writhed, so fraught with fear that she even tried to sink her teeth into her captor's skin. Nothing made her kidnapper loosen his grip; there was not so much as a wince from him as he wielded her back the way they had come, to where a horse and cart waited in the road.

With a grunt from her captor, she was unceremoniously thrown into the back of the cart. Two of the men clambered in after her, one sitting on her legs, the other pinning down her arms so she could not try to flee. But it was the final man who Betsy stared at, as he sat down just behind the driver's bench, like he was just hitching a ride to someplace else.

*I should have let you leave the courthouse on the day my father was sentenced. I should never have chased you. I should have taken the pocket watch and never thought of you again,* she seethed in pained silence, the pressure of a grown man's weight on her legs almost unbearable.

Clifford shook his head slowly as, at last, he deigned to meet her gaze. The snow drifted down around him, the glow of the nearby streetlamp casting him in a mockery of a bronze halo. Although, with that reddish hue, perhaps it was more befitting than it seemed.

*I didn't do this,* he mouthed in that low light. *I swear to you; I didn't do this.*

But she no longer believed him, and as she tore her gaze away and squeezed her eyes shut, she had just one thought: *I wasted my Christmas wish on you.*

## Chapter Sixteen

A beautiful dress lay on the bed in a room illuminated by a single candle, resembling a deflated body. Shadows danced menacingly on the faded walls, whilst the cackling laughter that echoed from rooms below seemed to come from those flickering demons, mocking the woman who stood staring at the gown.

Betsy had been carried from the cart in the same way she had been carried to it, over the shoulder of the man who had not said a word during her capture. She was not even sure if he *could* speak, but he certainly had not responded to her when she had pleaded with him to be set free. All he had done was grunt and point at the dress on the bed before leaving, slamming the door behind him.

She had tried the handle, only to find the door locked. It had not come as a surprise, for now that he had her, it seemed unlikely that Don would let her go again.

*I won't put it on. I won't obey. I don't care what it costs me.* She grabbed the dress, crumpled it into a ball and hurled it at the wall.

Something familiar fell to the floor, her heart sinking further into the pit of her stomach: a necklace that looked like a sapphire. 'Costume jewellery,' according to Clifford and Mr. Kimpton, so how had it found its way there, to Don's realm? She could think of only one reason: Clifford had cleverly conned her before, and she had fallen for it, and the cycle was merely repeating again.

But her eyes were open now.

She left the necklace and thrown dress where they were and perched on the edge of the bed, her ears pricked for any sound coming from the hallway outside.

Footsteps approached a few minutes later, followed by the *click* of a key turning in the lock.

The door swung open to reveal the blonde-haired young man from earlier, his smirk a leer in the sickly light of the lantern in his hand. "Don has invited you to dinner," he said, frowning. "Where's the dress he wanted you to put on?"

"I wouldn't know," she shot back.

The man's nostrils flared. "It'd go easier for you if you did what you were told."

"I don't want this to go easily," she replied. "And I'm definitely not prettying myself up for someone like Mr. Durham. If he wants to have dinner with me, he can have dinner with me as I am."

"He won't like it."

Betsy shrugged. "I don't care what he likes."

The man sighed, though she was under no illusion that his words were for anyone's benefit but his own.

He had likely been tasked with ensuring that she wore the gown, and there would be a punishment waiting for him when Don saw that it had not been fulfilled.

"Follow me," the man said grimly. "And I'd suggest you don't try running. It's a rabbit warren in here. You'll lose your way ten times before you find the door, and if you manage to, you'll only be caught again."

Betsy had caught glimpses of where she was as she had been jostled and bounced on her captor's shoulder. It was a large building in Whitechapel with candles flickering in almost every window, and lively music sweeping out into the street. The interior possessed a faded glory, everything steeped in shades of red and black, every doorway they had passed draped by heavy curtains, the air thick with the scent of overbearing perfume. Even someone who was unfamiliar with that part of London would have known what sort of building she was in by the sounds alone.

The man stepped back out into the hallway and held his lantern higher, waiting for Betsy to obey.

Straightening her posture and pulling her shoulders back, raising her chin in defiant readiness, she headed out to join him. But she would not be returning to that room; she did not care what Don wanted or what he threatened, she would not be another ruined bird in his twisted menagerie.

They traipsed through hallway after hallway, and descended staircase after staircase, until they came to a heavy wooden door at the end of a narrow passageway. A deterrent for any constables that might try to reach Don's most prized and illegal gains, no doubt, for no man of the law would be mad enough to try and attack a ruffian overlord at a bottleneck.

The door opened onto what might have been a cellar once, but had been transformed into underground quarters. There was a seating area off to one side, with brocade settees and armchairs, and a curtained area to the rear. In the middle, right ahead of her, was a long dining table, adorned with the most grandiose feast she had ever seen: a gleaming roast goose, golden potatoes and buttery vegetables piled high in large serving bowls, fresh loaves of bread, smaller roasted ducks and partridges, among countless other dishes.

Betsy had never had less of an appetite, especially as she noticed Clifford sitting to the right of Don who, of course, had taken his place at the head of the table. The Rat King and all of his Rat Boys, waiting for the entertainment to come and amuse them as they ate their festive feast.

Don's thin lips pursed as he looked at her. "Where's the gift I prepared for you?"

"I don't accept gifts from strangers," she replied coolly, refusing to let her nerves get the better of her. She had worked too hard, endured too much, to allow her fight to end like this.

A smirk darkened his expression. "A sensible girl."

"Not sensible enough to refuse brandy from the likes of you," she retorted, flashing him a sarcastic smile. "And not sensible enough to refuse the offer of charity from one of your underlings either."

Don reached over and clapped Clifford on the back. "Don't feel too hard done by. You're not the first to fall for one of his tricks, and I doubt you'll be the last. No one gets past our Cliff."

Clifford stared down at the empty plate in front of him, his expression blank, not even giving her the courtesy of meeting her gaze.

"Well, Mr. Durham, as pleasant as I'm sure this dinner must be, I'm not hungry," Betsy said. "I'll be on my way and the rest of you can enjoy what's left of Christmas."

Don smiled, but the devil danced in his eyes. "Not so fast, Miss Martin." He gestured to the empty seat on his left, directly opposite Clifford. "I've gone to the trouble of inviting you to dinner. The least you can do is sit. Maybe, you can sing a song for us whilst we eat."

"With respect, I'll stay standing," she replied, uncertain of how much further she could push him before he snapped.

Don's menacing eyes pinched. "I had hoped you might be more pleasant this evening, but it seems I was mistaken." He sniffed. "But you should know that it's in your favour to be a good girl."

"I'm very tired and my ankle is sore after your thugs chased me," she said with saccharine sweetness. "If you wouldn't mind, I'd like to know why you brought me all the way here, so I can decide if I want to try and run or if I'd rather take a goose bone and choke on it."

To her surprise, Don laughed at that: a great rumbling laugh that conjured stilted chuckles from the men around him.

"Mercy, you *are* an interesting girl," Don said with a sly grin. "The moment I saw you, I knew there was something... unique about you. Special, some might say. Either that or you're very stupid, but I'm going to give you the benefit of the doubt for now."

Betsy said nothing, letting the tense silence force him into speaking again.

"I've an offer for you," he said. "You know I loathe Christmas, but let's say it's a festive gesture of good will, considering your situation."

"My situation?"

Don leaned forward, steepling his fingers. "You've no father to help you anymore, and Mr. Crawley has decided that it'd be in everyone's interest if you didn't return to the music hall. Besides that, my boys have decided to give more of their efforts to mudlarking, so you'll not want to be digging at the riverbank of a morning anymore."

*You told him everything?* Betsy's sharp glower shifted to Clifford, but he still would not look at her. How long had he been informing Don? More to the point, why did Don care? She was no one; she was just a young woman, like so many others, trying to scrape a living.

"So, why don't you come and work for me," Don continued. "You'll be well cared for, with a roof over your head and food in your belly. You won't have to do much, just the obvious, and you'll have money aplenty in your pockets for when your poor father *finally* gets out of prison. Why, you'll certainly have enough stashed away to pay for a better lawyer, that's for sure."

"Why me?" she finally asked. "Why pursue me like this, when I've no doubt there are a thousand girls in this city who'd leap at what you're offering?"

Don reached for a glass of port and sat back in his chair. "Because I've been looking for you for a long time."

"Why?" she repeated. Clearly, she was missing something.

Don took a loud sip, his mouth curling into a sneer. "Because you're your mother's daughter."

"Pardon?"

"You look just like her," he said, eyes flaring. "When I saw you hiding by the courthouse, I thought I was looking at a ghost. It's remarkable."

A cold chill slithered into Betsy's chest. "How do you know my mother?"

"Everyone out," Don growled, downing what was left in his glass.

The Rat Boys scarpered in a cacophony of chairs shrieking against the stone floor, scurrying towards the door as if the constables were after them. The only one who walked slowly was Clifford, his head down, and as he passed Betsy, he whispered, "I swear to you; it wasn't me."

But the evidence was right there before her like a bit of silver sticking out of the river mud. There was no way that Don would know all of those things if someone had not told him, and Clifford seemed like the most obvious culprit. After all, he knew her—and her troubles—better than anyone.

"When I was just a costermonger's boy with nothing to my name, I loved her," Don began, once the door to the cellar was firmly closed. "I'd see her wandering in the market with her basket, and I knew I'd marry her. I went to her pa to ask if I could court her, and he agreed. For six months, I gave that girl everything she could've wanted.

I spent all I had on gifts and trinkets to please her. I was patient, I was generous, because I knew she'd be my wife.

"Then, she met your father," he continued, his voice barbed. "Did you know he had a stall at Covent Garden?"

Betsy shook her head.

"A butcher. Could get meat even when there wasn't any." Don laughed bitterly. "And your ma was smitten. A month later, they were wed. A pity his stall burned down, and his suppliers took his money and ran, or you and your ma might've had an easier life. Don't know where your ma and pa went after that. They went into hiding for a long time, but I never stopped looking. Funny, really, that you were right under my nose for all these years."

A lump formed in Betsy's throat as she pictured her mother and father amidst the warm Christmas glow of Covent Garden, decorating their own stall for the festive season. Her mother had adored Christmas, and Betsy knew she would have relished the opportunity to put wreaths and ribbons and tinsel everywhere. She might have carried a younger Betsy on her hip, to look at the twinkling candles on the Christmas trees in the piazza. All of that gone because of one man's bitterness.

"I heard she died, so I let it lie," Don carried on. "Having my boys take from the mudlarks was a happy coincidence. I didn't know it was you and your pa until later. Then, of course, I saw you... and it was as if I was staring right at her, no years having passed. Let's just say that my desire for reparation was reignited."

"And this is your idea of revenge?" Betsy hissed, wondering how scared her mother must have been for so many years, always looking over her shoulder.

Don shrugged. "It's as satisfying as any." He poured himself a fresh glass of port. "I rediscovered my taste for it after I spoke with that confectioner. Didn't take much to get him to demand a lengthy sentence. Hasn't taken much to keep your pa where he belongs, either. He might've stolen just a quart of sweets, but he stole what was mine long before then. *That* is what he's serving his sentence for, and I didn't think two years was nearly enough."

*And now you're going to tell me that, if I do as you say, you'll make sure he gets his freedom.* A younger, more naïve Betsy would have done whatever it took to get her father out of prison, regardless of what it cost her dignity and honour, but she had learned enough about the Rat Boys and their King. If she accepted, it would never end. If she submitted to what Don wanted, there was no assurance that her father would ever be released; Don would simply keep dangling the possibility over her head to get her to do whatever he asked. No criminal with half a morsel of intellect would give up leverage like that, and Don was not stupid.

"I suppose I shouldn't be surprised that you'd lower yourself to blackmail," Betsy replied as evenly as she could.

"It's a generous offer, Miss Martin," Don said, smiling as if he had already won. "Easy work, good food, a comfortable place to live, and your father's freedom."

A crack splintered down the centre of Betsy's heart, her hands curling into fists as she cleared her throat to say the most painful thing she had ever said. "Thank you for the offer, Mr. Durham, but I'm afraid I must refuse again. My pa would never forgive me."

She gestured around herself. "He'd throw himself *back* in prison rather than hear of me being in a place like this, and I assume you'd make sure he knew."

Don froze, his port glass halfway to his lips. His eyes pinched, his mouth flattening into a grim line as he observed her. Evidently, he had not expected his plan to fail, and though she knew he could easily trap her and force her to stay, she also knew that he would not be able to take any satisfaction from that. He *wanted* her to come crawling, he wanted her to fall to her knees and beg, he wanted her to have no choice but to obey and thank him for his generosity.

"You refuse?" he said with quiet menace.

Betsy forced herself to nod. "With regret, yes."

He shifted in his chair and drained his glass, clearly taking a moment to gather himself. When there was not even a dreg of port left, he put on a tight smile and shrugged. "I'll ask you again next year," he said. "See how much of your pride is left then. *Until* then, let's say you owe me half of whatever you make in the sewers and the riverbank. I'll let you keep your mudlarking, since it's Christmas and I'm no Scrooge, but it won't be worth your efforts. You'll be closely watched, and if you try to evade your taxes, you'll owe me more and more of whatever you earn until you don't have a single coin for yourself. But remember, my door is always open should you change your mind. Sorry—*when* you change your mind."

Betsy wondered if Don had ever actually read 'A Christmas Carol,' for he was the very epitome—*worse*, in fact—than Ebenezer Scrooge. She, herself, had only heard someone read it, and had not forgotten the story.

But Christmas Day was almost over, and she doubted that any persuasive ghosts would dare to visit this wretched creature who was, quite clearly, beyond all redemption.

"You'd be surprised how resilient I can be," she said defiantly. "I'll pay this 'tax,' and I won't change my mind. I'm my father's daughter as much as I'm my mother's—*you* should remember that."

Don's nostrils flared with irritation. "You owe me for the dress and the jewellery that you didn't wear. I'll dock the cost from whatever you scrabble together next week. Expect a visit, though I daresay it won't be long 'til you don't have lodgings at all."

"Very well." She put on a smile though, inside, her heart had sunk into her churning stomach, tossed like a pebble. "Can I leave now?"

Don waved a hand towards the door. "Be my guest."

Not trusting his word at all, she turned and made her hesitant way to the exit. She heaved the door open and looked out to find the Rat Boys waiting in the darkness.

"Kick her out!" Don's voice bellowed.

Clifford lunged forward before anyone else could, seizing her roughly by the arm. "I'll take her out. I brought her here, so it's only fair that I get the honour of throwing her back out."

He pulled her through the swarm of Rat Boys, his hand a shackle around her wrist as he led her up from the underworld and out into the bite of the night air. A few delicate flakes of snow continued to float down to the street, but there was no beauty in it anymore.

"I hope you're well rewarded," Betsy said coldly, wrenching her arm away from him.

He turned, his eyes burning as he gazed down at her. "Until those cretins burst into my lodgings, tonight was the happiest night of my life, Betsy." He grabbed her again, tugging her down the street to where the horse and cart still waited. "Get in."

"I'm not going anywhere with you," she shot back. "I'd rather walk and risk freezing to death."

He pinned her against the side of the cart, his hand coming up to cradle her face. "Betsy, I didn't trap you, I didn't trick you, I didn't... want this at all." He clenched his jaw. "I have tried to keep you away from this. You might not believe me, and I probably wouldn't blame you, but it's the truth. I *knew* who you were to him, and I deliberately didn't hand you over to him. For pity's sake, Betsy, if giving you to him had been my plan or whatever all along, I wouldn't have pushed you from the horse; I'd have kept riding, carrying Don's 'precious cargo' where he wanted whilst you still had that tainted brandy in your veins. I wouldn't have wasted time inviting you to my lodgings, cooking dinner with you, *sharing* Christmas dinner with you—none of that."

Her breath caught in her throat, her eyes meeting his. *Why* would *he have done that if not to try and save me?* She had been so caught up in the shock of *hearing* she had been betrayed that she had not paused to ask that question—why he had pushed her from the horse and told her to run. But that shock had not *quite* worn off yet.

"I don't know why you did it," she said uncertainly. "To amuse yourself, maybe. To make it more of a challenge.

Perhaps, you thought the tainted brandy made it too easy and wanted to toy with me some more, make me think I'd escaped that fate."

Clifford's shoulders sagged. "You've had a grim encounter just now. You're probably still reeling, so I'll pray that's all it is that's making you see me as a... monster who'd torment you for my own amusement." He brushed his thumb across her cheek, and she turned her face away sharply, recoiling. "For two years, Betsy, my sole purpose has been keeping you safe from him. May the Devil drag me down if I'm lying. I didn't know we were being followed. *I* thought we'd evaded trouble, and that was my mistake, because if I had known we weren't out of danger, I would have taken you by the hand and found somewhere for you to hide."

"And I don't believe you," she rasped. "I don't trust you anymore. I stopped altogether when I saw that necklace waiting for me."

He tilted his head up to the sky, a snowflake kissing his cheek. "It's still worthless. *I* bought it back from Kimpton, as the boys saw that you had it and might've said something if it hadn't ended up with Don."

"A likely story." A tale she simply could not, at that moment, believe to be true. Although, a few days ago, she would have.

"Do you trust me enough to let me take you back to your lodgings?" he asked. "After that, you never have to see me again."

"Is that my real Christmas gift?" she said sourly.

He looked back down at her. "If that's what you want, then yes. I promise you, if you let me do this, you'll never see hide nor hair of me again. A Christmas gift that lasts a lifetime."

Shoving him in the chest to make him take a step back, Betsy climbed up into the cart and sat down. She said nothing, but he clearly understood, as he went to the driver's bench and snapped the reins, taking Betsy away from Don and his brothel full of lost and desperate souls. A place where Christmas was just another day.

## Chapter Seventeen

The cold had made Betsy sleepy. In the back of the cart, she had promised she would just close her eyes for a moment, curling up on the hard planks and covering herself with a threadbare blanket. Soon enough, she would be at home in her own corner of her lodgings, listening to the familiar sounds of the Holbrooks and the Westons sleeping. Maybe, they would still be awake and willing to finish the day with a final sliver of festive cheer to try and raise her spirits.

So, when the sharp jolt of the cartwheel hitting a rut in the road woke her with a start, she had no notion of how long she had been asleep. A few minutes, perhaps? It could not have been more than that.

*Why are all the lights out?* She rubbed her tired eyes, confusion a hazy snowstorm in her mind.

There were dark corners of London, but London itself was never dark. The streetlamps and gas lights glowed through the night, whilst oil lamps and candles flickered in at least one window of every tenement and terraced house.

And there was a constant babble of noise from drunkards, quarrelling couples, Hackney carriages and carts rattling by, dogs barking—an ever shifting, strange orchestra of people going about their daily lives.

So, why was it suddenly so silent? Why could she not hear anything other than the turn of the wheels and the plod of the horse's hooves and the creak of the cart?

She blinked up at the sky, where swollen clouds scudded across a glittering backdrop of stars.

"Cliff?" she murmured, pulling herself into a sitting position.

Over the lip of the cart side, dark shapes smudged the landscape, rustling whispers soughing into her ears as if they were surrounded by a clandestine crowd. As her eyes adjusted to the gloom, she realised that they were trees and hedgerows, and that whispering sound was the wind through the wintry boughs.

*Are we in a park?* Even as she thought it, she knew she was wrong.

"Cliff," she said with greater urgency, praying that he was still the one driving the cart. "Cliff, where are we?"

The cart did not slow, but she saw the driver's head twist, glancing back at her. "We're not there yet."

"Not *where*?" On numb legs, she scrambled toward the bench. "Cliff, what is going on? Did Don tell you to do this? Does he want you to... kill me?"

Clifford made a disgusted noise. "If he did, I wouldn't do it." He sighed. "I'm not ready for Christmas Day to be over, and I have one last gift for you.

It was already planned before all of this unpleasantness happened, so just... humour me. We'll be there soon enough. After that, I'll take you home and I won't darken your door again."

"Cliff, where *are* we?" Betsy climbed over the back of the driver's bench.

"That's for me to know," Clifford replied.

"Stop this cart at once. Take me back to London. Whatever it is you have planned, I don't want it, and if you don't turn the cart around, I'm going to jump!" She tried to grab for the reins, but he was too strong and too quick, blocking her attempts.

He looked at her. "I can't stop you jumping off, but if you do, I'll just catch you and throw you back into the cart. You'll get lost in minutes out here." He returned his gaze to the road, faintly illuminated by the two lanterns that hung from poles at either side of the bench. "Just let me do this."

"Do what?"

He shook his head slowly. "You have to see it. I don't want to ruin the surprise."

"And I don't *want* your surprise! I've had enough surprises to last me a lifetime," she protested, but peering out into the darkness, where skeletal-limbed trees stood like otherworldly sentinels, she knew she would not jump. The world beyond the cart was too silent, too eerie, too filled with the unknown.

Folding her arms across her chest, she glared into the darkness ahead, a stilted silence crackling between the pair. It was bizarre to have such tension where she had grown accustomed to ease, as she remembered all of the mornings that she had peered up the riverbank, hoping to see him standing there.

*Was it really all a ruse? Is he telling the truth?* She scrunched her eyes shut, her brain fizzing with confusion and betrayal and regret.

"You've often asked why I work for Don in the first place," Clifford said suddenly, prompting her to crack open one eye. "It's a long story, but... I might as well tell you now."

Betsy suspected he was trying to soften her anger, and, to her annoyance, it was working. "I'm listening," she muttered.

"I have a sister."

"What?" She grabbed his arm. "But you said she wasn't real. You said you made her up! I *knew* it wasn't just a 'turn of phrase' when you said that your mother gave "us" up!"

He nodded. "No, it wasn't."

"Where is she? How come you've never introduced me?" As she spoke, she remembered the rest of their earlier conversation: How he had been handed over to an orphanage, and how the children there were just free labour.

Clifford rubbed the heel of his hand against his chest, like he was trying to loosen a knot there. "We escaped together on Christmas Eve, eight years ago. I was ten, she was five. But we were chased, and I told her to run. I gave her the money I'd collected for the stagecoach and told her to meet me at a friend's lodgings. She never showed up."

"Did something happen to her?" Betsy asked quietly, her hand still resting on his arm.

He shrugged. "I assumed she'd been caught and taken back to the orphanage, but when I asked one of the other children from that place whilst they were on their way to work, they told me she wasn't there. I must've searched Newcastle a thousand times from top to bottom, but it was like she just... vanished."

"Newcastle?" Betsy's eyes widened. "Is that where you're from?"

He nodded. "A lifetime ago."

"But... if you're from all the way up north, how did you end up here?"

She was invested now; she could not help it. For two years, she had begged him to tell her this story, and though she was still wary of him and his intentions, she needed to know what had thrown him into Don's path and kept him there.

He cleared his throat. "I had all but given up, when I thought about the stagecoach. I waited for an age until I found the driver who'd driven the stagecoach that night. He told me that a little girl had got on and insisted that she was going to London to meet her brother. *That's* where we'd planned to escape to. She must've misunderstood where I told her to meet me. I left that same day, and I haven't been back since.

"At every stage she would've stopped at, I asked again, and got confirmation that a little girl had continued on, all the way to London," he proceeded, his voice thick. "But once I finally reached London, her trail disappeared again. She was... swallowed up by that huge beast of a city.

I searched every workhouse, every orphanage, everywhere I could think of, but she wasn't anywhere. All the while, I was trying to survive, and, one day, I happened to pickpocket a coin purse from the wrong person."

Betsy gasped. "Don?"

"I thought he'd kill me," Clifford confirmed. "In a panic, I told him everything, and... his manner changed. He gave me food, clothes, and somewhere to sleep. I've since learned that's his trick—that's how he gets everyone into debt with him, so they feel obliged to do what he says. He asked me to go with some of the older men to rob a house in Mayfair. I refused at first, but he told me he'd help me find Athena if I did it."

"Athena?" Betsy's heart ached at such a beautiful name. "Is that your sister?"

Clifford smiled. "My ma, for all her faults, picked a good name. In my first weeks with Don, I begged one of the lads to teach me how to read so I would recognise that name, written down. Athena Kinross. I'd search every newspaper for it." He readjusted his grip on the reins. "Needless to say, I robbed the house in Mayfair, and I've been working for Don ever since."

"*Did* he help you find Athena?" Betsy suspected she already knew the answer.

Clifford tilted his head from side to side. "He's given me pieces of information here and there over the years, but then, a few months back, he told me..." He cleared his throat, shifting uncomfortably. "He told me she was dead. Apparently, she was found by a man named John Brookes when she got off the stagecoach in London. He ran an orphanage which no longer exists.

She... died there, a week after she arrived, of scarlet fever. I was still in Newcastle... while she was dying, and I don't know that I'll ever forgive myself for that. It's why I couldn't find her in the city, because she was already gone, and orphanages don't give out the names of dead children for obvious reasons."

Betsy's eyes stung with tears she did not dare to shed, but through the blur, she began to see the man she adored in the man beside her once more. She took hold of his hand, giving it a reassuring squeeze, but there was still one question that had to be answered.

"I'm so very sorry, Cliff," she murmured, hesitating. "But—"

"Why did I stay after I heard she was dead?" Clifford laughed tightly, staring down at her hand holding his. "I was already dedicated to keeping you safe, so I carried on doing what I could for you whilst you were waiting for your pa. You were, and are, my purpose. Obviously, things went awry, but... my heart was in the right place."

Betsy's breath hitched as she leaned into Clifford, her own heart sore that he had suffered so much.

He expelled a weary breath into the cold air. "But she's been guiding me, even though she's gone."

"What do you mean?" Betsy peered up at him.

"She's one of the reasons I helped you that day, outside the courthouse. *Inside* the courthouse too, I guess." He cast her a sideways glance. "All of a sudden, she was in my head, telling me off for being mean to you. She was a righteous little thing even before she could speak properly. If she was still alive, I know she'd adore you—probably end up adoring you more than she once adored me."

"Then, I'm grateful to her for guiding you," Betsy murmured, thinking of the robins in the cemetery, of her mother who, though gone, was still around somehow. The essence of her. "And I'm sorry I'll never get to meet her, and that you spent all that time hoping, only for it to be snatched away. Truly, I am sorry. I wish I had better words to say, to offer comfort, but I've never been much good with words."

She put her arms around him instead, hugging the side of him to the front of her.

Clifford twisted in his seat, eyeing her with suspicion as her arms shifted with him. "Does this mean you believe me—that I had nothing to do with Don capturing you?"

"I'm still deciding," she replied a note too quickly, having forgotten that she was supposed to be wary of him. "But... why did you keep her a secret?"

"It's easier not to talk about her. It was always easier to pretend she was working at the matchstick factory or that she never left Newcastle or that I just made her up, you know? After so many years, it was just... simpler." His voice hitched. "I didn't have to think about what *might* have happened to her, and once I found out, it was still easier to believe she was out there somewhere. I'd already trained my thoughts to believe it and saw no reason to stop."

Betsy understood that keenly. Grief was such a private, painful thing, and everyone carried the burden of it in their own way. Whilst she and her father had celebrated her mother, visiting her grave and talking to her as if she was still there, others chose to forget, or put distance between themselves and their loss.

She held him tighter, letting him know that she was there to lean on through whatever hurt he felt, letting him know that she could take some of that burden if he wanted her to.

She pulled back slightly, whispering, "You'd better not be lying to me."

"I wish I was," he replied, resting his cheek on her hair.

"Because it would be easier?"

He made a noise of assent. "Am I forgiven yet?"

"I thought you said you didn't do anything wrong," she pointed out.

"Not directly, but I was so... caught up in spending Christmas with you that I didn't stop to think we might be followed. Watched." A soft sigh made his chest rise and fall. "After eight years in Don's service, I should've known better."

Nestling further into the warmth of him, feeling his arm drape around her shoulders, Betsy mustered a sad smile that he could not see. "If that's all I have to forgive you for, consider it done."

In truth, she did not know how she could have accused him so vehemently, when he *had* spent the past two years showing her that she could trust him. At any point, he could have shown the Rat Boys where she was, but he had not. Instead, he had shared his breakfast with her, made her laugh, and brought a reliable smile to her face no matter how awful any given morning had been.

She supposed it had been the shock of the situation and her misjudging what had looked like clear evidence of betrayal. A simple enough mistake to make.

"To be clear, do you really think I'm capable of hurting you like that? Am I still the boy who stole your pocket watch in your eyes?" Clifford asked, a mite shyly.

She slipped her arms around his waist and hugged him close. "You look a little bit like him, but you're not him," she murmured, feeling sleepy again.

"Thank you."

"For what?" she mumbled.

But she did not hear his reply, as the heat of his body, the hearty Christmas dinner in her belly, and the swaying of the cart rocked her back into a deep and much-needed slumber.

And as she sank into that secret world of sleeping, she dreamed of a little girl with a purse full of coins and no fear whatsoever, demanding a ticket to London to see her brother. A little girl alone on the roads on Christmas Eve with a single wish in her heart that kept her brave: to be with Clifford in that far-off Capital, to start a new life.

*I hope she knew how loved she was...* Betsy prayed, knowing she did not need a spare Christmas wish for the heavens to be able to hear her.

# Chapter Eighteen

"Here." Clifford put a brown paper bag in Betsy's lap as she stirred to a lightening world.

The landscape around them had transformed from eerie shadows and smudged shapes to snow-heavy trees, their trunks glittering with frost. A blackbird pecked at a small mound of snow, kicking up a spray of white as it searched for a morning worm. A robin hopped along the still-green branches of a lone cedar and fluttered over to the hedgerow that flanked the other side of the road, balancing deftly on a tiny twig to snap off a bright red holly berry.

*Is that you, Ma? Or are you Athena, perhaps?*

"Ma used to say that was why they had such red breasts," Betsy said, smiling as she opened the paper bag.

Clifford chuckled. "Too many holly berries?"

"Don't laugh. It *could* be true, and I'm choosing to believe it." She flashed him a playful look of warning that swiftly turned into a gasp as she saw what was in the bag. "Where did you get boiled eggs? They're still warm!"

Clifford thumbed back over his shoulder. "There was a man selling them on the side of the road. He'd just come down from the farm nearby."

"How did I sleep through it?"

He shrugged. "You tell me."

Betsy plucked out one of the boiled eggs and cupped her hands around it, letting the speckled shell warm her skin.

Once it had cooled, she set to work peeling off the shells. That done, she handed one to Clifford and kept the other to herself, taking a big bite as she admired the beautiful winter wonderland around her.

In the distance, a woodland of pine trees made her heart sing, the triangular evergreens growing tall and proud. She could just imagine how extraordinary they would look, decorated in bows and ornaments and tinsel and little flickering candles that resembled constellations, each topped with an angel or a star.

*An entire forest of Christmas trees...* It made her so giddy she could barely sit still. Indeed, to anyone travelling through the night as they had done, it would certainly make the frightening shapes less scary. Instead, it would look like a magical realm on the horizon, where festive cheer and merriment reigned, and there was a roasted goose and crispy golden potatoes for everyone.

"You look heartened after your rest," Clifford remarked, chewing his mouthful of egg.

Betsy sighed and sat back against the hard bench, sweeping her hand out. "It's not the sleep, it's all of this."

"I thought you might like it."

"Did you know I've never been out of the city before?" she asked.

He swallowed his mouthful. "I didn't, but the look on your face is a bit of a hint. Your eyes are as wide as saucers."

"The air is... so much fresher, and everything is so green and alive." She grinned from ear to ear, sucking in a crisp breath.

He raised an eyebrow. "Everything is white, Betsy. Are you sure you're fully awake?"

"Oh, you know what I mean." She chuckled, batting him on the arm. "I can *picture* what it must look like in the spring and the summer, when the flowers are in bloom and the trees have all of their leaves. Oh, and in the autumn, with all the leaves changing colour! I doubt I've seen anywhere more beautiful, Cliff. I've never seen snow glitter like this before. It looks like millions of crushed diamonds, twinkling away."

He cast her a lopsided smile. "You don't want me to turn back then?"

"Not just yet, but I *would* like to know where we're going," she replied, suddenly aware of how far they were from London. Several hours at least. It did not frighten her anymore, but her curiosity could not stand the anticipation nor the secrecy.

Clifford put a finger to his lips. "We'll be there soon enough, so you just have some patience and wait. I've put a lot of thought into your last Christmas gift."

"The currant bun, the delicious dinner, the sweets, the beautiful little tree—you've done too much for me already," she insisted. "And I still haven't got you anything."

He looked at her, eyes gleaming, but his smile did not reach them. "This will be the last one; I promise." He reached for her hand. "Don't make me ruin the surprise, or you'll undo all my efforts."

"Very well," she mumbled, hiding a smile as he kept her hand in his.

---

The sun was just creeping above the horizon, casting shards of burnished orange and dreamy pinks and brooding purples into the sky, when Clifford suddenly pulled the cart to a halt at the side of the road. In the same spot, a couple of other horses had been left to wander at their leisure, nosing aside the snow to get to the grass beneath, and there were footprints in the fresh fallen blanket of white.

Looking ahead, Betsy could make out the wispy coils of chimney smoke in the near distance. A village or town of some kind, stirring with the Boxing Day dawn. Perhaps, some of them might have been granted the day off work to spend with their families, enjoying a gift of coin or food or something similar from their employers. Betsy hoped so, for she was not yet ready to relinquish *her* festive cheer, not after Don had stolen some of it.

"We're here," Clifford said, getting down from the driver's bench.

He came over to Betsy's side and raised his hands up to help her down. She shuffled forward, a flood of heat rushing into her cheeks as Clifford's hands settled on her waist. Her chin dropped to her chest as she braced her own hands against his shoulders, his strong arms lifting her to the snow-covered ground with ease.

"And where is "here" exactly?" she asked, though she did not really want the surprise to be spoiled.

He laughed. "And you call *me* the impatient one."

Taking her hand in his, he led her away from the road, along a woodland pathway that had been trodden into the snow by several other pairs of feet. Whenever they came to a low-hanging branch, he swept it aside to let her under, and as it sprang back, powdery snow sprinkled down to the earth to join the drifts below.

"It's like I'm in a completely different world," she gasped in awe, revelling in the fairytale of her surroundings, marvelling at the fresh crunch of snow under her shoes as she deliberately veered off to make her mark in an untouched stretch of white.

Clifford beamed at her. "I'm glad you like it."

But she had seen nothing yet, and as the trees began to thin out and the pathway began to slant downwards, the surprise was finally and exquisitely revealed to her spellbound eyes.

They had reached the bend of what was, quite obviously, a river, but the water was not moving. It was perfectly still and solid. Perfectly frozen. And though the sun had only just begun to rise, there were clusters of people setting up stalls on the ice whilst others sped around on thin blades of metal attached to their shoes.

A few others had no blade at all, skating around on just their shoes, all of them gliding with the grace of a swan.

She gasped as a child, no older than six or so, toppled over and two slightly older boys skated over to help. The air stilled as if waiting for the child's cry, but it did not come. Laughing merrily, the child took the proffered hands of the other two boys and got back up, skating again as if nothing had happened.

*Like Papa and his brothers.* Betsy had always prided herself on her imagination, but she had never quite been able to conjure clear enough images of her father's stories about the London Frost Fairs. Now, at last, she understood. She could see it all perfectly, picturing her father and his brothers skating around, causing mischief.

"I'd have taken you to our spot in Limehouse, but the river just refuses to freeze," Clifford said quietly, smiling.

Betsy peered up at him, tears pricking her eyes. "You... remembered this?"

"I remember every story you've told me."

He had asked to hear the tale of the Frost Fairs a few times since they had become friendly with one another, and she had told it eagerly, despite knowing that she could not do it justice. Her father was the storyteller, not her. But to think that Clifford had not only listened, but had remembered and sought out a real Frost Fair was enough to make her melt into a puddle of her own bittersweet tears.

"Don't cry, Betsy," he murmured, covering his palm with his sleeve to dab away the droplets that fell onto her cheek. "If you cry, I'll think you hate it."

She smiled through her tears, her heart so swollen in her chest that it threatened to burst. "This is... the nicest thing... that anyone has ever done... for me," she hiccoughed. "I... I... don't know how to thank you."

*And I'm sorry your sister can't see this,* she wanted to add, but did not want to upset him, so she held her tongue.

"Enjoy yourself," he told her, his voice thick as if he, too, was thinking about his sister. "That'll be enough for me."

Overcome, she threw her arms around him and hugged him tightly, burying her teary face into the shoulder of his greatcoat. He smelled of fresh winter air, sweet woodsmoke, and earthy soap. A perfect perfume that reminded her of home.

"Thank you," she whispered.

"Thank *you* for not jumping out of the cart," he replied, hugging her in return. His breath was hot against her neck, his arms so strong and safe that she did not know if she wanted to leave their embrace.

But as the laughter and happy shrieks of the skaters drifted up the riverbank, Betsy's envy proved to be a compelling thing. Weaving her arm through Clifford's, both of them bathed in the amber light that pierced the trees, they headed down to the ice to join in.

Betsy swiftly learned that the children who were speeding around the frozen surface, as graceful as ballerinas, made a very difficult thing look ridiculously easy. She was like a fawn on the ice, her legs slipping and sliding in every direction, her arms flailing wildly, none of her limbs doing what she wanted them to.

"How are they doing this?" she gasped, laughing through her embarrassment.

Clifford grinned and took both of her hands in his, walking backwards over the ice as he led her. "They've had years to practice, I'd wager. And you're not doing so bad for your first attempt. You haven't fallen yet."

"What did you say that for?" She groaned, certain that he had just doomed her to take a tumble.

Clifford held tightly to her hands as they made their way into the centre of the frozen river. With each push of Betsy's legs—trying to glide like the children who skated in smooth circles and figure-eights—her feet slipped less, and she thought she might be finding something of a rhythm.

"The ice won't crack, will it?" she wheezed, surprisingly breathless from the exertion. Bundled up in the old coat that she had found in the back of the cart, she was almost *too* warm.

Clifford shook his head. "There wouldn't be people out on it if it was too thin. You're safe, Betsy. I promise."

She met his gaze and knew he was right. As long as he was with her, she was always safe. It shamed her to think that she had spent so long doubting him, not just with Don but earlier too, forever wondering when he was going to give her a reason to distrust him again. Now, all of that seemed like such a waste of precious time.

"Shall I let go?" he asked.

"Not yet," she replied, gripping his hands more tightly.

He smiled, eyes twinkling. "Very well. If you fall, make sure you take me down with you."

"I intend to." She chuckled, her heart as full as a heart could be.

---

The breeze whipped through Betsy's hair as she glided across the ice, flying around and around the frozen river with cautious confidence. At the very least, she no longer resembled a staggering drunk.

She had blades buckled to her feet, borrowed from a young woman who had insisted on lending her the pair, and it had made all the difference.

Betsy was fairly sure that the woman had only lent the skates to her because Betsy had fallen quite hard, close to the stalls that were being erected, and had clearly wanted to give up. But she was more than grateful that the woman had taken pity on her and that she had not, in fact, given up. If she had, she would have missed out on a feeling that was the closest thing to freedom she had ever experienced. Even more so than the snowball fight on the bridge.

"Look at you!" Clifford skated up to meet her and took her by the hand. He had borrowed some skates too, his movements powerful and confident as if he had done it before.

"I can't believe it!" she panted in reply, as they skated the last circuit together. "I had so many dreams of doing this, and... I can't believe that I am."

They flew around the ice faster than before, her confidence bolstered by Clifford's presence at her side and his hand holding hers. And she wondered for a moment if this was akin to what the birds felt when they soared through the skies, utterly and completely at liberty to do what they pleased.

Presently, they slowed and skated towards the riverbank together, pink-cheeked, bright-eyed and smiling at one another. Betsy had thought that no Christmas could rival those of her younger years, but, despite everything, that year was racing to the very top of her most favourite. The only thing that would have made it better was if her father was there to share in it.

*Next year... I'll find a way.*

"I'm exhausted!" Betsy laughed. "Watching the young ones do it, you'd think it took no effort at all."

Clifford shuffled off his greatcoat and set it down on the snowy bank. "How are your bruises?"

"They'll be tremendous, I've no doubt," she replied. "But worth it."

He gestured for her to sit. "So, not such a terrible surprise then?"

"Not at all terrible." She peered up at him, not sitting just yet. "Thank you, Cliff. I know I've been saying it for hours, but... thank you."

He moved closer to her, tucking a loose lock of hair behind her ear. "Being here becomes you well. You look... beautiful, Betsy. Some colour in your cheeks, some life in your eyes, and that smile—it's brighter than the sun."

His gaze flitted to her lips. "I'll fetch us some mulled cider to drink, to warm us up."

"I'll come with you," she urged.

He smiled, shaking his head. "You need to rest your legs, or they'll seize up and you won't be able to skate again. You've got a whole day of it ahead of you, if you want." His arm encircled her waist, his hand cradling her cheek. "Please, Betsy, let me do this for you. One very last thing."

She sighed, her palms on his chest, feeling the wild thud of his heart. "Very well, but nothing more after this. And I'm going to find something at one of those stalls later to give you for your Christmas gift."

"Nothing more," he replied, and dipped his head.

His lips were on hers in an instant, her eyes widening in surprise. But like the frozen river and the ice skating and the Frost Fair, it was not at all a terrible surprise.

A moment later, she closed her eyes and kissed him back, looping her arms around his neck. The soft graze of his mouth warmed her to the soul, her skin tingling as if she had just walked in from the biting cold to the fierce heat of a fireplace, all of the frost of recent years thawing in that magical instant.

All at once, memories of him glowed in a different light—every kiss to her hair or brow, every time he had held her hand or put his arm around her, every time he had done something to make her smile; every breakfast they had shared, every bag of boiled sweets; the joy of last Christmas, where they had wandered together the way couples might, and he had peered through the bakery window at the currant bun, so close to her that she had not been able to breathe.

*I love him...* It was like thick fog clearing on the Thames, revealing all, where before she had only been able to make out shapes and the warning clangs of pans and bells. It had been there all along, hidden beneath everything else.

She melted into his embrace as their kiss deepened, the snowy trees around them creating a silent world just for the two of them, where no one could disturb them or hurt them.

Slowly, he drew back, a dazed expression on his handsome face. "I won't be long," he murmured, bending to place another kiss upon her brow. "You stay warm."

Speechless, all she could do was nod. There would be time for confessions later, once they both had a hot drink cradled in their hands.

"This has been the greatest Christmas of my life. Thank you for giving me good memories to hold onto; I couldn't ask for anything more," he said softly, before stepping back onto the ice and skating off towards the cluster of stalls that were now serving what appeared to be an entire town.

Giddy and flushed and breathless, Betsy sank down onto Clifford's greatcoat and tucked her knees up to her chest. An unyielding grin made her cheeks ache as she stared out across the frozen river, watching a young boy spin on his skates, while a short distance away, another boy slid through the legs of a friend or brother. Their laughter and their joy was intoxicating, but nothing could have been more potent than the kiss that still tingled on her lips.

Clifford really had saved the best Christmas gift until last.

# Chapter Nineteen

The sun had reached its highest point of the day, peeking through the grey fleece of thick clouds. More snow was on its way, but Clifford was still not back. Betsy had waited patiently, forced to pull the greatcoat around herself to feel the benefit of its warmth. However, with each ticking minute, the seed of worry that had been planted in her chest had begun to bloom into a terrible, thorned thing that pricked at her lungs with every anxious breath she took.

*What if he's in some trouble? What if he had no money and stole drinks for us, and now he's being chased?* Memories of the sweet air behind the confectionery soured her thoughts. *What if we were followed and Don's men have taken him? What if they're looking for me right now?*

"This is silly," she muttered, getting up on numb legs. She stamped on the spot for a minute to urge some life back into her limbs and blew her hot breath into her icy hands.

Indeed, there was no use fretting when the solution was painfully simple: she would go and find him.

Feeling less confident than before, the greatcoat swamping her, she skated out onto the frozen river, tilting her head up as the sky darkened and a snowflake kissed the tip of her nose. It would soon be falling heavily, and she intended to have Clifford back at her side before it did.

The scent of frying meat and sweet pastries and warming spices bombarded Betsy's senses as she reached the shacks, tables, and rickety wooden structures that had been hastily lashed together that morning. Her mouth watered, reminding her that she had not eaten anything but a boiled egg since yesterday. But food would have to wait. She would indulge in a mince pie or a piece of figgy pudding with Clifford, not without.

Stopping to remove her skates, she carefully wandered through the impromptu market until she came to a stall selling mulled cider.

"Excuse me," she said, approaching the woman behind the simple counter. "You haven't seen a man about this tall," she gestured with her hand, "with... uh... quite strange grey eyes and really dark hair. He was skating with me earlier. I think he borrowed skates from the man selling meat pies."

The woman's eyes widened as if she recognised Betsy. "Clifford?"

"Yes!" Betsy gasped, overwhelmed with relief. "Have you seen him? He said he wouldn't be long, and I haven't seen anyone else selling mulled cider."

The woman came out from behind her counter, her expression unnervingly sad. "He's gone, Betsy."

*How does she know my name?* Betsy's relief flipped into panic, a cold prickle beetling down her spine as she blurted out, "What? Gone where?"

"He's gone back to London, Betsy. He doesn't want you to follow him. Doesn't want you to ever go back there, for your own sake," the woman replied. "My husband—the man selling the meat pies—is an old friend of his. We're to take care of you now." She put a gentle hand on Betsy's shoulder. "He said to tell you that everything in his pockets is now yours."

Betsy stared at the woman as if a great monster were standing before her. "I have to go back. My father is there, Clifford is there—I can't stay here. I don't know you. I don't... I don't..." Her breathing came in fits and starts, like wrenching sobs without the tears.

"Clifford has promised to send news of your father, if it ever comes, and he has promised to do all he can to help your father's cause," the woman said. "But he said that's the deal—he'll help your father if you stay here, safe away from Mr. Durham. He said it was his last gift to you."

Betsy staggered back, her hand flying to her chest. She thumped her palm against it to try and get her breathing to even out, but the world around her was spinning and her heart was racing, and all she could think about was Clifford alone on the road back to London without her. Leaving her in safety whilst he returned to consequences that would probably be the death of him.

"I... have to go back," she wheezed. "Can someone lend me a horse or a cart? Is someone going in that direction? I can't... I can't let him do this. I can't let him. Don will kill him for this. I... I..."

The woman pulled her into a tight embrace, holding her there. "He said you'd say that," she whispered softly, soothingly. "So, he told me to tell you, "It's for my immortal soul." He said you'd know what he meant."

Betsy allowed herself to be held as a man came over, removing his cap from his head as he said, "Is this her?"

"It is," the woman replied.

Hot and furious tears welled in Betsy's eyes, frustration coursing through her veins like the current that swept beneath the thick layer of river ice. *He had no right... He had no right to do this... How could he leave me like that? How could he kiss me and... leave.*

"I have to go back," Betsy murmured desperately, clinging to the stranger who smelled of the sweet mulled cider that she sold.

The woman patted her gently on the back. "You can't, Betsy. Clifford told us everything." She sighed in sympathy. "I'm sorry. I'm so sorry, but you can't."

And though Betsy wanted to fight against that refusal, she could not. Deep down, past her sinking heart, she knew it was the truth. If she went back to London, her life would be a misery. She would fall deeper and deeper into destitution, starvation, desperation, until she had no choice but to accept Don's offer.

Clifford had given her a chance.

He had said that this excursion would be his last Christmas gift to her. With all her broken heart, she wished she would have figured out what he meant sooner—that it was not his last gift this year, but perhaps his last ever.

For if Don ever found out what he had done, that he had spirited Betsy out of London altogether, it surely *would* be the last thing Clifford ever did.

# Chapter Twenty

*Winterbrook, December 19th, 1852*

Betsy paused at the farmhouse door to kick the snow and mud off her boots, the moisture from her breath making the inside of her scarf feel wet against her chin. She sighed as she peeled off her gloves and coat, hanging them on the nearby hooks that always gave away who was in and who was out. Especially in autumn and winter.

The patter of tiny claws on the flagstones heralded the appearance of Bramble—a small but lively terrier who was solely responsible for the amount of rabbit that the household ate.

Betsy crouched down, scratching behind the terrier's ears. He thumped his back leg happily while his black, wet nose snuffled her hands in case she had brought home something delicious for him.

"Not today," she apologised. "But I'll bring you something from town tomorrow."

"You're back late," called a voice from the warm kitchen.

Betsy stood up and headed into the comforting heat, her nose filling with the mouthwatering aroma of stew and fresh bread. "One of the sheep got out of the barn again and led me on a merry chase through two pastures. Is there water out back?"

"Oh my!" The woman stirring the pot stared at Betsy in dismay, noting the smears of mud all over her. "I've just boiled some if you want it warm."

Betsy waved a dismissive hand. "The cold will wake me up in time for dinner. Are Thomas and the boys not back yet?" She already knew they were not, judging by their absent coats on the hooks by the door, but she liked to ask her friend, Florence, directly.

"They've not long headed up to town. I was going to join them, if you wanted to come with me?" Florence replied. "I'd be glad of the company and Bramble is itching to cause some mischief."

Betsy smiled. "Give me enough time to wash the mud and smell of sheep off me and I'll be with you."

"I'll have your stew waiting. I'll not have you keeling over in the market square 'cause I haven't fed you properly." Florence returned to stirring the mighty pot of stew and Betsy headed toward the courtyard at the back of the farmhouse, where a barrel of rainwater served as their bath. On special days, they had a tin tub inside by the fireplace, but that day was like any other.

In the year that Betsy had lived at Winterbrook Farm—one of three farms in the small hamlet of Winterbrook, just outside the town of Wallingford—she had found gratitude for Clifford's parting act of generosity.

She had thrown herself almost immediately into hard, backbreaking farmwork, eager to ensure that Florence and Thomas Moreley did not regret doing their friend Clifford such a great favour in giving her room and board. The work changed depending on the season, and she did it all without complaint, reminding herself that at least she was not waist deep in river mud.

Slowly but surely, she had become friends with Florence, and was well liked by her husband, Thomas. Their three sons had taken to her instantly, treating her like a long-lost sister. Betsy, in turn, liked the Moreleys, to the point where, sitting out in the courtyard one balmy summer's evening, she had not been able to imagine any other life for herself. Even through the winter, she could not argue with the impeccable beauty of the landscape around her.

But there was one thing missing. Two things, really. Always there in the back of her mind, smearing an indelible flaw through her new existence. The two men she loved above all else: one stuck in prison, one unaccounted for.

In eleven-and-a-half months, she had heard nothing from Clifford. As such, she had heard nothing about her father, either. For all she knew, both could be dead.

At the barrel in the courtyard, Betsy took up the pick that leaned against the puncheons and heaved the sharp end into the dense layer of ice that frosted the surface. It splintered into satisfying chunks, which Betsy heaved out and dropped onto the ground, watching as they fractured into a hundred sparkling shards.

Bramble raced out at the sound and, once he was certain there was nothing nefarious afoot, began to crunch on the pieces of ice.

"See, I said I'd give you a treat," Betsy said, chuckling at the adorable terrier.

Ten minutes later, soaked and shivering but scrubbed to a pink cleanliness, Betsy returned into the heat of the farmhouse and hurried through to the small annexe that served as her bedchamber. She changed into her only good dress with shaky hands and ran a comb through her hair, tying it up with a red ribbon before heading back out, feeling as awake as if it were morning again.

"Now, that's more like it," Florence said with a smile. "You'll have half of Wallingford proposing, and Amory's heart broken, by the end of the night."

Betsy grimaced. "I wish he'd stop asking."

"You could do worse," Florence pointed out.

Amory Spiggot was the eldest son of the nearest farmer and, at five-and-twenty with a respectable farm to inherit, he had decided the moment news spread of Betsy's arrival that she was going to be his wife. For a year, at least once a week, in every season, he had asked her to marry him. And every time, she had refused, for though he was pleasant, reasonably handsome, and well-stationed, he was not Clifford.

"He's persistent; I'll give him that," Betsy said with a sigh. "But there are countless women in town who'd give anything to marry him. What on earth does he keep hounding *me* for?"

Florence laughed as if it should have been obvious and dished out a bowl of piping hot stew. She set it on the long, timeworn kitchen table and hung up her apron. "I'm going to put another dress on. We'll make our way up to town once you're done."

With that, she left Betsy alone in the farmhouse kitchen to feast on the hearty stew. Bramble, however, stayed at Betsy's side, eagerly waiting for a dropped bit of meat or vegetables, or a crumb of bread.

As Betsy ate, relishing every spoonful of the savoury meal, her gaze turned to the windows. Frost spiderwebbed across the pane and, beyond, the trees that lined the first pasture had lost their leaves, standing stark and almost embarrassed in the muted, dark blue light of early evening.

Absently, she wondered if Clifford was looking at that same sky, thinking of her.

Within ten minutes, she had devoured the last of the stew and put the bowl on the ground for Bramble to lick clean. And not a moment too soon, as Florence breezed out of the door that led to her quarters, looking beautiful in a finely woven dress of claret wool.

"All done?" Florence asked, casting an amused glance down at Bramble.

The terrier licked his lips happily.

"All done," Betsy confirmed, smiling.

"Come on then, or we'll miss it all," Florence urged, a new spring in her step as she headed for the door.

Wrapped up warm against the bite of the wintry wind, it did not take the two women long to reach the edge of Wallingford. Bramble trotted alongside, diving into the hedgerows now and then if he heard a rustle, emerging quickly if Florence whistled for him to heel.

But as the town's lights grew brighter and the babble of chatter became clearer, Betsy's attention was solely fixed on what lay ahead.

"My goodness..." she gasped, as the market square came into view.

The town had been transformed into a festive wonderland, with neat stalls arranged all around the square. Smoke coiled up from a tray of roasting chestnuts, the heat blackening the shells to make the nut inside that much sweeter. Fragrant steam swelled from great vats of broths, soups, mulled wine, and mulled cider. Someone was stewing apples, served with a handful of currants and a hearty dose of cream. There were pastries of every kind, shaped like stars and flowers, giving off the most buttery-sweet scent.

A Christmas tree stood in the centre of the market square, ornamented with ribbons and glass baubles that tinkled in the breeze. They would not light the candles on the tree yet, but Betsy could already imagine how beautiful it would be.

*I wonder what became of my little tree...* She had not thought about it in a long time—that perfect little gift that Clifford had somehow found for her. If nothing had befallen him when he had returned to London, perhaps he had taken care of it. If something *had* happened to him, she supposed it would have withered and died in those lodgings, tossed out when someone else moved in.

"What's wrong?" Florence asked, nudging Betsy in the ribs.

Betsy smiled, shaking her head. "Just thinking about Christmases past."

"Your father?" Florence knew everything that had come before Betsy's appearance at the Frost Fair, the stories told in dribs and drabs across the dinner table or whilst out in the fields or whilst cleaning out the barn and stables.

"Partially." Betsy shrugged. "That guard said he would be released this year, but... I don't know if it's true. And I keep thinking that I should be there, but I can't bear the thought of being tricked again."

*And I don't know if Clifford is alive or dead, and it's eating away at me more than usual,* she neglected to add. Whenever she mentioned Clifford to Florence or Thomas, they would smile and reassure her that he was well, telling her there was no scrape he could not get himself out of. And she wanted to believe that, she really did, but there was something about that time of year that made it almost impossible.

"I really do love it here, Florence, but it has never felt quite so... so... far away before." Betsy stared at the Christmas tree, hoping to find some kind of answer in the swaying fronds. "I think what I'm trying to say is—if I'm to root my life here, I first need to know if there's anything still tying me to London, or I won't thrive properly. Like leeks in November."

Florence turned to face her with a fond expression, resting a hand on Betsy's shoulder. "Clifford charged me and Thomas with making sure you never went back there, but you're no prisoner here, Betsy. We can't actually make you stay if you feel there's something you need to do elsewhere. That being said, I hope you *do* choose to root your life here. Doesn't have to be with Amory, if that's what worries you." She flashed a sad smile, as if she already knew what Betsy would decide.

Betsy lowered her gaze, fidgeting with a loose thread on her gloves. "If I *were* to return to London for a short while, just to be sure one way or the other, how would I get there?"

"You have the coin that Clifford left for you," Florence replied. "I suspect it was meant to pay us for your keep, but you've done more than earn that with all your hard work. And if there's a time where we could spare you, it's now, when there's not much afoot at the farm."

Betsy's heart swelled with gratitude for the woman who had become her friend, giving her this opportunity without judgment. "I promise I'll come back," she said in earnest. "I'll go to the prison, and if my father is turned loose, I'll bring him with me. He has always been a steadfast worker."

What she did not add was that she planned to search for Clifford too, though she suspected that Florence already knew that he was part of her melancholy, and that he was another reason for her restlessness.

"You do that," Florence urged. "It'll save Thomas having to find another couple of workers for Spring, and there's plenty of room at the farmhouse. But... you'll not go tonight, will you? I'd been looking forward to showing you Wallingford when it's all dressed up for Christmas."

Betsy opened out her arms and her friend walked into them, the two women embracing one another fondly as carol singers shuffled into position in front of the Christmas tree.

"I won't go tonight. I'll leave on Christmas Eve," Betsy promised, the gloom lifting from her shoulders. "Tonight, I'm going to enjoy this town that feels like home with the people who have become my second family."

Florence hugged her tighter. "Oh, I am glad to hear that."

"Ma! Betsy!" Sweet voices called out above the chatter of the town, followed by the beat of footfalls as three figures came running, trailed by their bear of a father.

The Moreley boys skidded to a halt in front of the two women, their hands filled with treats from the stalls. Betsy inhaled the delicious scent of mince pies, fruity and spicy and buttery, all at once. And laughed as the oldest of the trio, Peter, thrust one of the tart-like pastries into her hand.

"We know they're your favourite," Peter said, grinning.

"We were all going to give her the mince pie!" one of the twins, Harry, complained.

The other twin, Arthur, puffed his chest. "I picked it for you, Betsy. It had the best star on top."

He took another mince pie and gave it to his mother. "And this one has the best star, too."

"You didn't pick them," Harry argued.

Peter nodded. "*I* was the one who chose them."

The three brothers muttered amongst themselves as Betsy and Florence turned to each other and, in unison, took a bite of the festive delicacy. Betsy's eyes closed in satisfaction at the sweet mincemeat—bursting with currants, raisins, and grated apple, combined with a hearty dose of sherry. The sugar might have been overwhelming had it not been tempered with lemon juice and zest, her soul tingling with happiness as the taste of ground ginger and nutmeg hit her tongue.

"It's perfect," she sighed, smiling at the boys. "Thank you."

They ceased their quarrelling, just as the carol singers burst into a jaunty rendition of 'I Saw Three Ships.' And as the entire market square stopped what they were doing to listen to the singers, Betsy realised it was not just the mince pie—it was all so perfect. Knowing that she would return to London soon, to put an end to the mystery of her father and Clifford, she could finally enjoy herself, savouring every bit of the festive cheer that now coursed in her veins.

Beaming from ear to ear, putting her arms around the boys' shoulders, she did what she had not done in a year and let the music pour out of her in song, joining in with the carol singers. Taking her lead, the boys sang with her, creating magic in the town square as everyone else—whether they could hold a tune in a bucket or not—raised up their voices, united in their joy for that one glorious moment.

As she sang, Betsy sent up a silent wish to the twinkling heavens, *Let them both be with me next year, standing in this very spot. My father and Clifford—next Christmas, let no one be absent.*

And though there was no way of knowing if a wish would be granted until it was or was not, there was such potent power in the sound of an entire town singing together, that her hope rose as high as their voices.

# Chapter Twenty-One

Betsy arrived in London in the small hours of the morning on Christmas Day, having travelled through the night in a cramped stagecoach, stuffed with merriment and food and gifts for the families that the other passengers were on their way to visit. Food and song had been shared generously, turning the journey into one of the rowdiest of Betsy's life. She had relished every second, telling herself that the good cheer could only mean that good things were coming her way, too.

But once everyone had trickled out of the stagecoach and gone in their respective directions, Betsy was left alone again in the freezing cold of pre-dawn, the cobblestones gleaming with black ice and frost glittering on the streetlamps and windows. Absently, she thought of Athena, wondering if this was what the little girl had seen when she arrived in London all those tragically fateful years ago.

*At least my belly is full, and I have people waiting for me if this comes to naught,* she told herself, checking Clifford's greatcoat pocket to make sure the coin purse was still there. It remained plump with money—more than enough to get her back to Wallingford safely.

The greatcoat did not fit her at all, the hem sweeping the frost from the ground as she set off for Pentonville Prison, but whenever she wore it, it was as if Clifford was there with her. And it was nothing that rolled up sleeves and a hitched-up hem could not solve, the finely woven wool keeping her warm against the bitter chill.

By the time Betsy reached Pentonville Prison, the sky had lightened to an inky grey, reminding her of so many winter mornings on the riverbank, digging through the mud for treasures.

Steeling herself, she walked the last stretch to the guard post. "Merry Christmas," she said as brightly as she could, surprised to find the same guard standing there. "You must've done something to annoy someone higher up."

"Pardon?" the guard replied brusquely, eyes narrowing. Clearly, he did not recognise her.

"A jest," she said apologetically. "You were here on Christmas Day last year, so I wondered if you'd done something to upset the higher-ups."

The guard relaxed a little, a smirk lifting his lips. "I don't bother with Christmas. Would rather be making honest coin, so here I am." He paused, observing her more closely. "I think I *do* remember you. Came to see about your father. The one what was in the papers a few years back for getting a hefty sentence, though he only nicked a quart of sweets?"

"That's him," Betsy replied, swallowing her nerves. "You told me he was due to be released today, so here *I* am, bothering you again."

The guard leaned on the ledge in front of him. "Well, he ain't here."

"What?" Betsy's heart stopped for a moment, frozen in the purgatory of not knowing if she was about to receive good news or bad.

"I thought of you, as it happens," the guard said. "He got turned loose on Boxing Day last year."

She stared at him, an invisible hand around her throat, squeezing it shut.

"Tomorrow, a year ago," he added, as if his first explanation was not enough. "I told him you'd been waiting for him, and off he went. Just assumed you'd have found each other, but I guess not if you're back here and he ain't. Unless he's got himself back in the clink, has he?"

Betsy's breaths came in ragged gasps as she braced her hand against the icy wall of the prison, stooping slightly to ease the dizziness that swirled in her head. She had been away for a year, living a hard working, relatively cheerful life, and all that time, her father had been free and looking for her.

*He must've feared the worst. I never went back to our lodgings. I never left word of where I was going. I didn't send a message back with Clifford.* There had been no time for any of that, considering she had not known that she was being taken out of London.

"Did he leave a message or an address or anything?" Betsy wheezed.

The guard shrugged. "Not with me, he didn't."

She turned without another word, walking as quickly as she could along the icy road. Nevertheless, it would be over an hour's journey back to Whitechapel, where she knew she stood the only chance of finding answers about her father. If Clifford was there, he might know of her father's whereabouts, killing two birds with one stone. If Clifford was not there, Don would certainly have answers for her about both of the men she sought, and she no longer cared what they might cost.

---

Betsy marched up the street where she knew Don's infamous brothel could be found, bent double against the sleet that pierced down like razor blades.

It had come out of nowhere, the tiny pellets of ice striking her with a vengeance, but she would not be deterred by a bit of bad weather.

She was almost at the front entrance, the swinging sign above the door depicting a black cat with a red bow around its neck, when a shadow lunged out of the nearby alley and grabbed her.

Her mouth opened in a scream, but a hand clamped over it, a strong arm dragging her backwards into the shadows of the alleyway.

But she had grown in strength and health during her time at Winterbrook Farm, and as she flailed and writhed and kicked out, she could feel her captor struggling to keep hold of her.

"Stop!" a man's voice hissed. "Stop wriggling!"

Betsy blinked. There was something familiar about that voice.

"For pity's sake, it's me," the man said. "Mercy, did they have you hoisting haybales at Thomas' place?"

Her heart leapt and she stilled in Clifford's rough embrace, waiting until she felt his grip loosen before she whirled around to face him. And as she gazed up into those striking grey eyes, she did not know whether to hit him or hug him.

He had not changed much, but there was a new, silvery scar across the lips that had kissed her before he abandoned her. And a smaller scar on his left cheek, the ragged end of it coming perilously close to his eye.

"What are you doing here?" Clifford asked, panic etched on his handsome face. A face she had dreamt about so often, not knowing if she would ever see it again.

Betsy raised her fingertips to his lips, touching that shiny scar. "I came to find you. I came to find my father." She sighed. "You must've known that I would."

"I *hoped* you wouldn't," he replied, flinching as she lightly stroked the injuries that were new to her, but must have been old to him. "We both did."

Her hand stilled. "Both?"

"Your father is here, Betsy. He works for Don now, paying off the imaginary debt that was conjured for him, for daring to marry the woman he loved." Clifford drew Betsy's hand away from his face, holding it tightly. "When I came back from Wallingford, he was already here. Don knew when your father was going to be released, so he had men waiting just out of sight of the prison. He hadn't been free for more than five minutes before they caught him and brought him here."

Betsy's mind drifted back to the year before, and the promises that had been made. "You said you'd send word of him if you received any." Her voice hitched. "All year, I've been waiting, hearing nothing. I thought... I thought you were dead! I thought Don had done something terrible. I thought my father was in prison. One message from you, and I... wouldn't have worried every bloody day for twelve months! I mean, of all people, you must know what torture that can be!"

"I know, I know," Clifford said softly, shamefully. "But I spoke with your father. I told him everything. And we decided it was better if you stayed where you were, where you could be safe and happy."

"That wasn't your decision to make! Neither of you!" Betsy hissed, her eyes prickling with tears. "I have been beside myself with worry. And yes, I was happy there, but I could never truly settle, not knowing what had happened to the both of you. One word, Cliff! One word could have set my heart and mind at ease!"

Clifford bowed his head. "In truth, *I* wanted to tell you. Your father told me not to. He knew you'd want to come back, and I suppose I did too, in the end."

He raised his gaze, his grey eyes gleaming with a mixture of fear and relief. "But you have to go back now, Betsy. We're both fine. *You* won't be if you stay, so why don't I put you on a stagecoach before anyone notices you're here."

Betsy squeezed Clifford's hands. "I didn't come all this way to not see my father, Cliff. I think you know that."

*And I didn't find you just to leave without you...* She could not admit that, could not admit that she loved him still, and had thought of him every day since the moment she realised that she loved him.

"I do, but I hoped I could persuade you," Clifford replied, a muscle tensing in his jaw. "I should've told you that he doesn't want to see you. Should've made up a story about him being angry with you for something or other, but... I can't do that today of all days."

Betsy frowned up at him in confusion.

"Merry Christmas, Betsy," he murmured, pulling his greatcoat tighter around her. "It suits you better than it ever suited me."

"Liar," she mumbled.

He sighed like a millworker trying to expel cotton from their lungs. "Come with me. But we can't stay long. Five minutes, then you leave, and you don't look back."

"Very well," she lied.

Glancing down the alleyway and poking his head around the corner to check the street beyond, he slipped his fingers into hers and tugged her deeper into the alley, where they were swiftly swallowed up by the shadows.

With every step, Betsy wondered if Clifford was taking her in the opposite direction, hoping to force her into leaving.

But, in due course, they stopped outside a narrow door—barely half the width of Clifford. It had seen better days, a sliver of wood missing, the hinges rusted over. From within, drifting out of that gap, she heard the harsh bark of someone coughing violently.

"Five minutes," Clifford repeated, easing open the door. It squeaked a little.

A smoky haze that carried the sour scent of sickness greeted Betsy as she stepped into the room beyond. A bunkhouse of some kind, it was tiny and overcrowded with beds and hammocks, and bedrolls on the floor in-between. Betsy had to pick her way across the slumbering, snoring bodies of men who did not stir at the intrusion. The reek of stale alcohol suggested why.

*Where are their families? Why are they not sitting around a table, sharing the day together?* She pushed the thought to the side as she noticed a single lantern burning on the far side of the small room, and in the hazy glow of it she saw the face she had not beheld in three years.

Her father leaned against the soot-stained wall, his cheeks sunken, his ribs showing in the wide gap of his open collar. His shirt was filthy—*he* was filthy—and he held a tattered handkerchief to his mouth, his eyes glazed over in the lamplight.

"Pa?" she whispered, stepping over a few more bodies to reach her father's corner of the awful room.

He turned slowly, his expression listless.

But the moment he saw his daughter standing there, a spark of life flared into his glassy eyes. He sat up straighter and hurried to pull his collar closed, as if he were ashamed. A second later, he was bent double, coughing and spluttering into the grubby handkerchief; his breaths a wheezing rasp, like he could not get air into his lungs despite mimicking the act of inhaling.

"Pa?" Betsy repeated, sinking to her knees on the dirty floor. She reached for her father, gingerly putting her arms around him in case she accidentally hurt him. "Pa, what's wrong?"

Over Betsy's shoulder, her father growled, "I told you not to tell her."

"I didn't tell her, Kenneth," Clifford replied, standing just behind Betsy. "She came back. She came to find you, and now that she has, she's leaving again. That was the deal."

He looked anxiously across the lumps of sleeping men, likely wondering if some of them were not sleeping nearly as deeply as they seemed to be. Betsy shared the fear, but she would not let it stop her from talking to her father.

Her father relaxed a little, his coughs receding to a rattling croak. "You'd best... be on your way, mouse. It's Christmas Day—if you hurry, I'm sure you can... make it back to where you've been... in time for... a feast and... celebrations."

"I'm not going anywhere." Betsy held him tighter, willing him to hold her back. "What happened to you, Pa? You need a physician. We should get you out of here right now."

He pushed her away gently, turning his face from her as he covered his mouth with the handkerchief. "Mouse, I don't know what's wrong. I don't know if it's catching, so you shouldn't touch me."

"I haven't seen you in years, Pa. I don't care if what you have is catching." She cradled his sunken cheek and when he made no move to push her hand away, she leaned in to hug him again.

This time, his thin arms encircled her and as he rested his chin on her shoulder, she could have sworn she heard him whisper, "Thank goodness." His raspy sigh was one of relief, his body trembling as he held her as tightly as he could.

"I heard you were there... last year," her father murmured, after a while. "They were... supposed to tell you that it was the day after, but... I know Don had a hand in it. I thought... I'd seen the last of him when... your ma died, but that's the... trouble with bad pennies. Always turning up when... they're not wanted. You can't be here, mouse. He likes to gloat... about the things he'll do if he ever finds you, and... it would kill me if he harmed you. You need to go back."

Betsy pulled back, tears in her eyes. "I'll go back," she said, her voice catching, "but not without you. I'm not spending another Christmas without either of you." She glanced back at Clifford. "If you want me to leave, you have to swear you'll come with me."

"Your safety relies... on me being here," her father insisted, turning his head to cough into his handkerchief. "As long as I'm paying... the debt, Don won't try... to find you."

She grabbed her father's hands. "No one will know where we are, and Don won't waste his efforts and coin in trying to hunt us down. If he cared that much, he'd have done it years ago. The only reason he sought me out before was because he knew I was in London. The only reason he sought *you* out was because he thought I was still in London. But we'll be out of sight, out of mind. I promise you." She paused to take a breath. "Failing that, we'll keep going, as far as we have to, to stop him coming after us. I have enough money now."

"I hate to rush this," Clifford hissed, "but someone's coming."

Sure enough, from the interior door—larger and more rickety than the narrow one they had entered through—came the sound of footsteps and a deep voice shouting, "Get Denby to do it. I'm getting some kip."

"Then help me," Betsy urged, staring up at Clifford with all the desperation that prickled in her veins.

He grimaced, his gaze darting between the interior door and the slim exit. A second later, he had Kenneth over his shoulder, his free hand grabbing Betsy's, all three of them pouring out of the bunkhouse before they were discovered.

Out in the alleyway, Clifford shoved Betsy to the right. "Go, Betsy," he whispered, eyes wide. "Run... and meet us by the trees in Covent Garden. The stagecoach stops there. Three o'clock. Run, love. Run."

He took off toward the brighter light at the left-hand end of the alley before she could argue, or process what he had called her. And as she heard the muffled growl of someone in the bunkhouse, she did not hesitate, sprinting deeper into the alleyway to her right, hoping it would spit her out somewhere she recognised.

It had been a long time since someone had told her to run, but she had not forgotten how. And with the hope of escape hanging over her, she prayed that the rabbit warren of Whitechapel would be no match for her.

# Chapter Twenty-Two

Betsy huddled on the steps of St. Paul's Church, making herself as small and unnoticeable as possible in Clifford's greatcoat. The most recent chime of the city's churches had marked the hour as three o'clock, and the day was already waning into evening. Sunset was, perhaps, an hour away, but it was not the encroaching darkness that worried Betsy—it was that the next stagecoach was due at any moment, and her father and Clifford were still not there.

She patted the greatcoat pocket, comforted by the rustle of the paper bag. Foolish though it might have been, she had not been able to help stepping into the confectionery that had begun her father's troubles to buy a quart of boiled sweets. Something to share on the road back to Wallingford. A tradition she had started with Clifford that warranted continuing.

*When we are safe, I'll tell him... When we're in the kitchen at Winterbrook Farm, warm and surrounded by good people, I'll tell him what my heart wants him to know.*

She hugged her knees to her chest and gazed up at that inky sky, where clouds that might be snow clouds scudded across the muted sun.

Watching her breath plume in the cold air, she turned her attention to the beautiful Christmas trees that stood sentinel on the piazza. A man with thick white hair and spectacles walked up to the first tree and struck a match, carefully lighting all of the thin, delicate candles that were tied to the slender branches.

Despite her worry, Betsy's eyes widened in wonder as the candles began to twinkle like stars, so perfect and magical that, if she had not already made a Christmas wish, she would have made it then.

Still, she supposed it would not hurt to repeat her wish, just in case those candles really *did* possess magic in their softly glowing flames. *Let them both be with me next year, standing in Wallingford's market square. My father and Clifford—next Christmas, let no one be absent.*

As if to prove that her wish was too great a request, blowing away her hopes before they had the chance to burn too brightly, the clatter of carriage wheels snatched her attention away from the beautifully decorated tree. The stagecoach had arrived, and though there would undoubtedly be another the following day, that might very well be too late.

Betsy ran down to the stagecoach, passengers filtering out and hauling down their luggage from the rack on top.

"Excuse me," she called up to the driver. "I need to be on this stagecoach, but my father and my... friend are meant to be meeting me, and they're... um... waylaid. Might you wait until they arrive?"

The driver, devoid of festive cheer, scowled down at her. "I leave in five minutes. If your father and your friend aren't here, I still leave in five minutes. Up to you if you're on it or not."

"I'll just... um..." Betsy kept glancing back, willing Clifford and her father to appear. "I'll just pay for three passengers now."

She passed up the money for three, praying he would not say that the coach was full already with passengers who had purchased their tickets already.

But he took the money and gave her three tickets, then stared ahead with his shoulders hunched, putting an end to any conversation she might have started in order to delay him. Perhaps, he had encountered such a trick before, or perhaps he just had no compassion to spare for a young woman on Christmas Day. Maybe, he had his own family waiting for him, and his eagerness to return to them was hiding in each crevice of his frown.

Those five minutes proved to be the longest of Betsy's life, her eyes fixed on the clock above the market. The hands moved silently but, to her, each tick was a deafening clang in her head.

"Are you getting on or not?" the driver asked, presently.

Betsy peered up at him. "Please, sir. Just a few more minutes. Please, I beg of you."

Other passengers were climbing aboard, stowing their luggage, chattering excitedly amongst themselves, oblivious to Betsy's turmoil. They remarked on the beauty of the Christmas trees and the delicious aromas that wafted from the stalls, brimming with an enviable cheer.

"I won't wait for one person," the driver snapped in reply. "You've got thirty seconds to decide if you're coming or going."

Panic bubbled in Betsy's chest, her fingertips pulling at the collar of her chemise in an attempt to stop it from strangling her. The air was frigid and heavy with the promise of snow—more sleet, at the very least—but the heat of her desperation had turned the greatcoat, her good dress, and all of her petticoats and undergarments into a fiery swathe that seemed determined to burn her up.

"Come on," she whispered, clasping her hands together. "Come on... Please."

"Ten seconds," the driver muttered.

Her father had taught her to count that high, and as she counted the precious seconds in her head, sweat beaded on her brow and her stomach roiled with nausea.

They were not coming. She should never have parted ways with them.

*It was a ploy...* Her heart lurched. *It was a ploy to get me to return to Wallingford, whilst they stayed here, trapped beneath Don's rule. How did I not see that before? Of course it is a ploy!*

She was about to tell the driver that she would not be travelling after all, and march her way back to Whitechapel, when two figures suddenly rounded the corner of St. Paul's Church. Both were hobbling, but one was helping the other along—dragging him, in truth.

"It's them!" Betsy cried to the driver. "I told you they would come! Please, just wait for them!"

The driver sniffed, narrowing his eyes at the two men as they shambled towards the stagecoach. His frown deepened, likely noticing the state of Clifford at the same time that Betsy did. The man she adored had a swollen eye, wore nothing but his trousers and a torn shirt, and had red welts all over his face that would soon become dark bruises.

*That* was when she heard it—a scream and a burst of angry shouts rising up from the opposite end of Covent Garden. Betsy's head snapped toward the noise, her heart dropping as she saw them: five other figures charging along the far side, knocking over anyone and anything that got in their way.

"Not the young one," the driver snarled, as Clifford and Kenneth reached the stagecoach.

"But... he has a ticket!" Betsy begged, her attention flitting between the grizzled man and the five that were getting closer and closer by the second. It would not be long before they saw Clifford and Kenneth, and knew they had their prey where they wanted them.

Clifford all but shoved Kenneth into the stagecoach, before dipping into his trouser pocket. He withdrew a fat coin pouch and tossed it up to the driver, proclaiming, "Go! As fast as you can!"

The driver mustered the ghost of a smile as he weighed the pouch in his hand, before looking back down at Betsy. "In or out, girl."

"She's going," Clifford urged, picking Betsy up and pushing her into the stagecoach.

She did her best to fight back, did her best to use the strength she now had to wriggle out of his grasp, but he easily overpowered her. And once she was in the stagecoach, he slammed the door shut behind her and thumped on the side. Still, she struggled forward, knowing she could get out before the coach started moving, certain she could help Clifford to safety.

But her father's hand was suddenly on her elbow, pulling her backwards. Following his lead for reasons Betsy could not understand, a few of the other passengers grabbed at her, holding her back while Clifford roared, "Go!" at the top of his lungs. Perhaps, they did it to save themselves, seeing the furious faces of the men who were barrelling up to the stagecoach. Perhaps, they could see that it would do Betsy no good to step back out.

"You have to come with us!" she shouted, yanking down the sliding window. "Clifford, please! Don't... don't do this to me again!"

He smiled at her as the coach began to move, and he trotted alongside. "I'll find you, love," he said. "It might take a Christmas miracle, but I'll find my way back to you."

"Please, Clifford," she gasped, a sob lodged in her chest as she stuck her head out of the window. "Please, just get in."

He shook his head, gazing at her whilst his pursuers were already halfway across the piazza. It would be seconds before they caught him. And he used those precious seconds to grasp hold of her face and press a quick, fierce kiss to her lips. It happened so fast that it was over before Betsy could kiss him back the way she wanted to, and as the driver snapped the reins and the horses quickened their pace to a jolting lope, he was out of sight before she could see what happened to him.

"Come away from there," her father said softly, but she could not listen to him. She had spent a year not knowing if Clifford was all right; she would not spend the rest of her life the same way.

A cold wind whipped the side of her face as she strained to try and see, but it was no good. They had turned the corner and gone past the church, the grey exterior blocking her from witnessing anything that might haunt her. And as she touched her fingertips to her lips, feeling the warm tingle of Clifford's rushed kiss, nothing had ever felt more like a goodbye.

## THE RAGGED MUDLARKE'S CRHISTMAS MIRACLE

# Chapter Twenty-Three

The hour was late, and the night was starless by the time the coach halted outside Wallingford, the bleak sky filled with swollen clouds, so thick that no moonlight could even hope to pierce through.

Betsy helped her father down, Clifford's greatcoat wrapped around his thin frame, and though some of the other passengers tried to offer help and gifts, she refused them all. She did not even bother to bid the driver a "Merry Christmas" for there was no festive cheer in her anymore; it had been left behind on the piazza of Covent Garden.

"He'll be all right," her father murmured, as they began the short walk to the gates of Winterbrook Farm.

Betsy cast him a sideways glance. "That's just what people say when they know the opposite is true."

"I... didn't know the two of you were..." Her father cleared his throat. "I didn't realise there was... affection between you. I'm... sorry, mouse. But I still don't... think you should give up hope. You shouldn't, ever, until you can't... deny it anymore."

Betsy swallowed thickly. "At least I have you." She readjusted his arm on her shoulder. "I've missed you, Pa. I think you'll like it here."

"If they've taken such... good care of you, I know I will," he replied, pausing to cough into his handkerchief.

They had just reached the gates when a burst of barks erupted into the silence, and a blur of fur and mischief shot down the path. Bramble bared his teeth, his hackles up, growling at the intruders... until his shiny black nose scented the air and realised who it was. Immediately, his barks became twice as loud, his tail wagging furiously as he waited for Betsy to push the gate open.

"Don't mind him. He's a sweet creature, really," Betsy said to her father, as the terrier charged back to the farmhouse.

Moments later, a cluster of figures came running down the path, lanterns held aloft. Bramble had sounded the alarm, and the Moreleys likely knew it was no ordinary vagrant at their gates.

"Betsy, is that you?" Florence called out.

"It's me!" Betsy called back. "My pa is with me. He's not very well, so I'd keep your distance."

"Nonsense," Thomas's voice boomed. "There's no one so hardy as farmers. It'll take more than a bit of sickness to make any one of us poorly, mark my words."

All at once, Betsy and her father were surrounded by the Moreleys. Thomas took her father from her and scooped him up, carrying him as if he weighed no more than a cat, back to the farmhouse. Florence caught Betsy's arm, as if she knew Betsy might be unsteady, while Peter took her other arm—ever the responsible oldest son. Meanwhile, Arthur picked up Bramble, who was desperately jumping up at Betsy's legs, trying to get her attention. And Harry moved ahead of them, lighting the way to the farmhouse with his lantern, casting the glow on the path so no one would stumble.

"Clifford?" Florence asked quietly.

That one word, spoken so softly, threatened to buckle Betsy at the knees. Sorrow swelled in her chest, rising up to her throat, tightening it until she could not get out a single sentence. All she could manage was a slow, resigned shake of her head.

This time, Florence did not tell her that all would be well. Instead, she gave Betsy's arm a comforting squeeze and murmured, "I'll open us a bottle of brandy when we get inside. Nothing better than it when you've had a shock." She cleared her throat. "And we'll make sure your pa is tended to, so don't you worry about that."

*Thank you,* Betsy longed to say, but the words would not come out. There was only silence and the starless, cloudy sky, and the feeling that the last ties she had to London had just been severed.

---

Betsy sat by the window in the farmhouse parlour, a plate of delicious food balanced on her lap. She picked at a piece of roasted goose, the meat succulent and glistening with savoury juices. It was a deal she had made an hour ago with Bramble, who sat patiently by her leg; she would have a piece, then he would have a piece. Otherwise, she doubted she would have eaten anything at all.

She popped the sliver of goose into her mouth and chewed slowly, and though it tasted wonderful, it might as well have been the remains of the ash pile. It took all of her willpower to swallow it.

Just then, the parlour door opened, and Florence came in.

"How is he?" Betsy asked, setting the plate down on the windowsill.

Florence smiled. "He's had some broth and some hot milk with brandy. Now, he's sleeping soundly." She gestured back over her shoulder. "Thomas thinks he knows what's wrong, but he's going to bring the physician in a couple of days anyway, to be sure."

"You should've let me feed him," Betsy said, her heart heavy.

Florence shook her head. "You need tending to as much as he does. And your pa has his pride—he'll prefer to have Thomas and me looking after him until he's a bit stronger. My pa was the same when he was sick. Couldn't bear to have me or my ma fussing over him."

"Well... thank you," Betsy mumbled, knowing that those small words were not nearly enough.

Florence came over, pulling a chair with her. "We're just glad you're back here safe. We all sat down to our Christmas dinner earlier and... it wasn't the same.

You were sorely missed, Betsy, even though you weren't gone long, just as you promised." She reached over and took hold of Betsy's hands. "How's the goose?"

"Wonderful."

Florence smiled. "And how's your heart?"

"Sore."

"I thought as much." Florence sighed. "We're going down to the Frost Fair in the morning if you want to come with us? Thomas has his pies to sell, and I'm hoping to just enjoy myself this year. I know the boys would be happy if you came with us. They've got skates for you."

Bittersweet tears welled in Betsy's eyes, hastily dabbed away with her sleeves. "I don't think I can be away from pa. He'll need someone here."

"He's already said you should come with us," Florence said, chuckling faintly. "I'm telling you—these men, they don't like fussing."

"I'll think about it," Betsy promised, though she already knew she would not be going. Visiting the Frost Fair without her father and Clifford would be like a knife to the heart that was already cracked beyond repair.

Florence sat back and drew a bottle of brandy and a pair of tin cups out of her deep apron pocket, flashing a wink as she poured out two healthy measures. She pushed one along the windowsill towards Betsy, and brought the other to her lips, taking a restrained sip.

Betsy followed suit with her own cup, swallowing a mouthful of the potent liquor. It tasted distantly of mince pies and warmed her belly, dulling the edge of her sadness for a moment.

"You're going to wait for him, aren't you?" Florence said gently.

Betsy glanced out of the window at the darkened world beyond. "If you don't mind."

"Not a bit." Florence paused, staring down into her cup. "What happened in London, Betsy?"

Betsy froze. "He... was right there. He was... by the stagecoach, and he... pushed me in and slammed the door. He... kissed me and then he was... gone." She had to fight to get every word out into the open. "And I don't know if... I hate him for it or if I should... be grateful. I was begging him to... come with us, but he... wouldn't do it. There were men—Don's men, I assume—chasing him and my pa, and... he wouldn't save himself."

"Only someone who loves you would do that," Florence said, sipping her drink. "And you'd only hate someone you loved for doing it."

Betsy blinked back perennial tears, wishing she was as strong as Florence. "I do love him, and... I don't think I'll ever get to tell him."

"Do you think he knows?"

Betsy shrugged. "I have no idea." She scrunched her face, her heart aching. "If it weren't for my pa, I'd wish to turn back the clock and never return to London. I'd have preferred the not-knowing of before to the not-knowing of now, you know? Something terrible has happened to him— I know it and I can't bear it. He always said that helping me was to help his immortal soul, but... I thought we had more time before he went to find out if... his soul was in a better condition."

"But you didn't know if you'd see him again before," Florence said carefully. "You got to see him again. That's something."

Betsy swallowed past the lump in her throat. "I suppose so, but... I can't think clearly."

It likely was not a good idea to have that conversation now, whilst visions of Don's men running up behind Clifford played over and over in her mind. Of course, she wanted to believe that he was all right, and that seeing him again *had* been a blessing, but she did not have the hope left in her veins for that.

"And I'm wondering if how I'm feeling is how he has been feeling for years, before he knew about his sister," she said. "He said that was the worst part—not knowing one way or the other."

Florence's expression softened as she poured more brandy into Betsy's cup. "He's a wily creature. You once believed that, once scorned him for that, but you won't now, not even a little bit?"

Betsy stared at Florence as if a light had just been sparked in an empty, dark house. It was not in Florence's nature to tiptoe around things, choosing tough love for those she loved the most, and, perhaps, that was exactly what Betsy had needed. It *was* ridiculous to believe that a sneaky Rat Boy who had survived everything life hurled at him could not evade his captors.

After all, Clifford had found a way to survive Don's wrath after taking her away from London. He had risked his safety countless times by fraternising with her, and he had done it so casually, so confidently, as if he knew that he would be fine.

Florence smiled. "Have some faith that he'll come to you, and don't give up hope. Not today." She downed what was left in her cup. "It's still Christmas Day, after all."

Glancing at the small clock on the mantelpiece, Betsy saw that the hands read twenty-to-midnight. Twenty minutes left of the day that had always been the most magical to her, even during the years where it had seemed impossible to find joy in that precious day.

"I'm off to bed," Florence said, padding to the door. "You should think about doing the same. You'll feel worse if you don't sleep in a proper bed tonight."

Betsy cradled her cup of brandy. "I'll just stay up a while longer."

"Very well." With a fond, sad smile, Florence headed out. To Betsy's dismay, Bramble went with her, leaving her entirely alone.

Returning her gaze to the wintry world outside, Betsy listened to the familiar creak of Florence crossing the kitchen to the sleeping quarters at the rear of the farmhouse and heard the patter of Bramble's paws as he undoubtedly made himself comfortable in front of the stove.

Then, there was silence. Minutes and minutes of silence, peppered only by the ticking of the clock on the mantelpiece, quietly mocking Betsy.

Drinking the last of her own brandy, the warmth in her belly turning to melancholy, Betsy took one last look at that wretched clock. It read five minutes to midnight.

*I'll just stay until the chimes, then I'll retire,* she told herself... and immediately froze.

There was another sound beneath that steady ticking. The *clip* of hooves somewhere out in the darkness, accompanied by the soft jingle of bells. And as she kept her ears pricked, her heart in her throat, Betsy realised that they were coming this way.

## THE RAGGED MUDLARKE'S CRHISTMAS MIRACLE

# Chapter Twenty-Four

Betsy flew out of the farmhouse door with a lantern in hand, echoing the welcoming gesture that the Moreleys had granted her earlier. She did not know who she might find on the road at the end of the path, but she could not rest until she had made sure.

She was halfway down when another lantern bobbed towards her, coming in the opposite direction. Someone was walking towards her and, in the amber light of the lantern in their hand, she could see that they were worse for wear. One eye was completely swollen shut, his face dappled with bruises, his gait taking on a pronounced limp, his torn shirt bloodied, revealing more bruises and cuts across the flesh beneath.

"There you are," Clifford's voice drifted to her on the frosty breeze, sighing from his lips like a prayer. And as he spoke, he opened out his arms, a smile turning up the corners of his lips.

Betsy ran faster than she had ever run in her life, sprinting straight into his waiting embrace.

She threw her arms around him and held him tightly, burying her face in his neck, inhaling the woodsmoke scent of him, praying to the heavens that this was not a brandy-soaked dream.

He winced as she hugged him, and she instantly tried to pull back, terrified of hurting him.

"Don't even think about it," he said, holding her even closer. "I'm fine. Bruises heal."

She embraced him more hesitantly, but no less gratefully, her lips finding the apple of his cheek. "I feared the worst."

"Whatever for?" She heard the smile in his voice. "I told you I'd come back to you, and I might be many things, but I'm not a liar. Now, the real trouble is, am I too late?"

Betsy frowned, pulling back slightly. "For what?"

"A Christmas miracle," he replied.

She shook her head. "You just made it. *Almost* midnight. Cutting it rather fine, actually."

"Apologies. I had a handful of ruffians to get rid of, a horse to borrow, and a lengthy ride to race through." He grinned. "And we both know that if you don't go to sleep, it's not the next day yet."

She lightly touched the swelling around his eye. "Does it hurt?"

"Not anymore." His hand came up to cradle her cheek, his thumb brushing gently across her skin.

And as his lips grazed hers, there was no frantic rush. His kiss was soft and slow, warming her far more than the brandy had done.

And as she kissed him back in kind, it felt nothing like a goodbye and every bit like a new beginning. He had found her, just as he had said he would, and she would not be letting him go again.

She sank into his embrace, savouring his kiss, until all of the wretchedness of the day faded into nothing, like salt scattered on snow. There was only the two of them in the quiet of the night, with the promise of a more peaceful, happier, joyful future ahead of them. At least, that was her hope.

Just then, the church bells at Wallingford began to chime.

"I didn't get you anything this year," Clifford said, chuckling. "But I hope a kiss is enough."

"Oh no, that's what *I* got for *you*," she replied, her heart full, all of the cracks healing over with each moment she spent in his arms.

He tilted his head to one side. "In that case, let me give you this—it's not much, but it might be enough."

"What?" she whispered breathlessly.

"Betsy," he said, a flicker of anxiety in his eyes, "I love you. For a long time, I have loved you. And it's my Christmas wish to be able to tell you, even if you don't feel the—"

She kissed him before he could think of doubting her, looping her arms around his neck to pull him closer. She felt his pleased smile against her mouth as he kissed her back, whilst the church bells tolled the twelve strikes of midnight... and something cold saw fit to place a smaller, stranger kiss on her cheek.

With a gasp, she looked up.

He followed her gaze, laughing as a snowflake landed on his eyelash.

"You brought the snow with you," Betsy murmured, awestruck.

He brushed a few flakes from her face. "No, love, you saved it for my arrival. A gift I won't forget."

"I love you," she blurted out, realising she had not said it back. "I love you, Clifford. You brought joy to my life when I thought it was impossible. Every morning, I hoped it would be one of the mornings where you'd come to see me on the riverbank, and I've never lost that feeling."

"Well, you won't have to wonder anymore," he told her. "Because I don't plan to leave your side again."

He dipped his head and kissed her once more, his lips more urgent, his arms holding her more tightly as the snow came down and the church bells chimed their last strike, transforming Christmas Day into Boxing Day. But the magic lingered between them as they kissed, and, just as Clifford had said, it did not feel like Christmas was over at all.

"Merry Christmas," he whispered.

"Merry Christmas," she murmured back. "You *were* just in time, and in that farmhouse, I have a bag of boiled sweets for us to share."

He blinked in surprise. "You do?"

"Of course, my love. It wouldn't be a tradition if we didn't keep doing it," she replied, slipping her hand into his and leading him up the path to the glowing, welcoming lights of Winterbrook Farm where, by the sound of it, the entire household had decided to wake up and greet the last visitor of the night.

# Chapter Twenty-Five

Betsy awoke sharply to the sound of something clattering on the flagstones of the parlour. It took her a second to remember where she was, not seeing the familiar surroundings of her annexe bedchamber.

She was in the parlour, curled up beneath layers of blankets on the old and battered settee. Across the room, someone was crouched by the fireplace, stoking it back into life.

"Cliff?" she croaked, her throat hoarse with all the happy tears she had shed the night before.

He turned, grimacing. "I didn't mean to wake you."

"I don't mind," she replied, her heart soaring at the sight of him there, in the house that had become such a home for her. They were not in London; they were not in danger anymore, or so she hoped.

She glanced at the bedroll on the floor where he had slept, wishing she had insisted more vigorously that he took the settee whilst she slept on the hard ground.

After all, he was the injured party: his eye was still puffed, his bruises maturing into purples and yellows and greenish-greys, his cuts healing over.

*But alive,* she reminded herself, gladdened.

"I'd hoped to get the fire going before you woke up," he explained, somewhat shyly. "I'm clumsy this morning."

She chuckled. "You're clumsy no matter what time of day it is."

"Since when?" He feigned affront and stood up, padding over to Betsy.

She patted the empty stretch of cushioning, and he sat down, reaching for her hand. He kissed it gently, his good eye not leaving hers.

"I was worried it was a dream," Betsy whispered.

He smiled. "Me too."

"You're not going to sneak away again, are you?"

He shook his head, keeping hold of her hand. "Not even if you chase me off. I can't return to London now, any more than you can." He grinned. "Truth be told, I've never been more relieved."

"Do you mean it?" She shuffled closer to him.

He tenderly pulled her blankets closer around her. "I mean it. The city wasn't serving me anymore, and it's probably good for a person to get fresh air in their lungs."

He gazed out of the window for a moment. "When I was younger, I'd take Athena to the town green on Sunday afternoons. We'd lie on the grass, and I'd tell her about forests and woodlands and lakes and all sorts, promising we'd see all those things one day, though I'd never seen anything of the kind. It was only when I first came to visit Thomas that I saw proper greenery."

"Do you think she'd have liked it here?" Betsy asked tentatively, aware that it was a sore subject.

Clifford nodded, turning back to look at her. "I reckon so."

His face clouded over, and Betsy knew he was thinking of that lost little girl, and of a very different Christmas all those years before. The Christmas they were separated, never to be reunited.

"You never did tell me how you came to know Thomas," Betsy said, nudging Clifford in a more comfortable direction.

"He used to bring his produce down to Borough Market at the beginning of the week," Clifford explained. "Had the best vegetables and a hearty supply of meat, too. There was nothing he couldn't get, so I befriended him, hoping I'd get first pick of everything for Don's benefit. A couple of years ago, he tells me that he's earned enough that he can send a lad down instead of coming himself. I think he just wanted to spend more time with his bonny family, and who could blame him?"

Indeed, the Moreleys had given him quite the reception the night before, welcoming as if he were a prodigal son, just returned. Florence had tended to his injuries with Betsy's help, Thomas had brought him food and good brandy, and the boys had begged him for stories, calling him 'Uncle Clifford,' though he was no blood relative.

"You'll have to learn to dig in the muck," Betsy teased lightly, nudging him in the ribs with her elbow.

He chuckled, his expression lightening. "You'll have to teach me."

"I'd be more than happy to."

He gazed at her, bringing his hand up to hold her face, his thumb brushing the apple of her cheek. "As long as we're both together, I don't care what I have to do. Nothing can be as difficult as the path it took us to get here, to this moment." His throat bobbed. "I love you, Betsy."

"I love you too," she murmured, willing him to kiss her.

But as he dipped his head to do just that, the parlour door burst open and Bramble hurtled inside, leaping up onto Betsy's lap and stealing kisses for himself. The Moreley boys followed behind the terrier, bringing in carefully wrapped gifts, with Florence hurrying in a few seconds later, shouting, "Goodness, I'm so sorry! I told them not to disturb you!"

Betsy could not help but laugh. "It's no disturbance, don't worry."

"Since you missed Christmas, we thought we'd have it today," Peter said proudly, standing right in front of Betsy so she would have to accept his gift first.

Florence cast her friend another apologetic look which softened into a smile as she noticed Clifford's hand resting discreetly against Betsy's back.

"And we're going to buy presents for you at the Frost Fair, Uncle Clifford," Arthur added.

Not to be outdone, Harry chimed in, "So don't feel left out. *I* think it's as much fun watching other people open their gifts."

Clifford laughed softly. "I couldn't agree more. Besides, I've got everything I could ever want right here."

"What do you mean?" Peter asked, clearly bemused.

"You'll find out when you're older," Clifford replied, bringing Betsy's hand up to his lips to kiss it.

The younger twins pulled a face, whilst Peter nodded in apparent understanding.

"Are you getting married, then?" the older boy asked outright.

Clifford and Betsy exchanged a look, but it was the former who spoke: "If her father agrees and she's not appalled by the idea, then I think it'd only be right to marry the most beautiful woman in the world, don't you?"

"Can we throw the wheat?" Peter said, eyes wide with eagerness.

Clifford nodded. "Who else?"

Excitable, Peter turned to his mother. "Ma, can we wake Betsy's father and ask him if she can marry Uncle Clifford?"

"Not right now," Florence said, stifling a laugh. "He's still resting."

Peter considered the rejection for a short while. "Can we ask him tomorrow?"

"We'll see," Florence replied, nodding towards the gifts that, as of yet, had not been given to their recipient. "For now, why don't you do what you came in here to do? Even though I strictly told you not to burst in like a bunch of wayward sheep."

Forgetting his quest for the moment, Peter shyly handed Betsy the brown paper package that he had clearly wrapped himself, using a considerable amount of twine.

She diligently unwrapped it, her heart aching with joy as she set her gaze upon a wooden carving of an angel that would look perfect on her windowsill. From Arthur, she received a rosy red apple, so pristine that she knew she would be sorry to bite into it. And, from Harry, she received a little green plant in a ceramic pot.

"What will it bloom into, sweetling?" Betsy asked, admiring its light green leaves.

Harry puffed up proudly. "Snowdrops. Ma says they're the first thing to bloom when the new year comes."

"A sign that winter is coming to an end," Peter interjected, "but my angel will last through all seasons."

"And you'll never forget an apple like that," Arthur argued.

Before a quarrel could break out, Betsy opened out her arms for the three boys, hugging them to her. "Thank you, dear boys. I'll treasure each gift with all my heart. Merry Christmas to you all."

"And to you, Betsy," Peter said, hugging her fiercely. "We opened our gifts yesterday, but we can wrap them up again and pretend if you'd like?"

Betsy chuckled. "No need. Did you like them?"

"Mine was the best!" Arthur crowed.

"No, mine was!" Harry protested.

"Actually, *mine* was," Peter insisted.

She had left the toys—three spinning tops, to avoid conflict—for the boys to open in her absence, but despite her careful planning, it appeared that the darling boys could argue over just about anything. Even three identical toys.

"Actually," Florence interrupted, "you'd all best be getting ready for the Frost Fair. Come on, out with you!"

The boys departed, their bickering following them out of the room. Rolling her eyes with a laugh, Florence went after them, leaving Clifford and Betsy alone once more.

"Did you really mean what you said?" Betsy asked, turning to Clifford.

Clifford cupped her cheek and smiled. "About marrying you?"

She nodded.

"Without doubt, my love," he replied, as his lips finally grazed hers in a sweet and hesitant kiss, as if he half-expected the door to burst open again at any moment.

---

Betsy sailed around the frozen river with all the same giddiness of the year before, feeling as if she were flying as the skates helped her to glide along. She flashed a bright smile at Clifford, who skated beside her with the same expression of joyful freedom, his hand clasping hers.

Meanwhile, the Moreley boys weaved effortlessly around the other skaters who had taken to the ice, their laughter and brotherly rivalry sounding out across the Frost Fair. They seemed to have challenged each other to see who could skate the fastest and, thus far, there was no apparent winner, as they kept insisting on beginning the race again for one made-up reason or another.

"I could do this all day," Betsy sighed, relishing the wind in her face.

"Until the river thaws, you can," Clifford told her, smiling.

She was about to respond when she caught sight of something that almost made her lose her balance. On the lowest part of the riverbank, seated with Florence and Thomas, who were in the midst of preparing a winter picnic, was Betsy's father. A man who should not have been outside at all in his weakened condition.

Without a word, she tugged on Clifford's hand and skated over to where her father sat, wrapped in so many blankets that he *almost* looked like the sturdy man from her memories of three years ago.

"Papa, what are you doing?" Betsy began to chide, her heart thumping with panic.

Her father raised his gaze to her, a warm smile brightening his grey complexion and still-glassy eyes. The sort of smile she had rarely seen since her mother passed but had savoured endlessly when he had graced her with one.

"Don't scold me, mouse," he said quietly. "I've waited most of my life to see one of these again.

Never thought it would ever happen, and nothing was going to keep me away."

All of the bluster went out of Betsy, charmed by that rare smile and the happier ghosts that danced in his eyes, no doubt playing out memories that even his stories of the past had likely not been able to describe to their fullest.

"Well then," she said thickly, "you have to promise me that next year you'll join us on the ice."

Her father nodded. "I swear it, mouse. There's no medicine in the world as healing as watching you skate, seeing you happy, seeing... all of this again. It's smaller, granted, but... it's exactly as I remember."

"Your old man is stubborn as a mule," Thomas said wryly. "I told him he shouldn't come, and he threatened to walk here himself if we wouldn't bring him."

Betsy allowed herself a smile. "I suppose there's no harm in it, as long as he stays bundled up in those blankets."

"And I suppose, while you're in good spirits," Clifford chimed in, his hand still holding Betsy's tightly, "there's no harm in asking if I might marry your daughter?"

Betsy stared at Clifford, then back at her father, worried that he would not consent.

But her father's rare smile only widened, his hand coming to rest on his heart. "I lied before," he rasped, clearing his throat. "*That* is the best medicine, and the finest gift a father could ask for, even though it's not Christmas anymore." He paused. "As long as that's what you want, mouse?"

"I do," she gasped, echoing his gesture with her hand to her heart. "My goodness, I do. I know of no man better than Clifford, nor do I know of any man so willing to tolerate me." She flashed Clifford a grin, a rumble of laughter sounding in the back of his throat.

"It has been the greatest honour of my life to be with her these past few years, and it has been my hope, for quite some time, that I might spend the rest of my life never far from her side," Clifford said, his laughter fading into a sincere expression. "I love her, Kenneth."

Betsy squeezed his hand. "As I love him, Papa."

"In that case," her father said, "it would be *my* honour to see you married. I'm only sorry that you'll have to wait a while."

Betsy frowned. "What do you mean?"

"Well," her father replied, his eyes shining with absolute joy, "I won't have anyone walk you down the aisle but me, so you'll have to give me a few weeks to gain back my strength."

At that, Betsy knelt in front of her father and threw her arms around him, hugging him fiercely. Not merely because he had consented to the match, but because they were attending a Frost Fair together at long last, and he was free, and would never have to set foot in a dank jail again. And though he might not have been in good health yet, as she held him close, she knew without doubt that he was going to be all right. He would make sure of it, because he was her father, and that was what he had always done: persevered, for her.

He hugged her back in kind, whispering, "Your ma is smiling down on us. Truth be told, I wouldn't be surprised if she's the one who threw the two of you together."

"I couldn't agree more," Betsy whispered back, at the exact moment that she spied a robin hopping along a tree branch up ahead, the little bird watching over the scene before it fluffed its feathers and burst into song.

# THE RAGGED MUDLARKE'S CRHISTMAS MIRACLE

# Epilogue

*Oxford, Christmas Day, 1855*

"They'll be here at any moment!" Betsy shouted down the stairs, before hurrying back into her bedchamber to check her reflection one more time.

"So you keep saying!" Clifford shouted back, laughter in his voice.

Betsy turned this way and that in front of the cracked mirror, admiring her new dress of claret red wool, and the short, fur-trimmed shawl that draped over her shoulders. She had a matching red ribbon in her hair and her cheeks were still pink from the wind chill of hurrying to the shops that morning, giving her a rosy appearance.

"We'll get you a mince pie or two," she said quietly, resting her hand on her abdomen, feeling the slight rounding there. She had not yet begun to show to the point where it was obvious that she was with-child, but she was ever aware of the life growing inside her.

"Next year, she or he, will be here too," a voice said from the doorway, startling Betsy just a little.

In the mirror, she saw Clifford standing there, a fond smile on his lips.

She turned. "I can't stop thinking about it. When I was setting the table earlier, I kept wanting to put down another plate. Is that strange?"

"Not at all." Clifford approached her from behind, sliding his arms around her.

They gazed at one another through the mirror's reflection, Clifford swaying Betsy gently from side to side, one hand protectively placed on her belly. It had been a relief when the town doctor had informed her that she was with-child at last, after three years of hoping and praying, and to receive the news just a week ago had been the most wonderful early Christmas gift. More to the point, it had been nice to understand why she had been so tired of late, when she used to be able to till and pick entire fields, carry haybales, wrangle sheep, and turn soil all day without so much as a yawn.

"You look beautiful," Clifford said, bending his head to place a kiss on her shoulder.

She beamed with delight. "You look rather handsome yourself."

"Nonsense," he mumbled, smiling against her skin as he pressed a fluttering kiss to her neck.

It had truly been a wonderful three years. Once the physician had come to tend to Betsy's father after the Frost Fair, he had recovered quicker than anyone could have anticipated, determined not to delay his daughter's wedding for too long.

Indeed, Clifford and Betsy had been married shortly after New Year's Day at the nearby church, beginning 1853 as they meant to go on, with most of the town filling the pews as happy witnesses. Only Amory Spiggot had watched the proceedings with a sour face and, even now, he would not deign to greet Clifford if they passed in the street when they visited Wallingford. But the rest of the town had taken to Clifford with the same eagerness and warmth that they had given to Betsy when she had initially arrived in their town in tears and despair.

For the first year, Betsy had continued to work at Winterbrook Farm with Clifford joining in. Eventually, Betsy's father had grown strong enough to help in the fields too, his weakness of the lungs only ailing him in cold weather.

But the joyful couple had soon grown restless, and after Clifford had found work at a jeweller in Oxford, becoming famed for his keen eye, they had decided to move into a quaint little cottage on the outskirts of the beautiful town. Meanwhile, Betsy had taken work as an assistant in a confectionery, spending her days with a contented smile on her face, inhaling the sweet scent of sugar and revelling in the joy of everyone who came into the shop. Although, they made sure to visit the Moreleys and Betsy's father, who had stayed on at the farm, most Saturdays and Sundays, having the best of both worlds.

Indeed, they were happy in a way that neither of them could have predicted, and now that they had a child on the way, their contentment seemed to know no bounds. They had sown their seeds of hope in the ground of Oxford, and roots had slowly begun to form, anchoring them to that peaceful corner of the world.

Just then, a knock came at the cottage door.

"They're here!" Betsy cried, smiling from ear to ear as she grabbed Clifford's hand and pulled him out of the room and down the stairs, excited to share the day with her father and the Moreleys.

But when she wrenched the front door open, her giddy cheer arced back down to earth in a flutter of confusion.

Standing on the street, fidgeting awkwardly with the collar of her burgundy, woollen cloak, was a young woman. She appeared to be well-to-do, wearing a bonnet with an expensive lace trim that matched her cloak, while locks of raven-black hair lightly curled to frame her face. A pretty face. Uncommonly pretty, with big grey eyes and thick, dark lashes that she peered through, chewing on her lower lip as if overcome with nerves.

Frowning, Betsy noticed the three other figures standing behind the young woman: a handsome young gentleman with flaming red hair, and an older lady and gentleman in smart winter attire.

"Good day," Betsy said brightly. "Are you carolling?"

The dark-haired young woman shook her head shyly. "Excuse me, but... is this the residence of the famous appraiser of fine jewels, Mr. Clifford Kinross?"

Clifford's laughter boomed from behind Betsy, as he wedged himself into the doorway to be at his wife's side. "I'm afraid I can't take a look at anything until after Christmas. I've made a promise to my wife to *not* think about my work until at least Boxing Day."

The young woman's big eyes widened, brimming with unexpected tears as she stared at Clifford.

Her bottom lip trembled, her hands clasped together as if in prayer. And the longer that Betsy looked at the woman, who had gone rather pale, the more she realised that there was something familiar about her. The colour of those eyes was so... known to Betsy, but her mind could not pinpoint why fast enough.

"I am not here with jewellery," the woman said, her voice shaking. "I am here to see if... you are who I hope you are."

Clifford tilted his head to one side, squinting at her. "And who might that be?"

"My name is... Athena Merryweather," the woman choked out. "But I was once named Athena Kinross, of Heaton, Newcastle-Upon-Tyne. I journeyed alone to London on Christmas Eve when I was five years old, to rendezvous with my brother. I did not realise I had made a mistake, and by then I had been taken into the care of one John Brookes, owner of Brookes' Orphanage of Saint Pancras. I was adopted on the same day that I arrived at the orphanage by these two fine people, who happened to be leaving as I was being brought in."

The older woman dabbed a handkerchief to her eye. "It was love at first sight for us, Mr. Kinross, and we have loved her as if she was our own flesh and blood ever since." She paused, sniffing. "But, to our shame, we did not tell her she was adopted until a year ago. She had always had dreams of her brother, and of escaping somewhere unpleasant. We thought they would fade, but they plagued her more and more as she got older, turning into night terrors. Eventually, she asked if that Christmas Eve, all those years ago, was real... and, under the advice of a physician, we told her the truth."

"Forgive us," the older gentleman said, bowing his head. "We were instructed not to speak of it by Mr. Brookes. We were told it might send her into madness. We did not know any better, but the moment she said she wished to find you, we have done nothing but support and encourage her."

The older woman nodded. "Indeed, we think Mr. Brookes told us that because he was not at liberty to have her adopted from his establishment. The document we received about her was hastily written and sparse in detail. Much of what we know came from Athena herself, once we brought her home. Indeed, we were surprised by how talkative and well-spoken she was for her age."

Betsy peered up at her husband, Clifford's face frozen in shock, his grey eyes as wide as those of his sister, his mouth open. He had not yet blinked, all the colour draining out of him as though he were looking at a ghost. A Christmas ghost, not appearing to teach Clifford valuable lessons, but to grant him an impossible miracle.

"Where did... we go on Sunday afternoons?" Clifford rasped, as though all of the air had been knocked out of him.

Athena smiled, a tear rolling down her cheek. "A big field in the middle of the city. We would lie on the grass, and you would tell me about the forests up in Northumberland, conjuring stories about woodland creatures and fairies that hid in glens and glades. You always promised you'd take me there one day."

Clifford swayed, and Betsy lunged to wrap her arms around him, nudging him up against the doorframe to ensure he did not fall.

For a moment, he looked like he might be sick, but he took deep breaths and kept looking at Athena, rallying slowly.

"It's really you?" he whispered.

Athena nodded. "I have been looking for you since I found out you were not just a dream. But... finding you was something of a fateful accident." She gestured to the flame-haired gentleman. "My betrothed, Ronan, was a student here in Oxford. We came here to visit some of his friends for Christmas, and one recommended a jeweller here who could adjust his grandmother's ring for me. It did not fit, you see, and he was afraid it would slip off and I would lose it.

"We went into the shop just yesterday, and the fellow there urged us to get the ring appraised, to ensure the diamonds and emeralds were real. I refused, but Ronan was interested to find out, so the jeweller gave us your name and told us to return after Christmas." Athena's voice caught in her throat. "The moment he said that name, I *knew* it was you. I knew fate had guided me back to you, as I had long hoped for. I knew it was a wish coming true."

Ronan offered a kindly smile. "I made up some tale about needing the appraisal more quickly, and the fellow gave us your address. We intended to come yesterday, so as not to intrude upon your Christmas Day, but my darling needed time to gather her courage. We hope it is not an inconvenience."

"An inconvenience?" Clifford's throat bobbed as he took a step out into the street, a step closer to the sister he had thought was dead. "That couldn't be further from the truth. I've... searched ever since I lost you.

A few years ago, I was... told you... died of scarlet fever. I never thought to question it. I should've checked. I should've kept looking. I should've—"

Athena closed the gap between them, throwing her arms around her brother, silencing his frustrated rambling. She held him with the fervency of someone who had waited a long time for that moment, her eyes squeezing shut, sending more tears rolling down her cheeks.

A moment later, Clifford held her in return, his shoulders shaking as he hugged her tightly. Betsy spotted the glisten of a tear beading on his eyelashes, and clasped a hand to her heart, overwhelmed with joy for the man she loved. She had made no wish that year, but it seemed that Clifford's years' long wish had finally come true, even after all hope had been lost. Whether it was Don who had lied, or John Brookes who had lied to Don, she did not know and, right now, it did not matter. She was only sorry that so much time had been taken from them, but they would have the rest of their lives to make up for it.

"I've missed you," Clifford mumbled.

Athena hugged him tighter. "As I've missed you. Honestly, I am mostly glad that you are real, after all." She pulled back, wiping her eyes with the edge of her cloak. "And who is this?"

"My wife, Betsy," Clifford replied, reaching for Betsy, pulling her forward. "And *you* are to be married?"

Athena nodded, as Ronan came forward to put an arm around her. "In January. You will attend, will you not?"

"I wouldn't miss it," Clifford replied.

Betsy rested her hand on Clifford's chest, as the sound of familiar voices clamoured up the street, heralding the arrival of her father and the Moreleys. "Do you have any prior plans today?" she asked Athena and her adopted parents.

"Not at all," Athena replied.

Betsy grinned. "Then, please, join us in our Christmas Day tradition, with my friends and my father. In fact, let's start a new tradition, where everyone is together, and no one is absent."

*Let no one be absent...* The memory of Betsy's Christmas wish winged back into her mind, making her wonder with an awestruck heart if, perhaps, she had helped Clifford to get his miracle after all.

"I should like that very much," Athena said quietly, eyes gleaming with happiness.

"*We* should like that very much," her adopted mother, Mrs. Merryweather, chimed in, stifling her sobs.

At the edge of the market square, Betsy took a deep lungful of the fresh air, laced with the fragrance of spices and roasting chestnuts and the sweetness of stewed apples and confections. In moments like that, London truly felt like a different, faraway world: a prison that they had successfully escaped.

That *all* of them had escaped, for it turned out that Athena had been raised in Hampshire, her fleeting adventure in the Capital little more than a bad dream that she had now awoken from.

Don had never attempted to pursue anyone and, a few months ago, Clifford had heard from his informants that the Rat Boys and their Rat King had been usurped by another, more vicious gang. The new 'king' had the city magistrates in the palm of his hand, resulting in Don being sentenced to transportation for his crimes. As such, they knew they never had to look over their shoulders again, allowing them to truly think of Oxford as home, not worrying about having to flee northward at a moment's notice.

"I'm going to get the mince pies for Athena!" Peter shouted, running off into the crowds that milled about the festive market.

Harry and Arthur darted after him, while Clifford and Betsy, joined by her father, Thomas, Florence, the Merryweathers, Ronan, and, of course, Athena made their slow way towards the centre of the market, where the grand tree stood proudly over the proceedings. The little candles had been lit already, illuminating the tinsel, ribbons, glass baubles, and golden stars that hung from the branches.

"I think the boys have a new favourite," Betsy whispered to Clifford.

He smiled down at her, pulling her into his side. "Well, you'll always be mine."

Leaning into him, they both glanced back at his sister, who beamed with happiness in the golden light of the market, chuckling every time Ronan pressed a sweet kiss to her hand and asked if she was all right. Evidently, her betrothed was as protective and attentive as Clifford was to Betsy, and Betsy could tell that her husband was glad of it. Relieved, as any brother would be.

When Athena caught Clifford's eye, she smiled wider, holding a hand to her heart as if to remind him that she had always carried a place for him in there, for all those lost years.

The brother and sister had talked some on the way over to the market, sharing stories of the very different paths their lives had taken. Athena was well-educated, had wanted for nothing, had been loved and cherished by her adopted parents, living the sort of life that the five-year-old her probably could not have imagined. And she had found herself a pleasant, cheerful, adoring gentleman who would continue to offer her a good, comfortable life, with all the love and affection she could want.

Meanwhile, Clifford had given an abridged version of his own history, conscious of leaving out the less respectable parts. But when it came to Betsy, he waxed poetic, prompting his wife to blush furiously at all the compliments and rosy tales of their shared past, especially in front of her father.

"Are you happy, love?" Betsy murmured.

"Happier than I have any right to be," Clifford replied, sighing. "I thought you were my only Christmas miracle, my love. I never thought, not even for a moment, that a person could be granted two in one lifetime."

She rested her head on his chest, listening to the steady beat of his heart. "I think this means your immortal soul is safe. The heavens don't just smile on anyone."

"I hope you're right," he said, looking up at the magnificent tree. "I still prefer our little tree."

She chuckled. "As do I."

"Although, if I could fit one of these in our cottage, you'd best believe that I would."

"If anyone could, it's you," she told him, patting him lightly on the stomach as she peered up at him.

He paused, his brow furrowing. "Is it... strange to be grateful for the way things turned out?"

"What do you mean?"

He scrunched one eye, as if trying to find the right explanation. "Well, if she hadn't fled Newcastle on the stagecoach, she wouldn't have been in London when John Brookes found her, and she wouldn't have met the Merryweathers, so she wouldn't have had the kind of life that I would never have been able to give her. In turn, if I hadn't gone to London to try and find her, and been roped into Don's gang, I wouldn't have met you." He hesitated. "I missed her, I grieved her when I didn't have to, but... I don't think I'm sorry that she got to have such a lucky upbringing."

"I don't think that's strange at all," Betsy reassured. "I think it's... a complicated feeling, to want the best for someone even if it costs or cost you personally. It *is* one of your bad habits, though, and I hope you've grown out of it, because if you ever try to send me away again, I'll cling to your legs like a monkey."

She laughed softly, a sly smile quirking Clifford's mouth.

"I promise, I'll never send you away again," he told her, holding her closer. "I couldn't if I tried."

Just then, Athena pulled Ronan to where Clifford and Betsy stood, her eyes bright, her demeanour bristling with excitement. "I am going to fetch mulled wine for us all. Do you like mulled wine?"

"I have developed a taste for it," Clifford replied, nudging Betsy playfully in the ribs.

Athena clapped her hands together. "And you, Betsy?"

"I love it. Always reminds me of my mother," Betsy said, her heart so full she thought it might burst.

"Excellent!" Athena cheered. "Now, Ronan and I were just saying that, next year, perhaps you might join *us* for Christmas Day. Do you think that would be possible? Indeed, I am absolutely desperate to meet my niece or nephew, and I can think of nothing better than to have a child in the house at Christmas. Although, I do not suppose they will be old enough to understand what is going on, but... maybe that does not matter. *We* can enjoy it as a family until they *are* old enough to understand, and then, if I am blessed with children, they will be able to play together and we could visit the seaside together, or the forests of Northumberland to search for fairies and woodland creatures."

She halted, blushing intensely. "Apologies—I am getting ahead of myself, aren't I?"

Clifford shook his head, his gaze warm as he leaned over and pressed a kiss to his sister's forehead.

"Not at all, my dear sister. I'd like all of that very much. Plus, I *did* promise to show you those forests, and I'm not an oath breaker."

Athena mustered a relieved breath. "Good, then it is settled. New traditions, new memories, new... adventures to make up for all of the time we were apart." She nodded in agreement with herself. "I shan't be a moment. Ronan, my darling, come and help me fetch the mulled wine."

"Of course, sweetling," he replied, flashing an amused grin.

The happy couple wandered off toward the stalls, while the Merryweathers and Betsy's father appeared to be deep in conversation. Thomas and Florence were off to one side, holding one another, dancing slowly to music that only they could hear, lost in one another before their sons came back to squabble over mince pies.

Following their lead, Clifford turned to face Betsy and slipped his arms around her waist. "I love you so much, Betsy."

"As I love you," she murmured, melting into him.

With a nervous smile, he dipped his head and kissed her softly as the church bells chimed. She kissed him back, savouring the moment, thanking every festive spirit and heavenly force for not only bringing *them* back together when it had seemed impossible, but for reuniting Clifford and his lost sister on that day of all days. Christmas Day had always been Betsy's favourite, now more than ever.

And as the peaceful, lucky pair held one another, warm in their tender embrace, the carol singers from the university began a melodic rendition of 'Silent Night' that tingled pleasantly down Betsy's spine.

In the cold air, brimming with the scents of the festive market and the chatter of everyone's good cheer, she felt that particular, inexplicable magic once again, crackling in the air around them. She had always believed in the magic of Christmas, and for as long as she lived, she hoped she never lost that wonder and faith in Christmas wishes and miracles. It could not be mere myth and fantasy; they were all proof of that.

The End

I hope that you enjoyed this book.

If you are willing to leave a short and honest review for me on Amazon, it will be very much appreciated, as reviews help to get my books noticed.

Subscribe here to receive Nell Harte's newsletter.

**Over the page you will find a previews of some of my other books**

NELL HARTE

*PREVIEW*

## VICTORIAN ROMANCE

# THE LITTLE ORPHAN'S
## *Christmas Miracle*
# NELL HARTE

# The Little Orphan's Christmas Miracle

THE RAGGED MUDLARKE'S CRHISTMAS MIRACLE

# Chapter One

**London**

**1852**

The carollers had all gone home, the Christmas Eve dinners had all been eaten, the wreaths had all been frozen stiff on the doorways, the Nativity scenes were all slumbering in dark living rooms, the sun had been gone for a very long time, the kisses had been exchanged under the mistletoe, and the whole city of London had fallen dark and silent as though it was any other morning.

The grand new clock tower that people called Big Ben tolled out four long, sonorous notes. Its sound was almost the only sound in the entire city, except for the shriek of the wind around corners and under eaves, rattling every one of the small, squinting windows of the workhouse.

Even on a street as poor as this one, Christmas could still be found. The church on the corner was all lit up with candles, every surface bedecked in ribbons and holly, great drapes of mistletoe hanging on the backs of every pew.

It seemed as though the day's carols still hung somewhere in the rafters of the church. Up and down and across the street, too, stockings hung on mantelpieces and wreaths bumped and crunched on doors, every leaf edged with a pure white border of frost.

But in the workhouse itself, deep inside its dank halls, hiding in the women's dormitory that at that moment echoed with screams, in the heart of the old matron crouched at the foot of one of the narrow beds, Christmas was something that had perished a long, long time ago.

"Stop your noise, girl," growled Rosalyn West. "You'll wake the whole house."

In response, the girl that sat on the bed with her knees drawn up to her chest let out a long, keening moan against gritted teeth. A slip of a girl, she was. Her shoulders jutted hopelessly against the rough cloth of her white nightgown. Her cheeks were scarlet, sweat trickling down them as she panted. How old was she? Sixteen? Seventeen? If that.

Mrs. West pulled back the hem of the nightgown for a better view. "The baby's crowning. You'll need to push soon."

"I can't," sobbed the girl. She fell back against the pillows, her fingertips white where they clutched her legs just below the knees. "I can't push anymore."

Mrs, West resisted the urge to rub her burning eyes. "We don't want to be here all night," she barked.

The girl raised her weary head and looked around at the silent audience that surrounded her. Every woman in the workhouse was staring. She glanced at Mrs. West's face, as though to ask for a little privacy, but then another long, shuddering contraction gripped her body, making her curl in half and let out a primal shriek.

"Push. Push!" barked Mrs. West.

The girl's scream rose to an inhuman pitch, her toes curling deep into the straw mattress, and a rush of fluid gushed over the bed. The babe's face appeared, scrunched up, purple and blue. Perhaps it would be dead. It would be better, in a way, if the child was dead.

The mother was sobbing. "I can't. I can't. I have no strength left." Her fingers were starting to go limp.

"You can't give up now," Mrs. West ordered. "One more push. One more *good* push."

"No. No, I don't have it in me." The girl's tears mingled with sweat and soaked into her nightgown. "Make it stop. Please, please, please, make it stop." Her sobs were desperate and childlike now. Begging.

Mrs. West glared at the girl. What was her name? It took her a few moments to remember. Joanna. Joanna Gray.

"Joanna," she snapped. "Open your eyes."

Joanna did so, more out of the long habit of dreading obedience than anything else.

"You shall push. Now." Mrs. West reached for a towel and held it out, ready. "Or you and your child will both be dead before the hour is out."

Joanna's eyes widened in terror. Another contraction washed through her body, and she threw back her head and screamed, a raw and hoarse and despairing sound, and her entire body curled. The baby was shooting towards Mrs. West then, a rush of blood and fluid and purplish skin.

She caught it, wrapped the blanket around it and lifted it from the soaked bedclothes.

Joanna fell back, her limp arms collapsing on either side of the narrow bed, and for a moment Mrs. West was certain the girl was dead.

It was at that moment that a feeble cry rose from the bundle in her arms. She looked down to see that the babe was not dead after all. Tiny fists were outstretched on arms thinner than a man's fingers, and the little mouth was wide open, colour flushing into the baby's face as it screamed, drawing frigid air into tiny lungs for the first time.

For a few seconds, Mrs. West felt something other than the chaos of roaring pain that had been tearing her apart for so very long. At that moment she was no longer an exhausted and angry widow crouched on a cold workhouse floor, holding a baby that no one had planned and nobody wanted.

She was a young mother herself, although not as young as this one, sitting up in a warm and clean bed, holding in her arms a baby that she had longed for since she could remember. She looked down not into the face of this emaciated, undersized baby, but into the face of the baby she herself had prayed for, for so many years.

And she was not in a great workhouse dormitory surrounded by desperate women, but in a bedroom with a midwife washing her hands in the corner and, beside her, a man whose eyes were filled with love and pride.

Then, Joanna Gray sat up, sucking in a long and desperate breath, clawing her way back to life. She reached out, her pale eyes crazed, as though the sound of that cry had awakened her from the brink of death. "Give it to me," she croaked. "Give it."

Mrs. West looked into the girl's eyes and saw not maternal love but a fierce, base instinct clawing to the surface. She held out the baby, and the girl grabbed it awkwardly, and as it was lifted from Mrs. West's arms, it was as though it was all happening again.

Driving home from church that Sunday, laughing together. Little Miss West's eyes round and bright. Mr. West at the reins, his smile wide. The out-of-control brewers' dray barrelling around the corner. There had been splintering wood, screaming, and a terrible, terrible silence. A silence that followed widowed, childless Mrs. West into this very room, into the centre of her very heart.

Mrs. West did not scream or cry. There was no point. She had screamed and cried until it seemed her very spirit had been poured out of her along with her voice. She cut the cord, covered up the new mother, wrapped a clean towel around the baby.

She moved Joanna and the child onto the next bed and stripped the soiled one. She stood over them both, amazed that they were alive, this young woman whose ribs showed plainly under her skin as she fed the baby, this infant whose fingers and toes were blue already with the pervasive cold that seeped into the stones of the warehouse.

How was it that these two were alive, when her dear John and her sweet Anna were dead?

Joanna closed her eyes and leaned her head back against the pillow, her arms limp around the baby.

"What's the child's name?" Mrs. West asked.

Joanna's eyes opened. "What?"

"You have to name the child. I must write it down in the ledger and arrange for the christening." Mrs. West snorted a little, looking away at that last word. As if this wretch deserved such grace. The irony that she herself deserved no grace, that perhaps nobody did, that perhaps that was the very nature of grace, did not occur to her.

"Oh, I... I..." Joanna looked down, parted the blankets slightly. "A girl," she breathed. "A little girl." She stared down at the baby as though it was the whole world.

"A name," snapped Mrs. West.

Joanna raised fevered eyes upon the world and gazed through the one tiny window of the room. The church was just visible, all lit up with candlelight, a wreath hanging from the door.

"It's Christmas," she said, surprised.

"Yes." Mrs. West folded her arms.

Joanna was silent for a long moment, staring at the baby. "I have no family name to give you," she whispered, tracing a finger along the tiny cheek. "So let's name you something happy. Something Christmassy."

Mrs. West waited without patience.

"Holly." Joanna looked up. "Holly Gray. That's my baby's name."

Mrs. West nodded briefly and turned to leave.

*Let's name you something happy.*

A pathetic attempt, she thought, at believing that Christmas meant anything and that this little girl's life would be anything but misery.

Mrs. West had slept barely an hour when she had to rise again, wake the inmates, bully the staff into getting their breakfast ready, and start the day. A day like any other, until she flung wide the workhouse door and heard the lively sound of the church choir singing "Joy to the World" in the church next door. The sound sickened her. What joy was there in this world, she wondered, looking up and down the bleak and grey street? What joy was there in a world that could take everything from you in one heartbeat, in one collision, in one fell swoop?

She was the one who had wanted to take that route home from church that morning.

The wind was freezing. She was grateful for its howl in her ears as she walked down the short path to the gate of the workhouse grounds; it drowned out some of the Christmas carol. She unlocked the gate with a giant key on a heavy iron ring, but before she could turn back into the workhouse, a voice reached her ears.

"Hallooo, Mrs. West! Wait!"

She looked up. The familiar figure of a cheerful, portly policeman was strutting up the street towards her, and she groaned inwardly. The last thing she wanted to do this morning was to deal with happy people.

Happiness grated on her pain, like salt in a wound. And Constable Joey Mitchell was one of the happiest people she knew. His jolly red cheeks were, as always, squashed by a wide smile; a tumult of golden curls peeked out from under his hat, and, to her immense disgust, he was towing a very small boy along by the arm.

The boy was one of the scruffiest children that Mrs. West had ever seen, and she had seen a good many scruffy children. The tiny bones in his thin arms jutted against pale skin stretched tight over his frame, as though he had nothing to spare, not even skin.

His eyes were deeply buried in great hollows in his face, and they were a brown so dark they were almost completely black, like great pits of need staring up at her. Though he could not have been more than three years old, his black hair hung in awful mats, reaching just beneath his chin.

An oversized shirt hung from his bony frame, covered with holes, and his tiny feet were bare. He had two toes missing on each foot, the little toe and the one beside it. Frostbite, Mrs. West knew, without having to ask; some of the skin was still blackened. She wondered how he had survived this long.

"Found this little chap wanderin' around all on his own, like," bubbled the constable. "Told him you'd take good care of him, didn't I, little man?"

The boy regarded them both speechlessly. His tears were washing down his neck, black with dirt.

"Good morning, constable," said Mrs. West stiffly. "Where did you find him?"

"Oh, down by the slums, poor mite. Scratchin' around in the rubbish for something to eat." Joey beamed at her. "He'll be safe with you."

"I'm afraid so," Mrs. West sighed. "Do you know his name?"

"He says it's Theodore and he can't find his mam. I'd wager he's been abandoned." He ruffled the boys head "Theodore's quite a big name for such a little chap, isn't it?"

The child continued to cry, slowly and continuously, as though he had been crying for as long as he could remember.

"I suppose he has to come in, then," said Mrs. West with distaste. She held open the gate. "Come on."

Theodore hesitated.

"Run along, lad." Joey disentangled his hand from the boy's and gave him a friendly little shove. "Mrs. West will take care of you."

Theodore stared up at her for a long moment. Then, shoulders slumping, he shuffled through the gate.

She slammed it behind him. "Good day to you," she said to Joey.

Joey grinned and doffed his hat. "Merry Christmas, Mrs. West!"

Mrs. West gripped the boy by the arm and marched him up to the workhouse. No day could be merry in which she had two more mouths to feed.

And to Mrs. West, there was no Christmas.

READ THE REST: FIND IT ON AMAZON

THE LITTLE ORPHANS CHRISMTAS MIRACLE

# PREVIEW

VICTORIAN ROMANCE

# The Midnight Watchers Christmas

## NELL HARTE

# THE RAGGED MUDLARKE'S CRHISTMAS MIRACLE

# The Midnight Watcher's Christmas

# THE RAGGED MUDLARKE'S CRHISTMAS MIRACLE

# Chapter One

*Edinburgh, 1856*

Snow lay thick on the ground, blanketing the cobblestones. Fat flakes floated down from heavy laden skies, kissing the nipped cheeks of those hurrying home to warm fireplaces and warmer families. Giddy students from the university hurled snowballs at one another, oblivious to the cold, for they wore coats of potent brandy and merriment, their hearts full of the promise of Christmas. And across the city, bells chimed ten o'clock, while sweet voices rose up to the heavens from St. Giles' Cathedral, practicing hymns for the Christmas evensong.

It was Fiona McVey's favourite day—not Christmas itself, not Christmas Eve either, but the night of the 21st. Her father liked to say they were keeping with old traditions, celebrating Yule the way their ancestors might have, but Fiona had always suspected there was more to it, for her mother and father never missed a Sunday at church and her mother prayed every night by the bed. Not exactly the actions of a pagan.

"He's late," Fiona said, drumming her fingertips against the worn surface of the kitchen table.

Her mother, Beryl, chuckled brightly. "You shouldn't be starting the celebrations in a foul mood, Fiona." She had an Edinburgh lilt, a far cry from her husband's broad brogue. "He'll be up when he's up. Mr. Walker will be having him working his fingers to the bone, right up 'til Christmas Eve. You know what it's like at this time of year."

"I know." Fiona puffed out a breath, her twelve-year-old heart eager to begin the celebrations... and to devour the huge feast that her mother had spent the past two days cooking.

It had all been laid out on the kitchen table: little cheese and onion tarts, boiled, sweet langoustines fresh from the sea, a dressed crab, an entire ham studded with cloves, and flaky salmon that would melt in the mouth. Places had been reserved for the hot dishes that were keeping warm in the wood stove: the crispy potatoes, honeyed carrots, and the crown of the feast—the roast goose. Even hidden from view, the smell was a torment, making Fiona's mouth water.

"Can I have just one mince pie?" she pleaded, eyeing up the puddings at the farthest end of the table: a figgy pudding that would flicker with blue flames when her father soaked it in brandy and lit it; a whole plate of sugar dusted mince pies; a pyramid of spiced apple puffs, and currant dotted Bannocks, among so many more. They would be eating it all for days, and nothing would make Fiona happier.

Beryl plucked up a mince pie and handed it to her eager daughter. "Just the one, but if you don't eat your roast goose, I'll not be pleased."

"I haven't eaten all day to prepare!" Fiona took the delicacy gratefully, saying a silent word of gratitude before biting down. The taste of dried fruit and spices and butter and sugar melted on her tongue, her soul singing along with the choir in the distance.

Beryl untied her apron and hung it by the kitchen door. "Is it nice?"

"Heaven, Mama," Fiona replied with her mouth full, crumbs tumbling. "I could take one up the street to Pa. Might encourage him to come home quicker."

"You stay where you are. He'll be done soon enough," Beryl insisted, sitting opposite.

Fiona's father, Donal McVey, was the finest clockmaker in all of Scotland, employed by a wealthy man by the name of Mr. Walker at a prestigious shop in the New Town, aptly—or rather unaptly—named *Walker's Clocks and Clockworks*. Mr. Walker himself, on the other hand, would not know what to do with a cog or a dial if his life depended upon it. That was what Fiona's father said when he was at home, knowing he could not be overheard, but the work paid well and allowed the McVeys a comfortable existence in their cosy New Town apartments, overlooking the greenery of Princes Street Gardens.

"Eat your mince pie and be grateful," Beryl said, not unkindly, as she dabbed the sweat of the kitchen from her brow. "We'll have our merriment soon enough."

Fiona relented. "Why is he so busy at Christmas? You'd think he'd be less busy, since the shop is shut for two whole days!"

"He's just... a very dedicated man," Beryl replied with a secret smile.

As if summoned, the rattle of keys jingled through the apartments, followed by the strained squeal of unoiled hinges. Fiona sat bolt upright, her heart leaping as she listened to the familiar symphony of her father stamping his boots on the mat, scraping off the outside world, and the thudding rock of the coat stand as he hung up his coat. Softer footfalls crossed the entrance hall, and then, to Fiona's delight, the kitchen door swung open and her father poked his head around.

"I heard there was some sort of hootenanny here tonight," Donal said, grinning. "I dinnae have me an invitation, but I'm hopin' ye'll take pity on a lad with a growlin' stomach."

"Papa!" Fiona jumped up and flew at him, throwing her arms around his waist and hugging him tight.

Donal hugged her back, pressing a kiss to her wild, dark hair that desperately needed a brushing. "Sorry I'm late, me wee ducklin'."

"You're not late," she hugged him tighter, "you're just in time. I had a mince pie."

"Ye did? Eeh, ye wee imp!" He chuckled. "Ye'd better eat all yer goose, else yer ma willnae ever make us a feast like this again."

Fiona peered up at her father's face, pinched red by the cold. "I told mama already; I've been preparing for this all day. Haven't eaten a thing."

"Ye're a wise one, lass," Donal said, pressing another kiss to her brow, before he made his way to his wife, who stood waiting with her arms wide open.

Fiona pulled a face, turning her gaze away as her father swept her mother into a fond embrace, bending his head to kiss her deeply as if they had only married yesterday instead of five-and-ten years ago. Beryl melted into her husband's affection, the two of them dancing slowly around the kitchen for a moment or two, their lips never leaving one another's. It was the same every night and every morning, and though Fiona knew she ought to feel lucky that her parents loved one another so much, and so openly, she wished they would not show it in front of her quite so often.

"Can we eat now?" she said grumpily. "I've been waiting *forever*!"

The besotted pair parted, save for their clasped hands, casting adoring smiles at one another as they took their places at the table, prompting Fiona to slide back into her usual chair.

"It looks wonderful," Donal said, leaning over to kiss his wife's rosy cheek. "The feast doesnae look too shabby either."

Beryl batted him playfully away. "Fiona will kill us if we don't start eating soon." She shot up. "I'd forgotten the goose! You're a mischief, Donal McVey—all that kissing, and I'd forget my own head if it wasn't attached to my neck."

"I cannae help meself." Donal grinned, reaching across the table for a bottle of red wine that a client of the clockmakers had given him as a gift for fixing a very old grandfather clock that everyone else had said was beyond repair.

As Beryl fetched the warm dishes, placing them reverently into the empty spots on the feasting table, Donal poured two hearty glasses for him and his wife, while fresh-pressed apple juice was Fiona's chosen tipple. She did not like the taste of wine, and though her parents said she would when she was older, she doubted it.

"Hands together," Beryl insisted, the trio joining hands, though it meant Fiona awkwardly raising her elbow above the glistening ham. "Say your prayers, and once you're done, we can begin."

It was the same every time they dined, even if it was just a simple breakfast, the three of them closing their eyes and silently saying whatever was in their hearts, keeping their prayers to themselves. Sometimes, Fiona cheated and did not say a prayer at all, but that night, she *did* have something to say.

*Thank you for everything we have. Thank you for giving us good fortune from my father's hard work. Thank you for honouring us with your kindness,* she thought as loudly as she could, hoping, that way, it might reach the heavens. *Thank you for this glorious feast, and I hope there are many others tonight, and in the days to come, enjoying warmth and joy like this. To those who can't, I hope there will be happiness for them soon, and I hope that, one day, I will have enough to share to everyone I meet.*

They were the hopes of a naïve girl, but she meant them keenly, even if she did not know how she might make that happen. At her age, with no dream insurmountable, anything was possible as long as she believed it was.

"Are we all done?" Beryl asked.

Fiona opened her eyes and nodded effusively. "I wished for everyone to be this lucky. I wished that everyone could be happy this Christmas. And I wished that, one day, when I'm older, I might be able to make lots and lots of people as happy as I am now."

A strange look passed between Beryl and Donal, their sparkling eyes speaking a secret language that Fiona did not always understand. She ignored it and jabbed a slice of ham with her fork, flopping it down onto her plate.

"Thank you, Mama," she said, about to take her first delicious bite of the salty sweet ham that had been brined and baked and glazed to perfection.

She had just popped the morsel into her mouth when her father said, "Fiona, there's somethin' we should tell ye. Somethin' we've nae told ye because we were nae certain ye were ready." He paused. "I think ye're ready now."

"What is it?" Fiona chewed contentedly, washing the ham down with some apple juice.

Donal glanced at Beryl again, who nodded her encouragement. "I think it's time ye learned what it is I do on Christmas Eve and Christmas Day—why we celebrate tonight instead of then. And why I... work so late in the weeks before Christmas."

"Because Mr. Walker is a crank," Fiona said.

Donal erupted into laughter, while Beryl pretended to disapprove, smiling all the while, as she served her husband and daughter with thick, juicy slices of roast goose and golden potatoes.

Fiona's eyes widened. "What? That's what you always say."

"It's naught to do with Mr. Walker, for though he *is* a crank, he's more generous than most when it gets to Christmas," Donal explained, dabbing at his amused, teary eyes. "Truth be told, I wouldnae be able to do what it is I do if Mr. Walker had me workin' like the lads at the factories or the fellas at the mills."

Fiona cut into her goose, inhaling the tantalising smells. "What is it you do? You don't go drinking like those noisy students, do you?"

"I daenae," her father replied, grinning. "I... make toys, and I give 'em out to those who need 'em the most."

Fiona paused, a forkful of goose halfway to her mouth. "Pardon?"

"All through the year, I spend a few hours in me workshop after I'm done at Mr. Walker's, makin' toys. Wooden toys, mostly, but if I can find enough clockwork pieces that nay one is usin', I'll make some clockwork toys too. Mr. Walker doesn't miss the parts he doesnae need, and he wouldnae ken what he needed even so. But I *do* buy some of me own parts when I can," her father said, between mouthfuls of his own goose and potatoes. "Late on Christmas Eve and all through Christmas Day mornin', I put 'em all into sacks and I take 'em through the Old Town, handin' 'em out for the bairns who might nae have anythin' to look forward to."

Fiona stared at him in disbelief, so shocked she had to set down her fork and knife. "You do that every year?"

"This'll be me seventh year," he told her with a nod. "And if ye're willin', I wondered if ye might help me this year. We can always use extra hands."

Fiona looked to her mother. "Do you help, too? I've never seen you sneak out."

"I stay with you," Beryl replied, taking hold of her husband's hand. "But I am always proud of my darling and his tireless work. His toys are beautiful. Absolutely beautiful. Better than anything you can find in the toyshops."

Donal blushed. "Och, I do me best with what I have."

"And you want *me* to come and help?" A shiver of excitement ran through Fiona, tinged with an undercurrent of fear, for the Old Town was a dark place across the divide of Princes Street Gardens. A place she would never have dared to tread alone, for all of her friends at school told stories of that sprawling slum, filling her mind with terrifying tales of robbery and murder and worse.

*But if pa goes there every year, and he's not afraid, why should I be?* she told herself, bolstering her courage. Indeed, how bad could it be? She knew nothing of poverty, not really, and had always assumed that the stories of her school friends were deliberately farfetched. She could already imagine the stories that *she* would tell her friends, when she discovered that they were sorely mistaken, and that she had gone there with her father, completely unafraid. They would think her the bravest girl in Edinburgh.

"If ye'd like to," her father urged. "Ye said ye wanted people to be happy, and when they see them toys, ducklin', they *are* happy. There's nae sight more pleasin', I promise ye."

Chewing heartily on a carefully constructed mouthful of goose, redcurrant jam, crispy potato, honeyed carrot, and a little bit of ham, Fiona nodded with all the mettle of a twelve-year-old who had no idea what she would face in that shadowed realm beyond the pleasant park. "I'll do it!" she cheered, raising her glass of apple juice. "Merry Christmas to all, and to all a Merry Christmas!"

"Merry Christmas!" her mother and father responded, clinking her glass with theirs.

And as they ate and drank and truly were merry, while snow fell beyond the frosty windows and the bells continued to chime, Fiona's fears faded to nothing. For at a time like this, when all was right and beautiful with the world, how could there possibly be any darkness within it?

READ THE REST: FIND IT ON AMAZON

THE MIDNIGHT WATCHERS CHRISTMAS

Printed in Great Britain
by Amazon